GIIN
THE LAST REMAININ
THE HUMAN W

Thank you for reading n

you, I work for SITEL andrew.colley@sitel.com, I'm a Coach Admin. These days I work from home and writing is my passion in my free time. It's available on Amazon UK on paperback and Kindle. If you enjoy the story, please write a review for me on Amazon and email any feedback , it's worth more to me than the tiny amount of money I get for each copy. Oh! By the way – there will be a sequel. **GIIN 2 (The curse)** on Amazon just before Christmas. Thanks Again Andy .
www.andrewmcolley.com

GIIN

THE LAST REMAINING GENIE
IN THE HUMAN WORLD

By Andrew M Colley

Published by AMAZON

Cover artwork © 2020 by Rafaël Colley

Interior illustration © 2020 by Jan Jones

.

DEDICATION

GIIN - is dedicated to my husband Rafaël for his endless patience and unwavering support and to thank him for designing an amazing book cover that far exceeded my expectations.

Table of Contents

CHAPTER TITLE   **PAGE NUMBER**

Foreword

A British family with a long history of a tradition spanning hundreds of years, pass an ancient vase on to the first-born daughter of every second generation. The present-day recipient, Patsy Akilah Miller, hits on a release mechanism for a Genie who has been held captive in the vase for centuries. While trying to find a method to release the Genie, Patsy inadvertently draws attention to his unique DNA that has incredible powers to heal and rejuvenate human cells. In an attempt to escape from those who are hunting him and to protect the Genie from the atrocities of the modern world, Patsy and her family embark upon a journey, resulting in a strange and wonderful lifestyle that is sometimes terrifying.

The Vase - Chapter 1

Patsy arrived home with the same thrill she felt when she first moved into her new flat only two weeks ago. If she only knew the amazing adventure that would begin in the next few days she would also have been nervous, a little afraid and several other emotions besides. An unimaginable magical force was about to enter her life, and everything was about to change for her, for her family and even her cat Willam.

She was proud of her new home because she saved hard for several years for the deposit and was finally here. On the seventh floor, it had views across London, and it was her own space. Until she moved, she spent her whole life living with her parents Jean and Alec Miller in a large house in Wimbledon Village. She was sad to leave but excited to have her independence at last. She brought her cat Willam to live with her because she couldn't bear to leave him behind. Her mother said it was cruel to keep a cat locked in a flat in a busy city all day when he's used to a lovely garden in the suburbs. Her father had similar feelings but agreed to fit a cat flap in the balcony door so Willam could go outside if he wanted. She opened her front door to find a single letter on the doormat and knew immediately the brown envelope was her amended driving licence. She walked through to the living room and could see Willam sunning himself on one of the chairs on the balcony. As soon as she called him, he came darting through the cat flap and brushed lovingly against her legs. After giving him a few cuddles and a plate of food, she sat with a cup of coffee to check over her new licence. Patricia Akilah Miller, that unmistakable collection of names. Her middle name had been a great source of amusement at school and sometimes she'd resented it until she was told by her Grandmother that the first daughter of every second generation had been given this name and it was a great honour she should be proud of. The story was that they'd been named after a princess from ancient times. The name should be continued through the family as one day in the future, a treasure would be revealed to a woman bearing the name Akilah. No one, including her Grandmother, had any idea if the treasure was a pirate map or the deed to a gold mine, but it was exciting and made it easier to accept the name. Her mother was from the skipped generation and didn't want to give her child that meaningless weird name, just to carry on the old-fashioned tradition. Grandma had been named Margaret Akilah Stewart and was fiercely adamant. Throughout her daughter's pregnancy, she insisted if the baby was a girl then Jean would have to give her the name. They had fought, had periods of not speaking, being angry and a range of other emotions. One day Jean's husband Alec asked her why it was such a big deal to give the old lady what she wanted. Jean could find no real reason and knew it would not make much difference to the baby, so she agreed. When she was born Jean could see the family resemblance to her mother and it seemed natural to give her the weird name.

It was Jean who decided on the name Patricia although to her dismay, everyone who knew her daughter, including her father, called her Patsy. Patsy was a beautiful girl with long curly dark hair, olive skin and deep brown eyes. She looked very much like her grandma although Margaret now had greying hair and kept it somewhat shorter. Margaret was eccentric and wore strange hats with feathers stuck in the top of them. When she was younger, Patsy asked why she had a cushion on her head, much to her granddad Andrew's amusement. Margaret remained confident and happy when her husband died but she missed him and there was a sadness behind her eyes that Patsy could always see.

She surveyed her small domain with great pride, she had bought most of the furniture herself, she avoided allowing her mother to choose more traditional items and instead purchased a modern Italian style that she adored. Her Gran had kindly given her some money as a moving-in present, and the odd vase that Patsy had seen throughout her childhood. It was kept high on a shelf, but she'd never been allowed to look at it. Grandma explained part of the tradition was that the vase should be handed down from every second generation. It was quite a plain-looking thing with a normal vase shape, no handles just straight but sloping sides. It was made of metal with a finish that looked like velvet. No one had ever recalled seeing it before, causing wonderment as to how such a finish had been achieved. She wondered if it was only the finish and suggestion of velvet that made it feel warm to the touch, unlike most metal objects. It had a kind of sand inside that you could shake about but it would never tip out no matter how you shook it. It was an oddity that caused a lot of attention over the years, but no one knew its origin or ages except for Gran who wouldn't talk about it. Patsy treasured it, mainly because she had desperately wanted to look at it when she was a girl, and because it reminded her so much of her eccentric Grandma Margaret. Also because of the history of it having been handed down through the family and because of its odd design. She wasn't allowed to play with it as a child so she gave it pride of place at eye level on a shelf in her living room where she could see it.

Willam came to join her on the sofa and pushed the paper licence away to get himself onto her lap. She stroked him and he purred contentedly. She told him she hoped he was alright in his new home; she would take him back to Wimbledon if he was unhappy. For a few nights, since they moved in, he was restless, walking about making strange clicking and meowing noises that kept her awake. Even when she put him next to her on the bed, he only stayed a while then went back to his wandering, making his noises.

Tonight, Patsy was determined to get him settled because he was keeping her up every night. It was worrying to her, and she was trying to hold down an important job in the laboratory of University College Hospital London. She had been working there for the last seven years on the analysis of the human endocrine system and genetics, but she also performed DNA analysis on a variety of tissue samples on behalf of the hospital. Her work was important and took a lot of skill and knowledge, not to mention several years of study and the all-important qualification. She had to be able to concentrate on her work, but a lack of sleep was making it hard to do so and people had noticed. Until now she had an impeccable reputation with her colleagues and was highly respected by her boss Evie. It was mainly because of her intelligent approach and her uncanny knack for spotting patterns or sequences in her results that would probably have escaped others.

Unfortunately for Patsy, it was going to be another disturbing night with Willam again wandering around the flat making his mewing chattering and clicking noises. Not only that but a strange whispering noise seemed to wake her up just as she was falling asleep, although she could hear nothing when she woke herself. That night Willam knocked the vase off the shelf making a loud noise. Patsy woke immediately, ran into the living room in shock fumbling to switch on the main lights. The vase was on the floor in the centre of the room and Willam was staring into it making his weird noises and patting something with his paw. Patsy saw what looked like a strange grey stick being pulled back into the vase. She grabbed it looking into the top and she could swear there was a sad face made of mist or sand that gradually disappeared. The smoky vision completely disturbed her, so she put the vase into one of the drawers and took Willam to bed. Although she tried her best to sleep, she was unable to do so. Suddenly, she realised she could hear Willam making his chattering noises back in the sitting room. Annoyed, Patsy went to find him, ready to put him on the bed and shut the bedroom door but she found him on the floor with the vase again and the drawer open. Again, he was looking into the top of the vase and making odd noises. Patsy grabbed at the vase and looked inside to see the same sad face disappear like smoke. Eventually, with Willam safe and the bedroom door closed, she convinced herself it was a half-dream or imagination. Willam eventually cuddled next to her on the bed and they both fell fast asleep.

She was shocked to hear her alarm clock buzzing loudly; it had been buzzing for some time and when she checked the time was ten thirty-seven. She was two hours behind and she had to get washed and dressed and travel to work which would take at least another forty-five minutes. She dashed around and dressed, not forgetting to leave food and water for Willam who was still selfishly luxuriating on the bed. She scruffed him gently as she walked by and berated him for keeping her awake, but he simply made a gentle trilling noise and rolled over. It was Friday and although her boss Evie was normally gentle with her, she would be annoyed with her for being so late.

That night she decided to have an early night and watch TV in bed until she fell asleep. She had supper and gave Willam a good feed, then carried him to the bedroom and made sure the door was shut. Earlier in the evening she put the vase back into the drawer and was determined he wouldn't get to it. That night they both slept although she still had vague feelings that someone was whispering to her on the edge of her dreams. When she woke on Saturday

morning she was feeling much better for a good night's sleep.

Willam was off the bed in a flash and from his actions, Patsy knew he needed to go out on the balcony to his litter tray. She opened the bedroom door and noticed that the vase was in the middle of the living room floor. She was stunned because they had both been on the bed for the whole night with the door closed. When she thought about it, she realised a cat couldn't open a drawer anyway. She picked up the vase and put it back into the drawer then went to take a shower. She was deeply worried. Was she losing her mind because of the lack of sleep? She began asking herself if she really did see a face in the vase, what it was made of and where it came from? She would talk to her Mum on the phone, that would usually help to ground her, just listening to her mother talking about everyday things would bring everything back to normal.

Patsy called her Mum who spent the first ten minutes or so, as predicted, chattering on about their noisy neighbour and that vile woman in the post office. Jean was a sixties chick, but she'd kicked against sixties fashion and style and kept to her own taste. She wasn't against free love and peace, hippies and bells but she just couldn't wear the fashion herself. She didn't follow popular bands like the Stones and the Beatles, instead, she listened to classical music and dressed very smartly and formally for every occasion and never owned a miniskirt in her life. She was still an attractive woman and although she didn't have the dark brown eyes of her mother, she was lucky enough to have the dark hair and curls that made styling it so much

easier. She was very self-contained and had been lucky enough to meet her husband Alec who truly was her soulmate. Jean was an amazing cook and an even better baker who loved nothing more than having Alec's friends or colleagues round for dinner. She'd always wanted a son but instead had given birth to a beautiful daughter although she was never disappointed because they loved each other dearly. Her daughter was not only attractive but highly intelligent like her father and Jean was very proud of her.

Jean's only problem was that she had become bored with life and had begun to get irritated and obsessed with other people, particularly neighbours who she felt were inconsiderate, badly educated and aggressive. Sometimes she caught herself complaining to everyone about a trivial matter and for a while would try to stop herself. As there was nothing else happening in her life, she would inevitably return to her only source of interest. This was one of those times, she had been complaining about something trivial when she realised that Patsy was noticeably quiet. She stopped mid-sentence and asked if anything was wrong, apologising for not asking before. Patsy attempted to explain but she realised it sounded weird and crazy. In the end, Jean couldn't be bothered to listen, she couldn't understand anyway, so instead, she continued with her gossip.

When Patsy put the phone down, she couldn't tell if she felt better or worse for having talked to her mother, but she resolved herself to just get on with things. When Jean put the phone down, she realised that Patsy was deeply

troubled about something and felt guilty for not taking her seriously.

Within an hour of her call, the phone rang, and Patsy half thought it could be her mother calling back to check what she'd told her. Instead, it was Phil, a work colleague, calling to ask her out on a date as he had several times before. Patsy couldn't think why Phil would be so persistent because she'd done nothing to encourage him. He was a nice guy and whenever they went out, she had a good time, so she agreed.

The rest of the day was uneventful and when Phil came to collect her, she was ready and waiting and looking forward to going out. As Patsy was getting her coat and settling Willam down, Phil noticed the vase on the shelf and picked it up to study it. He was immediately struck by the way it felt and asked Patsy where she had found it. Patsy told him the history of how the vase had been handed down for generations. She decided to tell him how she had been finding it in the middle of the room with her cat talking to it. Halfway through she suddenly felt foolish so instead, she implied it was only a dream she'd had and smiled at the confusion on Phil's face.

Phil took Patsy to Chinatown, they had delicious food then went to a local comedy club. The show was exactly what Patsy needed, she laughed loudly and soon forgot about her sleepless nights. They had a lovely evening, a few drinks to round things off then headed back to Patsy's apartment for a nightcap and coffee. At her front door, they heard Willam making noises, but Patsy also heard the strange whispers and creaking voice. She turned the key in the lock quickly and they both burst into the hallway switching on the light almost in one movement. Directly in front of them on the floor in the hall sat Willam and the vase. She caught sight of the same grey stick-like object pulling back into it and quickly bent down to grab the vase. They both peered into the top of the vase and Patsy again saw that strange smoky face slowly disappearing. Phil could neither see the face or the grey stick and could only hear Willam chattering strangely. He was completely spooked, although he tried not to show it. He reminded Patsy what she'd said earlier about dreaming of the vase and she trembled visibly as he spoke. "It wasn't a dream Patsy, was it?" She couldn't answer because she was afraid to say it, so she just shook her head.

They went through to the living room and Phil took the vase from her and placed it on the shelf where it normally sat. Patsy asked him to put it into the drawer instead and went into the kitchen to pour them both a stiff drink. She was obviously shaken, and Phil asked her a hundred questions about the vase. Did her grandmother have any problems with it and was it just the cat being unsettled that was causing the problem? She gave him one-word answers and was afraid she had already said too much, thinking he would assume she was weird, a freak or something. He knew she was afraid of something and agreed to stay the night with her. It delighted him as he'd never been asked to stay before. Unfortunately, Patsy was too tense for anything more than hugs and no one could sleep properly except the cat who lay on top of the bed with them and curled up peacefully. Although she didn't tell Phil, she could still hear the whispering voice. What she didn't realise was that although Phil couldn't hear it, he was listening to her whispering answers all night in her broken half-sleep. The next morning, he rose early, took a shower and made her a coffee before setting off for a football match. Neither of them spoke about the previous night but Phil was convinced it wasn't only the cat who was disturbed by the move to the new flat, Patsy was also unsettled and maybe a little afraid of being on her own. He put the whole thing down to her getting used to being on her own and dismissed the vase thing as just Willam being playful and maybe a bit vengeful because he'd been left alone. He gave the cat some food and fresh water, then kissed Patsy tenderly on the forehead and silently crept out. She had finally fallen asleep without drinking her coffee.

When she eventually woke, she felt quite groggy and wondered if Phil was still there. She wandered into the living room and found a note from him on the table that simply said, "Thank you for a lovely evening and I'm sure both you and Willam will settle in your new home soon enough." Willam was outside on the balcony sunning himself with his eyes closed. She tapped on the window and he jumped from his perch on one of the chairs and came in through the cat flap to rub around her legs. She lifted him carefully and hugged him, putting his head under her chin the way he liked it. He rubbed his face against her cheek, his way to kiss her and Patsy kissed the top of his head. "Willam, what is your fascination with that old vase, can't you just leave it alone and go to sleep because I'm so tired I've started seeing things?" He just purred even louder and gave her a squinty-eyed smile.

She decided to wrap the vase in several layers of newspaper and put it in a trunk in the hall cupboard. Her plan worked and for several nights both Patsy and Willam had slept soundly with no disturbance. Willam seemed to be settled, he was eating like a horse and back to his normal self. She fell into a routine of work, shopping, and eating and began to enjoy living in the centre of the city. Her mother called a few times and was more attentive than usual, but Patsy assured her everything was fine. Jean decided she'd merely been homesick in the early days and she was convinced that all was now well.

At work things went back to normal except Phil seemed a little less interested in her since that night. Previously she would catch him staring at her across the room but now he only looked at her occasionally. When she smiled back at him, he still grinned but Patsy was sure he turned away much sooner than he used to do. Evie came to talk to her one day and she'd been talking to Phil. She made suggestions about extra bolts, chains on her door and how they were good for making you feel safe and secure. It explained why Phil had been sheepish with her, he knew she'd be annoyed that he'd discussed her personal life. Then one evening when she arrived home from work, she found Willam talking to the vase again on the hall floor with its newspaper wrapping undone. Her first reaction was to be cross with him. She picked him up and scolded him for getting the vase from the trunk in the cupboard and his little face showed discomfort. As she said it, she realised how absurd it was of her to suggest that a cat could open the hall cupboard then a trunk and lift out a vase. "I'm sorry Darling," she told Willam and kissed his head which he responded to by nudging her under the chin. She then worried that someone had been in her flat and moved things around. Nothing else appeared to have been moved and she looked cautiously around the rest of the flat, subconsciously carrying Willam as protection. She heard a noise in the hall and realised it was the vase rolling around the floor. She peered around the door and watched it pulling itself along, heading for the sitting room using the strange grey stick-like finger, sticking out of the rim. She dropped the poor cat in shock and backed away but Willam casually walked up to the vase and sat talking into it in his weird cat chattering and meowing voice. Patsy could hear responses coming from the inside the vase and was both shocked and terrified. In one quick movement, she picked up the vase holding it at arms-length and wrapped it tightly in the sheets of newspaper, threw it back into the trunk and slammed the cupboard door. Her heart was beating out of her chest and she realised she was panting with fear.

Her fear of the vase was growing, and she spent the evening with the door between the hall and living room firmly shut. Willam seemed quite happy and not at all disturbed by the weird events in the hall. Nonetheless, she was going to make sure he kept away from the vase from now on. She suffered another sleepless night and was sure she heard that creaky voice and whispering. Willam slept blissfully on the bed and only moved to stretch out periodically. The next morning Patsy was feeling awful, so she called Evie to tell her she was feeling too unwell to come to work. She felt and sounded awful, so she had no problem convincing her. She then called her Grandmother

Margaret who had given her the vase. They chatted normally for a moment and then Patsy became serious. "Gran," she said, "You may think this a little strange, but I need to ask you if there's anything weird or mystical about the vase?" Her Gran was silent for a while then quietly she said, "Patsy there are things I need to tell you and I have some documents I need to show to you but we'll have to meet somewhere private. I've been waiting for the right opportunity to talk to you about all of it." "I called in sick today," said Patsy. "If it's alright with you I could catch the next train to Edinburgh and come to visit?" Her Gran agreed and said she'd collect her from the station when she arrived. Patsy packed an overnight bag and booked her train ticket online, leaving herself enough time to take Willam to her mother's house.

Her mother was concerned and knew it wasn't like Patsy to take a day off work, let alone catching a train to Edinburgh so spontaneously. Patsy couldn't reassure her because it was obvious that she was behaving in an agitated and anxious way. She held her mum's hands, looked her in the eye and said, "Mum, I need to talk to Gran about something that only she knows about but I promise I will explain everything to you when I return." Jean wanted to ask why she couldn't tell her mother what was wrong, but she thought better of it, she knew that Patsy was already very afraid of something. If talking to her Grandmother would help that, so be it and she would wait until her return for an explanation. In the meantime, she consoled herself that she would have Willam for company.

History lesson - Chapter 2

Patsy picked up her ticket at the station and caught the train as planned, even managing to sleep for some of the journey, which was a great relief. She arrived in Edinburgh late that night and was met at the station by her eccentric old Gran, smiling sweetly in a bright red coat and weirdly placed hat. It was only a fifteen-minute journey from the station to Gran's big old stone house but there was enough time for Patsy to tell her everything that had happened. They both agreed they should go straight to bed and talk properly the next morning as it was so late, and Patsy travelled so far.

They both woke early, and Margaret cooked a lovely breakfast as Patsy took a shower. As they were eating Patsy added a few details to the information she'd already given in the car. They cleared the table and washed the dishes then went through to Margaret's beautiful library with a cup of coffee. Margaret began. "Before I tell you the family stories, I must warn you that some of the things you are about to learn are probably thousands of years old as incredible as that may sound." "We both share the name Akilah which is Egyptian and was the name given to a Princess." A serious look appeared on her face as she told her, "Some of the stories involve a Genie." However, Patsy had recently experienced events that made her open to any information that could explain them, so she just nodded acceptingly.

Then Margaret opened an old and tattered book with several loose pages, many of them written in vague foreign languages that had been translated many times over. The most recent transcript was from a Victorian woman called Sarah Akilah who was Margaret's grandmother. Margaret began to read out loud the story that had been handed down over probably three thousand years.......

******

Princess Akilah

Princess Akilah was the only daughter of ancient Egyptian King Izates and he adored her. They lived in a beautiful palace named Malkatah that was made of marble and stone and had green and lush gardens with trees and fountains. They had many servants; wore beautiful clothes and jewels and she was also incredibly beautiful. It was many centuries ago, in the days when the GIIN lived among men. The GIIN is a race unlike any other and over the decades they became known as Genies. They are made of fire, sand and smoke and were the servants of the great Kings of that time.

One of them, a half GIIN with a human father, was given a great honour. He was assigned to Princess Akilah to tend to her every need and serve her in any way she wished. His name was Adiim Ben GIIN Labet. From the first moment, he met her as a young girl he loved the young Akilah. Over time his feelings grew, until he became jealous, even of her own father's attention towards her. These feelings are strictly forbidden and Adiim was wrought with anguish and despair, he suffered from terrible guilt, but he had no one he could tell of his plight.

Akilah thought of Adiim as a brother and loved him in that way, she showed him great affection and always treated him with great kindness.

One day, one of the many cats in the palace gave birth to one single beautiful kitten with extremely soft grey fur and the most piercing blue eyes. Everyone in the palace was fascinated by this as most kittens were born with short flat fur and would normally have amber eyes. Her father gave the kitten to Akilah as a gift and asked her to care for him so that she would learn from the experience of caring for another. She named the kitten Shu after the god of the air and promised to keep him safe. The GIIN have been gifted with language and can speak to cats and other animals in their own tongue. The King ordered Adiim to help Akilah to look after the kitten and enable the two of them to communicate.

From the first moment he saw her with Shu the kitten, Adiim flew into a jealous rage and charged out of the Palace as he could not bear to see Akilah hug and stroke this small creature. His anger spilt out and one day he even shouted at Akilah which only made her fear him, so she began to avoid him which fuelled his fury. One day while Akilah was still sleeping, he took the kitten and drowned him in one of the fountains. As the kitten Shu was about to die, its eyes pierced Adiim and asked him why, and he suddenly realised what a terrible thing he had done. Not only was kitten Shu an innocent creature but the death of her pet would devastate Akilah and cause her terrible sadness. He began to wail with anguish and a Palace guard saw him with the wet limp kitten. In a blind panic, he ran and tried to dry the dead kitten's fur, but the guard had already reported the matter. The King knew that his daughter Akilah would be devastated when she learned that her kitten had drowned, and he ran to comfort her. Akilah knew nothing about it as she was still sleeping and when her father woke her, they tried to find Adiim and the kitten Shu. When they eventually found him, Shu looked as though he was merely asleep on a silk cushion but when the princess tried to wake him, he was quite dead. The King noticed a trickle of water running from the cat's ear and was immediately suspicious. However, he comforted his daughter and tried to shield her saying that Shu had simply died in his sleep and she was devastated.

The King returned to his chambers and called for the guard who reported the matter and sent for Adiim. There was an argument but Adiim lied and denied the allegation, he could not bear the thought that Akilah would hate him. Around the fountain, there was a good deal of water which added to the evidence and the King became terribly angry and ordered Adiim to tell the truth. He was sworn to obey the king, so he had no choice and he confessed. As he did so, Akilah crept into the King's chamber and heard what was being said. She sobbed so loudly that Adiim turned and on seeing her, fell to the floor with shame. The King was now bursting with anger and sent for the court magician. Adiim was forced into a small vase as a punishment and was condemned by the King to stay there forever.

The Princess fell ill because of her grief and in her weakened state caught malaria and died before she was able to help Adiim *by persuading her father or the magician to release him. However, her mother had observed everything and understood how Adiim had become jealous as he was so in love with Akilah and had no family to help him understand and control his human feelings. She promised to try everything in her power to help him.*

Eventually, the wife of the King's oldest son gave birth to another beautiful daughter and she was called Akilah as insisted by the King. When she was sixteen years old, she was told about her namesake and her grandmother Queen Laylah, told her about Adiim. The young Akilah was fascinated when she learned of Adiim and the vase and persuaded her grandfather the King to give the vase to her. She talked to Adiim every day and wanted so badly to set him free but did not know how to break the spell and neither did Adiim. Several years passed and eventually, her grandmother became ill but just before she died, she managed to tell her granddaughter that the only person who can free Adiim is one named Akilah. This was the reason why the name was transferred down the line. Over the centuries, many daughters have been born and the first female of every second generation is always called Akilah and the vase containing Adiim is given to them for safekeeping.

****

Margaret explained that the story has been passed on to every second generation, each Akilah has felt a sense of sadness and has wanted to care for Adiim but not all of them have been able to see and hear him and no one has been able to release him. All they have ever known is that a woman named Akilah will eventually break the spell and will become wealthier than she could ever imagine. Over the centuries the information became a story and as only a few Akilahs were born who could hear Adiim's voice, the story has become vaguer and more unbelievable. Margaret had never heard Adiim's voice, but she had heard whispering and had seen the face in the smoke a few times. She was sure no one had ever seen the grey finger, seen a cat talking to the vase, heard the whispering and the creaky voice like Patsy had, at least, not for very many years.

Patsy and her Gran travelled back to London together on the train without talking very much, both deep in thought. They went to collect Willam from Jean's house and while having coffee tried to tell her about the recent events. Jean has a stubborn streak and acted as though she couldn't hear and continued to speak about mundane things, almost ignoring what they said. Patsy was frustrated because she knew how important this information could be. When she tried to push her mother to listen, she became annoyed and shouted at them, "Stop these childish games immediately, you know I don't believe in any of this old mumbo jumbo and all you are doing is making me feel left out." She continued, "You know why I'm annoyed; it was because of this old fairy tale that I was forced to give my daughter that stupid and ridiculous Akilah name." "I don't believe in such things and I don't want to hear anything more about your ridiculous stories." Both Patsy and Margaret realised that it was pointless trying to convince Jean and decided to let it drop for now. They put Willam into his travelling basket and set off on the journey back to

Patsy's flat without talking very much, both worrying about how Jean would be feeling.

When they opened the door to Patsy's flat and walked through, the vase was again in the middle of the floor in the sitting room. Unafraid, Margaret picked it up and stared into the top of it. She could see the smoky face again and held it to her so that Patsy could also see it. This time the face seemed to be staying there and a creaky noise came out like a voice inside a rusty lock. Patsy could hear it, but it was obvious that her Gran could not. Willam could hear it though and as soon as Patsy let him out, he leapt from his carrying cage and up onto the back of a chair chattering and mewing oddly. Margaret was surprised to see him do this and asked Patsy if she could hear anything which she confirmed she could. Then Margaret took the vase again and looked inside. This time she could not only see the face with its mouth moving and speaking but she also began to hear the creaky voice however, distant it seemed. "Are you Adiim?" she asked and was shocked when the rusty voice repeated, "Adiim, yes I am Adiim, help me please."

Over the next few hours, the two women had an intense conversation with the face in the vase and established that Adiim has been aware of everything outside the vase over the centuries. The vase had moved to many countries over time and each time the Akilah of that period had kept it in their Palace, House or even for a while inside Bedouin tents, as one of them had lived as a Nomad. Only nine of them had been able to hear him and none of them had known a way to release him from his prison. One of the last to hear him had taught him to speak English and he had learned many things about successive Akilahs because of this.

Adiim told Patsy that her cat was special and was able to communicate with him, it was rare and had enabled him to attract her attention. He told the women that Willam is very brave and fiercely loyal to Patsy, he told Adiim he would kill and eat him if he ever hurts her. Patsy was overwhelmed to hear this and she could see Willam in a different light. It was Willam who was the first to know that Adiim was there and to investigate the vase. Adiim started to speak to him in the ancient cat language and he understood. Willam knew more about the world than Patsy could have imagined.

Eventually, Margaret built up the courage to ask Adiim about the first Akilah and he began to give his version of events. Although it was so long ago, Adiim remembered it vividly and confirmed the story passed down through the generations. He was still heartbroken and sorry that he had killed the kitten and caused so much pain to the princess. He described the look in the eyes of Shu the kitten as he died and said he was unable to forget it. He also told them that before the second Akilah was born he was cared for by the King's wife Queen Laylah who was also the princess's mother. She was kind to him and showed him great mercy as she understood his great love for her daughter. In her view, they had failed him by not helping him to understand such intense feelings, The GIIN were treated like children and never given information to help them with their lives, but he was half

GIIN and had human feelings. She told him he would eventually be let out as there was a secret way to break the spell, but she was unable to tell him what it was, or it would never work. Then he would be trapped forever. She could only say that a woman named Akilah held the secret that would eventually free him.

Both Patsy and Margaret assured him that they would try anything to help him as he'd suffered too much for his crime. Adiim told them many things had been tried from sorcery to witchcraft, burning the vase, freezing it, filling it with water, rubbing and scratching it. Both women told him of stories about the Genie in the lamp and how Aladdin would rub the lamp to let the genie out. Sadly, they had tried that many times in different places on the vase and nothing happened. Victorian Akilah had taken the vase back to Egypt to try to release him but sadly nothing happened there either. Margaret realised that this had been her Grandmother Sarah that Adiim was referring to and she was proud of her attempts.

Two weeks later, Margaret had to go home, although she'd spent every day talking to Adiim, including the times when Patsy was at work. She'd asked him a million questions and tried to find something that would help him. She talked about her late husband Andrew Stewart and was surprised how much Adiim knew about him. He'd spent all his time in their house listening to them as he had nothing else to do. Adiim was sad when she left because he hadn't had more than one person to speak to at any time for centuries and he'd loved being able to interact with the two of them and a cat at the same time.

GIIN DNA - Chapter 3

One day as Patsy was daydreaming about Adiim while completing another set of tests in the lab, she began to form an idea. What kind of DNA would Adiim have and how could she collect a sample from him? Thinking science and modern methods of exploration could help to find a way to release him she decided she would tell Adiim that evening and see what he thought.

That evening she persuaded him to poke his long grey finger out of the top of the vase. She was shocked by how withered and corpse-like it looked but she said nothing of this to Adiim. She told him she needed to touch him and to take a scrape of his flesh to examine at the lab. Adiim laughed and told her that Willam had already taken a sample from him the first time he put a finger out of the vase. Willam bit him but later apologised and explained that he did it out of fear. Patsy took hold of the finger and was surprised how fleshy it felt and there was an unexpected residual warmth to it. She took a small scalpel and scraped it down the side collecting a small bunch of grey cells in the process. Adiim made a small noise, although he explained it wasn't painful, he just wasn't used to feeling anything.

She spent the evening telling Adiim about her work and how their research had led to amazing treatments and drugs that were helping mankind to overcome diseases. He told her the GIIN were natural healers and could mend broken limbs and rid humans of any sickness. The King refused to release him so that he could cure her sickness and Princess Akilah died from malaria, which he bitterly regretted. Patsy was intrigued and asked how the healing worked but all Adiim knew was that he could move his energy into another and take away or repair anything sick or damaged.

The next day at work Patsy found a gap in her normal schedule and tried a standard DNA test on the sample from Adiim with astonishing results. His DNA, if you could call it that, was unlike anything she had encountered before. Under the microscope, his cells were constantly changing from solid to liquid, then to gas and back to solid again. At times they almost seemed to combust, but the resulting gas would then turn to liquid and then solidify again. She was tempted to tell Evie about it, but she realised it could lead to a complicated set of explanations and may lead to even more suffering for Adiim. She thought of telling Phil, but he already thought she was a freaky bird with an even freakier cat. So many things like freezing and heating the vase had been tried but none of them had succeeded. Sometimes this whole experience was mind-blowing, and she wondered who she was, where she was and what on earth was happening to her.

That evening she told Adiim what she'd found although she was no nearer to an answer. He had thought there was hope and let himself believe he would be released soon. It was just another idea that had been tried and failed as far as he was concerned. He was suddenly sad and spoke about regretting the day when he killed the poor kitten.

When Patsy asked him if Akilah had ever forgiven him, his voice shook as he sadly told her, "No, the Princess quickly became sick, she was unable to open her eyes and she died very soon after." Patsy suggested that perhaps she would have done if she had not become ill. Adiim considered this for a moment but dismissed the idea and the smoky face went back to looking sad again. Then Patsy said exactly the words needed. Wanting to ease his pain and guilt she said, "Adiim, all I can say is that I would forgive you any time for what happened to the kitten and for the sadness of the poor princess."

There was a flash and then a swirl of sand or smoke and suddenly a handsome young man stood in front of her wearing nothing but a broad smile. Patsy quickly pressed one of the cushions from the sofa into his hand and gestured for him to cover his private parts. Adiim was so excited he dropped the cushion again, gathered Patsy into his arms and spun her around shouting a jumble of foreign words as he did so. She pressed the cushion against him again and told him, "Adiim you must cover yourself, it's rude to stand there naked in front of a young woman in her own home." He laughed long and loud, but he did as he was told and continued laughing as Patsy went and found her dressing gown for him to wear. She found it hard to believe that the handsome tanned and healthy-looking young man could be the owner of the grey finger that was poked out of the vase. When she asked, Adiim explained that the GIIN need to take nourishment with food and with other elements that he had not been able to obtain inside the vase. He had been turned into sand and smoke to fit into the small space, but he had been able to collect enough strength to hold a finger out. Now that he was free, he had been returned to the exact age, shape and size he had been before he was cursed. Although Patsy was saddened by the thought, she could see that Adiim was excited, not resentful, and was only glad to be free.

Margaret was arriving this morning because Patsy called her immediately to tell her what had happened. She was excited but unable to get a train until early the next day. In the meantime, Adiim was enjoying everything from TV and food to playing with Willam, although his favourite thing was looking out of the seventh-floor window at the strange world going about its business. He agreed to Patsy's wish that he must stay in the flat and avoid meeting anyone else for now, but he was excited that Margaret was coming. She'd almost forgotten that Adiim, or at least the vase, had lived with her Gran for years so he knew her better than Patsy, even though they hadn't spoken until recently. Last night Adiim had stayed awake watching TV but Patsy had to go to bed.

First thing this morning she had nipped out to the local shops and purchased a pair of jogging bottoms, t-shirts and hoody tops for him to wear, rather than her feminine dressing gown which he wore with no thought to modesty. He loved the clothes, frowned at the concept of underpants and socks but he put them on as told. He was unable to tie his laces on the trainers she'd found although she guessed his shoe size and they fitted. When he stood, he looked like a regular modern Middle Eastern guy from London and she was delighted with the result. Anyone who saw him wouldn't think him out of place.

Patsy went to collect her Gran from the station and told him not to answer the door to anyone. Her train was on time, they were both excited and, in the car, Patsy explained how the spell had been broken. Both were glad but sad that no one had thought of that in all these centuries. When they reached the flat neither of them was prepared for what they found. Adiim had been making food for them, although Patsy had no idea where it had come from. He'd set the table and laid out the most delicious lunch they'd ever seen. Adiim and Margaret hugged each other, and she kissed him gently telling him how glad she was that he was free. You are also a very handsome young man she told him and winked her eye at Patsy smiling.

Their lunch contained bread and sweet pastries that neither of them had ever seen before and Patsy was curious about how he had made them in such a short time. The flat was filled with the delicious smell of spicy food and baking goods. Adiim explained that the GIIN were required to provide food as part of their duties and he had learned how to cook many centuries ago so he used GIIN magic to blend ingredients he found in the store cupboard and cooked them. Patsy looked afraid and horrified and he asked if he'd displeased her in some way. They quizzed him about what he meant by GIIN magic because they were both afraid of what he could do. They'd read stories of Genies and how they could fly and conjure up treasures and Palaces and all sorts of things. Adiim laughed loudly when they told him and explained that all he was able to do was to use the law of attraction to make things happen. He could turn himself into a sort of cloud and fly, he could cook things by making his type of controlled fire, he could even freeze things and mould earth and stones with just a thought. He was unable to create a mountain, at least not quickly although he could find the treasure hidden in the earth.

Patsy asked him to promise that he would never use GIIN magic to do anything unless he discussed it with her first. His reply astonished her. "I will obey you as you are my joined one and mistress, but I am unable to promise that I will not use GIIN magic if I believe you are in danger." He then turned to Margaret and said, "I will also obey you as you are a mother of my joined one and I will use my GIIN magic always to protect you both." They both stood with mouths open looking at Adiim who held them in a serious glare. Then he broke into a broad and beautiful smile and they all began to laugh. As they sat down to eat, they asked him about his magic and the kind of things he had done for the princess. He gave a list of times when he protected her from evil forces, he talked about the food she loved to eat and how he would help her to talk to and understand the animals she loved so much. They all ate far more than they should and both women agreed that the food was so delicious that they couldn't stop themselves. Adiim was delighted to have their approval and asked if he could be allowed to look at the TV again.

Margaret planned to stay with Patsy and Adiim for several weeks as they considered it would be wrong to leave him alone all day while Patsy was working. He had been content to stay in the flat and talk only to them, including

Willam who adored him and spent most of his time sitting on Adiim's knee. Over the last week or so both Patsy and Margaret had been out to buy clothing for Adiim and a sofa bed with new duvet and pillows so that he could have a good night's sleep. He insisted he didn't need any of those things and was happy to catch what sleep he could on the floor. His bed at the King's palace had been just a hard tray lifted slightly off the floor with a thin mattress and woollen blanket to keep out drafts on a cold desert night. However, when Patsy made up his bed and he climbed in, he realised for the first time what a luxury it was and slept like a baby.

Margaret was highly amused when Adiim asked why they would keep collecting up his clothes and pushing them into the machine with the circular window. They just came out wet and then had to be dried. She explained that in the modern world it was important to keep oneself and one's clothes clean and not to smell. He asked for permission to show her how GIIN magic could clean clothes and she agreed on the condition that he would tell her what was going to happen before he tried the magic. He explained and then showed her how he could rub the clothes between his hands and then pull them straight to show that they were completely clean and free of any stains or odours and in fact, they looked brand new. Margaret examined several items and then fetched a dirty overcoat that Patsy had been using to help her mother with the garden. When he had finished it was like new, and even the cuffs and collar were unmarked and looked as if they had never been worn. When Patsy arrived home Margaret gently told her about the agreement she had made with Adiim, to use magic to clean their clothes. Patsy was so angry that she shouted at them saying she forbids any magic to be used in her house except that which she agreed to, like cooking meals.

They both apologised and after a while, Patsy returned to her calmer self and stroked Adiim's arm to let him know she was no longer annoyed with him. Margaret left the room and returned with Patsy's overcoat which she handed to her. Patsy, thinking it was brand new, thanked her Grandmother and tried on the coat looking over the new fabric and admiring herself in the mirror as she did so. She loved the new coat and exclaimed that it was just exactly like her old favourite and where did she find it, she thought they were no longer being made. When Margaret explained that it was her old coat, Patsy couldn't believe it and went instinctively to check her pockets. Inside she found a packet of her favourite sweets that she always sucked while they were gardening and her woollen gloves that were also in pristine condition. Although Patsy's mouth opened and closed, nothing came out and Adiim and her mother both laughed. In the end, she had to agree that the GIIN laundry system was infinitely better than electric. Adiim suggested that he could keep their bodies clean in much the same way but both women said NO! very loudly and made Adiim agree that he would shower normally using soap and water.

One day Patsy's mother Jean came over to the flat to see what was going on. She always felt very left out when the two of them got together and she really couldn't deal with their nonsense chatter about princesses and Egypt and stuff. She received a telephone call from a friend of her father in Edinburgh, worried that Margaret hadn't attended the Rotary Club meetings for several weeks. Jean knew she went to visit Patsy, but she had no idea she was still there. Not only that, but she'd also spoken to them both on the phone since then and neither had said anything. When she was about to knock on the door, she heard her mother laughing loudly and the voice of a man talking very quickly about something.

When Margaret answered the door, she looked surprised and guilty to see Jean standing there with a stern look on her face. They went inside but Margaret was surprised that there was no sign of Adiim. She guessed he'd hidden and played along with that. Jean was having none of it and started searching every room, behind doors and under the bed looking for the owner of the male voice she distinctly heard from the other side of the door. Adiim had used GIIN magic to disappear and Margaret was relieved because she hadn't considered how to explain the handsome young man in Patsy's flat.

Jean noticed the sofa bed and pillows and sarcastically asked: "Moved in have you mother?" Margaret realised that it must look as though she'd been sleeping there although, in reality, she'd been sharing with her granddaughter which they both found great fun. Jean demanded, "Where is the man that you were talking to when I arrived?" Margaret calmly told her, "You must have heard the TV show I was watching, there is no man here and as the flat is on the seventh floor so there would be nowhere for him to go." After considering this she became slightly less annoyed but then asked, "Why are you still in London?" Thinking quickly Margaret told her she'd been so lonely on her own in the big house and when Patsy visited her in Edinburgh, she suggested a visit and purchased a sofa bed so Margaret could stay as long as she wanted. Meanwhile, Patsy was still at work and knew nothing of what was going on at home. During the afternoon she went into the small kitchen and made coffee for everyone. It was a tiny room at the end of a long bending corridor making the journey back with several scalding cups of coffee hard to manoeuvre. As she was checking the list of who wanted what, a face appeared in one of the mugs and she jumped almost screaming it was so unexpected. She realised it was Adiim and asked what he was doing there. He explained what was happening at her flat and that he'd hidden from view. He told her what Margaret said to Jean and brought Patsy up to date so she wouldn't say the wrong thing when she went home. She thanked Adiim, told him to stay out of sight and he left smiling.

It was hard to concentrate on work for the rest of the afternoon and Patsy was on the starting blocks as soon as the clock reached five to five. Evie noticed her behaviour and came over; it was unlike Patsy to be a clock watcher. It was some appointment that had distracted her all afternoon, she just wanted to make sure everything was alright. When Patsy saw her approaching, she was worried Evie would hold her up. To get away as quickly as possible, she told her she had to run for an urgent appointment. Evie asked if she was okay, said she was fine. She asked if it was to do with a young man Patsy nodded and it wasn't really a lie. Evie grinned and asked if it was Phil but Patsy shook her head, "That's a big part of the problem, I need to go before Phil tries to arrange a date, I don't want to hurt his feelings." She gave her a sisterly hug and then pushed her towards the door.

As she left, Evie began to wonder what was going on with Patsy. She hadn't been fully committed to work for a few weeks and that was very out of character. She decided to have a chat with Phil on the way out of the office. "Are you still keen on Patsy?" she asked. Phil thought for a moment and then said, "I was but, to be honest, she's been behaving a bit freaky lately." He thought about telling the vase story, but he felt a sense of loyalty towards Patsy even though she seemed to have dropped him. Instead, he explained, "I think she's worried about her cat, he hasn't settled since she moved him to the flat, he's used to a large garden in the suburbs." Evie seemed to ponder this for a moment and Phil wondered if she was satisfied, he knew she was an intelligent woman who couldn't easily be fobbed off. She decided she would come to the Lab early tomorrow and see if there were any clues at Patsy's workstation to explain her strange behaviour.

When Patsy arrived home her mother was sitting with a cup of tea and one of Adiim's lovely pastries. "Patricia Darling," she said, "these are so delicious, and this is my third, wherever did you buy them?" Patsy gave her a tender kiss and said, "Mum I'm sorry for not telling you that Gran had come to stay." Margaret was anxious because she had no way to tell Patsy what had been said. Patsy soon put her at rest by saying, "I asked Gran to come and stay as long as she liked since her last visit because she has been very lonely in the big house on her own" Jean had already calmed down but asked her mother, "Why didn't you feel that you could tell me you are lonely?" Margaret just said she had many times, but she hadn't listened. Then Jean began suggesting she'd have to sell the big house in Edinburgh and move south so that they could be near to her. Margaret always thought the house would go to Jean and ultimately to Patsy and that Patsy would live there but now that idea seemed distant. Jean hugged her mother tightly and said she was so sorry for not listening and promised she'd try harder in future. Margaret didn't reply, instead, she asked her to sit down and listen to something that would change everything for all three of them.

Patsy bit her lip and Margaret began her explanation of how Adiim's vase had been passed through every second generation and it was not that they intentionally missed her out, but it was just part of the tradition handed down. She told her about Patsy hearing voices, her visit and the subsequent release of Adiim from his tiny prison. Jean listened and smiled but she didn't believe most of it. When she asked them to produce Adiim they called him, but he was too afraid to show himself. They tried everything to prove his existence from showing the overcoat, the pastries and producing a chest full of men's clothing. She was not convinced and as Adiim was still too afraid to show himself a sadness came over the three of them and Jean again felt that she was not part of their secret life.

Just when they thought it would never happen Patsy remembered what Adiim said. He would obey her. Without saying another word, Patsy went into the kitchen and said quietly, Adiim I ask you to obey, make yourself visible to my mother and do not be afraid. He appeared before her like a cloud and then became visible.

She took him by the hand and led him into the other room where she watched her mother's face as she tried to fathom out how this young man could have been hiding in the kitchen when she had checked everywhere.

He introduced himself to Jean as Adiim Ben GIIN Labet and shook her hand gently. Jean could hardly speak, instead, she looked at each of their faces with her mouth open. Eventually, she realised what they'd said was true, although she still couldn't believe it. She asked a million questions and became extremely excited. Margaret warned her that she mustn't tell anyone about Adiim, he was new to the modern world and couldn't cope with too much attention. Jean agreed on the condition that they tell her husband Alec everything because she was unable to keep secrets from him. Margaret and Patsy agreed although Adiim was afraid, he hadn't had contact with any man for centuries. All three women assured him that Alec was one of the kindest men on earth and he reluctantly agreed to meet him.

Everyone believed that Alec was a banking official, but he had worked in a highly secret role since leaving university over thirty years ago. Even his wife thought he was a boring little man in a boring little job, but he was happy about that. She was a real busy body and a terrible gossip so he knew he could never tell her anything about his work. If the money kept coming in, she was happy and didn't care much where it came from. Alec loved her and only ever wanted her to have everything she wanted. Jean was quite an old-fashioned girl but that suited him, she stayed well under the radar and was as unnoticeable as he was himself.

His daughter was more like Jean's mother, eccentric and intelligent but as crazy as they come. She'd often asked him about his work, but Alec knew she was just trying to show interest in him because she loved him so much. She always came home with the craziest bunch of friends, who were just the type Jean didn't want her to mix with. She always referred to them as student types, but Alec knew they were intelligent young people with fresh ideas and a sense of fun and he loved to meet them. Over the years Jean had often felt pushed out by Patsy, mainly when she got together with her Grandmother. Alec knew that wasn't the case, she just had a different sense of humour and couldn't relate to them. He thought himself lucky to have Margaret as a mother in law and he loved her dearly.

When he drove up the driveway to the house, he knew Jean was out as her car was missing. That was unusual for her because she liked to be home to greet him after work and give him his usual whisky and soda while she finished serving his evening meal. The house was empty and there was no sign of anything cooking, which gave him a slight pang of concern because Jean is such a creature of habit. He poured his scotch and soda and was making his way to the study when he noticed the answerphone flashing like crazy. The answerphone counter said there were seven messages. He pressed the play button and listened to them one after the other as Jean left instructions for him to come over to Patricia's apartment immediately. The next one said that there was nothing seriously wrong so as not to worry him by the way. Then the rest just repeated Alec where are you and will you hurry up and get yourself over here. Poor Alec had a tough day, he was starving hungry and just wanted to crash out for the evening but now he had to get back in the car and go over to sort out some domestic issue with his daughter. When he arrived, he was surprised to see Jean, Margaret and a young friend of Patsy's were sitting waiting for him anxiously in a row on the sofa. Patsy took his coat and handed him a plate of sandwiches and pastries along with a nice cup of tea. That helped no end and as he sat down to munch on the food Patsy introduced Adiim who very politely stood and shook his hand and bowed to him. Alec felt a slight trembling in the young man's hand and instantly added two and two to make nine. Thinking Patsy had become pregnant by this young man Alec gazed into his eyes which only made Adiim more nervous.

Slowly as he sat and ate his food, first Patsy, then Jean and then Margaret ran through the whole series of events. His eyes grew wider all the time and eventually, he forgot to eat anything more. The story was so incredible but the mere fact that Jean was involved almost proved it without question.

Plan of action - Chapter 4

When everyone had finished their part of the story Alec looked at them one after the other with a stern look on his face, then he stood and put his hands on Adiim's shoulders. "Young man," said Alec, "I 'm sorry for the terrible suffering you've experienced, I'm glad to meet you and I will do everything I can to keep you safe." Adiim relaxed visibly and thanked him quietly then stayed silent. Alec began to point out all the dangers of having Adiim staying in a small apartment in London. He asked them to imagine what the media would write if they discovered there was a real live Genie living in London and the subsequent mass hysteria. Not only that but Government departments would be interested in him and where he had come from, scientists would want to study him, the whole world would want to look at him, prod and poke him and they would probably be afraid of him.

Alec began forming a plan of action, it was what he did every day at work and everyone was impressed by his authoritative approach and quick thinking. His first suggestion was to move Adiim to Margaret's house in Edinburgh where there was much more space for him to move around and separate rooms for privacy. "It's hardly fair to keep him cooped up in a small apartment after thousands of years in confinement." Margaret's house is in a quiet district, it has private gates, a long driveway, and ten bedrooms. It also has a private walled garden and a state-of-the-art security system. Alec arranged for it to be installed after Andrew died, leaving Margaret living on her own. The three women had never realised, Andrew also held a prominent role within the same service. He arranged for Alec to meet his daughter, as he'd taken the young man under his wing. After a few family meetings, everyone thought that they had only recently met but they had formed a strong friendship, no one realised they worked together beforehand.

Patsy asked what she should do about her job and Alec explained that it was important for them all to carry on as normally as possible for now. Jean and Margaret were to take it in turns to teach Adiim how the modern world worked as neither of them had to hold down a job. They would say that Adiim was the grandson of Margaret's old friend from boarding school. He was in the UK to learn English and wanted to study as a doctor when he'd learned enough. Patsy hated the idea of Adiim going to Scotland while she continued with work as though nothing had happened. Alec assured them it was the right thing to do and would give them time to plan what to do next.

The next big problem was how to get Adiim to Scotland without drawing too much attention to themselves. Patsy suggested she could just drive them all there which would mean they did not need to talk to anyone except at the petrol station when they filled up the car. Alec told her it was too long a journey to travel in one go and they would have to stop over for food anyway. He asked Adiim if he could make himself small enough to fit back into the vase but Adiim wailed with despair at the very idea. All three women chastised Alec for even suggesting it and he apologised to Adiim. However, Adiim did suggest he could become a cloud and then hide inside Patsy's pocket or bag, but Alec shook his head. When he arrived earlier in the evening, he assumed that Adiim was an ordinary guy from London. He told them no one would notice him on a train if he behaved the way Alec instructed him.

They all agreed that although it was risky it would be the fastest and easiest way to get Adiim to Margaret's house. They explained that the train was like a carriage that could travel great distances and would move extremely fast so he wouldn't be alarmed. He surprised them by telling them that Sarah Akilah had taken him on trains many times and ships and other carriages and he'd been on a journey to Egypt. Although he'd been inside the vase, she told him everything that happened on the journey. He had to admit that he was excited to be catching a train again, but he promised to be as quiet as possible, sit as still as he could and not do anything to draw attention.

Alec went home with Jean so that she could pack a few things, Margaret gathered her things together and Patsy packed a suitcase for Adiim. She was secretly saddened, she was already very fond of him and didn't want to see him go, although she knew it was for the best. She could visit the weekend after next and spend some time with him again in a more relaxed environment. As they were packing, Adiim asked if Willam could go to Edinburgh and no one answered.

Margaret eventually suggested it would make sense, she had a lovely garden, Willam loved being with Adiim and he wouldn't be on his own all day while Patsy was at work. It would make things much simpler if Patsy wanted to visit regularly. She was sad but she asked Adiim to speak to him and see what Willam wanted to do. The answer was more detailed than she expected. He wanted to go to Scotland, it was nothing to do with houses or gardens, but he felt that Adiim needed him. He would be sad not to be with Patsy, he loved her very much, but she would be visiting regularly so they'd see each other often. To reinforce what he'd said, Willam climbed on her lap and nudged her under the chin in his special way. She hugged him and kissed his head agreeing with that decision. Not long after that, Jean and Alec returned to pick up Margaret, Adiim, and Willam. As she was leaving, Patsy realised her apartment would be very empty when they left but she smiled sweetly and helped to carry their things down to the car park. She suggested that there was no point in her going to the station because there was not enough room in the car with four people a cat carrier and all those bags. Alec would have to go out of his way to bring her home. They were having none of it and insisted she should get in the back with the others.

As they drove up the ramp from the underground car park, Patsy realised this was the first time Adiim had been out of the apartment block and she knew he'd be thrilled. He hooted and laughed with excitement and everyone pointed things out to him on the journey. Alec told him to be sure to let out his feelings in the car because no matter what happened on the train, he would have to stay quiet, but he knew that and understood the reasons why.

Alec ordered their tickets online as Jean was packing as they had to dash to catch the 7:30 pm from Kings Cross station and had little time to spare. As they neared the station, Patsy jumped out of the car with Alec's credit card to collect the tickets while they parked and retrieved the luggage from the car. She yelled that she'd meet them at the information desk. Alec drove around desperately looking for a parking space and eventually just parked in a loading bay illegally. They rushed into the station with bags on a trolley and caught up with Patsy as planned. Adiim's eyes were everywhere, he'd never seen so many people in one place, but he stayed calm and didn't react, just as he'd promised. The train was already on the platform, they marched quickly down the ramp and Alec found their coach with allocated first-class seats. Margaret was impressed with him and thanked him, knowing it would have cost a fortune, but it would give them slightly more privacy. Margaret put Adiim on the inside next to the window and Jean sat opposite him with Willam in has carrying case on the seat next to her. Lucky for them there was no tag on the spare seat at their table, indicating that nobody had booked it and there were many vacant seats in the carriage anyway.

Patsy and Alec helped them with their luggage and into their seats and Patsy kissed them all goodbye which tickled Adiim and he laughed loudly and had to be shushed by everyone. They waited on the platform and Patsy used sign language for telephone with her thumb and little finger to tell them to call when they arrived, so they'd know everyone was safe. They waved to each other until the train was completely out of sight and Patsy let out a big sigh which Alec responded to by hugging her tightly.

The first part of the train journey was uneventful and the three of them had some food from the menu and settled down to have a little sleep. However, just past Newcastle, another train travelling in the other direction tooted its horn as they passed each other. Adiim was so shocked by the noise and the thunderous rush of the train next to his head rattling the window that he shouted loudly and climbed over the table to get away from it before either Jean or Margaret could do anything to stop him. The steward ran over to them to see what the problem was, and they had to grab Adiim and hold him to calm him down. Willam was also disturbed by the noise and Adiim's reaction from within his carrying case.

People throughout the carriage stood up to see what was going on. Margaret faced them and with a big smile on her face said there was nothing to worry about it was just her grandson having a nightmare. To emphasise the point, she chuckled and pretended to biff him around the ear. Adiim was shaking visibly but he began to settle down as Jean explained it was just another train coming in the other direction. Willam gave a few little squeaks to ask him if he was alright. Adiim told him he was just shocked by the noise but then he asked Willam if he wanted to be released from his confined space as he knew how that felt. Willam explained that he felt safer in the carrying case and he knew the women would look after him. Secretly Adiim was annoyed with himself for being caught off guard when he was supposed to be protecting the two women instead of the other way around. He stayed awake for the rest of the journey and made sure not to rest his head on the glass but Willam soon curled up again.

They arrived in Edinburgh and by the time they'd walked through the station to the taxi rank, it was almost one o'clock in the morning. Adiim managed to find a trolley and after he worked out the complicated braking system on the handle, he pushed all the luggage with Willam perched on top of it through to the street level without a hitch.

They waited in the rank and a driver pulled up and came over, reaching for the bags to put them in the boot. Adiim had no idea what his intention was and assumed he was trying to steal from them. He and the driver had a short tug of war with one of the bags before Margaret told Adiim to let the driver put the bags into the back of the car as she placed Willam on her lap. The driver eyed Adiim cautiously as he drove them to Margaret's house and threw the bags on the floor in an angry strop when they arrived. The house was completely dark but Adiim could see the great stone building perfectly in the moon and starlight and he imagined it was a great Palace. Although he had spent many years at this house, he had never been able to see the outside, only one or two rooms with no clear view. Once inside they had a cup of hot chocolate which Adiim had never tasted before and he loved it.

Willam was given sardines as a little treat because there was no cat food and he explored the house with gusto. He had stayed before with Patsy and loved the big house and especially the garden. Jean called Alec and Patsy to tell them they'd arrived safely. In the meantime, Margaret showed Adiim upstairs to his room which she'd chosen for its size, comfortable bed, private en-suite bathroom and views over the garden. Adiim couldn't believe that this whole space was for him alone and he thanked her over and over for her kindness.

Alec dropped Patsy outside the development where her flat was located and carried on for Wimbledon to have something more substantial to eat and get an early night. He assumed he wouldn't sleep too soundly until he heard from Jean that they'd arrived safely. By the time Jean did call he'd fallen asleep with the TV on which Jean immediately told him off for. Alec was amazed and asked if she was using a videophone because that was the only way she could have known. After he'd spoken to her, he dozed off again and began working out how to make sure Adiim and his family remained safe. He also wanted to know what GIIN magic was and what other things Adiim could do besides cooking and cleaning.

Meanwhile, Patsy arrived home to a quiet empty flat, and not even Willam was there to greet her. Without really meaning to she shed a silent tear then realised she was feeling sorry for herself and pulled out of it, just the way Jean had taught her. She went to bed early and watched TV until her mother called to say they were all safe. By that time, it was two o'clock in the morning, so she switched off the TV and light and was soon sound asleep.

Retrieval - Chapter 5

When Patsy arrived at the lab Evie peered across the room at her in a strange way over the top of her glasses. It gave her a shiver down her spine, and she wondered what it was about. She got down to work and briefly forgot about it until she suddenly looked up to find Evie standing next to her. She smiled but there was something in the way she did it that made Patsy feel uneasy. "Good morning Patsy," she said, "could we have a word in private?" Patsy's heart began to race but she tried to stay calm and not show it. They went to one of the small meeting rooms along the corridor and sat down.

She produced a file and opened it before looking back at Patsy. She explained, "For a couple of weeks now I felt that you've been unhappy about something and I was worried that something was affecting your work." She continued, "You've been late for work and you race home as soon as the day ends, which is not something you've ever done before." Patsy started to explain but Evie asked her to wait and listen to everything she had to say before responding.

She went on, "One morning I came to the lab early and looked through the various tests and results around your workbench and the records kept on your computer. One of the DNA tests had no label or markings, and this immediately drew my attention. I examined it under one of the Pro X microscopes. What I saw was both shocking and highly irregular and so far, I have not been able to explain the way the cells were behaving." Patsy's eyes were wide, and she had blushed fiercely. Evie then asked, "Why didn't you come to me to discuss these unusual cells Patsy, you would normally be buzzing with excitement by such a find?"

Patsy didn't answer, her mind was reeling so when Evie asked where the sample came from, she lied. "I found it on my desk one morning." Evie shook her head; the response was not what she had hoped for. "I have watched all the CCTV footage for the last few weeks and no stranger has been in the lab, not only that but apart from the regular cleaning woman, no one else has either touched anything on your bench or been near it apart from me." She shrugged and tried to look puzzled, but she was not good at lying and Jean had always told her so. Evie asked, "What did you think of the cells and their strange behaviour?" Patsy said, "I noticed they were unusual but not that strange and I was going to have another look at them sometime when I had a few moments to spare."

Evie told her the CCTV footage showed her placing a DNA testing kit into her handbag and retrieving it the next morning. Patsy made a face as if she was suddenly realising and said, "It was a small creature my cat caught, and I wanted to identify it, but I didn't think it was that important." "I want to apologise," she said, "for taking the testing kit I know it was wrong, but will I be fired for stealing." Evie asked, "Is THAT the reason you lied about where the test had come from because you thought you'd be in trouble for stealing the kit?" Patsy nodded and tried to grin in an embarrassed schoolgirl kind of way. To her relief, Evie seemed to buy this and smiled back telling her, "Don't be so silly, don't you know yet that staff from this lab are always encouraged to look for anything unusual and examine and analyse it however or whenever they find it?."

Patsy's stomach stopped rolling over quite as much so she told her, "I came home from shopping one day recently to find Willam, my cat, with a weird creature which I tried to retrieve from him but he quickly ate it and all I managed to gather from it was a few cells. I picked them up with a clean cloth and kept them in a sealed plastic container intending to test the sample the following day when I had a kit." "I wasn't too concerned about them. I was only trying to find out what my cat had eaten in case he became ill." Evie was silent for a while and was thinking through everything Patsy just told her. "Patsy," she said, "I think you should know that the cells were completely alien and not from any species known to live on Earth." Patsy pretended to be shocked and again Evie seemed to buy this. She asked, "Do you still have the rest of the sample or the cloth?" Patsy, she said she had thrown it away the same day which was now over a week ago. She asked, "What has happened to the test kit?" Evie told her, "I sent it up the line to be tested by senior scientists, but it should come back to this lab later next week." At that, Evie closed her file and in doing so closed any further conversation on the matter. She asked Patsy to go back to her workbench, Patsy nodded and walked back to her section. As she turned the corner at the end of the corridor, Evie called a number on her mobile phone and told whoever answered, "I've spoken to her as you asked she gave me a story but she was lying."

That night Patsy called her Dad and told him about their conversation including everything she'd said. He told her to stay calm and try to find out where the DNA test had been sent. Patsy suddenly realised how fortunate it was that both Adiim and Willam had gone to Scotland, or perhaps it was great foresight on Alec's part, Patsy wondered? Alec said he was coming over and to prepare something to eat while they decided what to do next.

When he arrived, he told her it was vital to find out where the test had been sent because he knew people who could make it disappear if they knew where to find it. Patsy couldn't believe what he was saying at first, but he was very sincere, and she had no better idea. They both knew there would be an enquiry to find out where the alien cells had come from and Alec told her they would be swarming all over her apartment soon. Patsy hadn't considered that and shuddered at the thought of it. They ate their meal and Alec gave Patsy a list of things she needed to do. He asked her, "Have you made any notes relating to Adiim's DNA, either in your own handwriting or on your PC?" "No Dad," she told him, "I didn't record anything and there's nothing on my PC either." This seemed to please Alec immensely.

They discussed possible scenarios, such as, what Patsy would say if anyone came to the lab. They both agreed she needed to stick to the story that Willam had caught a creature and eaten it, but they had to protect poor Willam too. Alec told Patsy, "You will have to act as though

Willam has been missing for several days and if anyone asks you should say he was last seen on the balcony when you went to work days ago." To make it more realistic Patsy went and knocked on her neighbour's doors to ask if they had seen him. Meanwhile, Alec went on her PC and printed off a lost cat poster to fix to nearby lampposts. That done they called Margaret and Jean and told them what had happened. The next few days were uneventful and if anything, Evie was extra nice to Patsy. She tried asking where the DNA sample had been sent several times, but each time Evie's answer was very ambiguous. She did her research online to try to determine which labs were linked to theirs, but it was impossible to identify where the DNA was sent.

Every night she let Alec know that she'd drawn a blank. Then on Thursday afternoon, she went to make a coffee and met Evie's assistant Beth in the tiny kitchen. Patsy took the opportunity to find out what she may know. "Hi Beth, how are you? I'm glad I've seen you, I wonder if you've heard anything about my DNA tests that Evie sent off recently, do you know where they were sent; I can't wait to hear the results?" "I only know that they are normally sent by post and that is usually determined by the label attached to them," said Beth. Patsy pushed further, "I hate the suspense of waiting for research results and I'm especially keen to get any news on a really interesting sample that Evie sent off recently." Beth didn't register any awareness of it on her face and Patsy was about to give up when Beth suddenly said, "It may have been in that special batch of tests that Evie took directly to the Institute for further analysis." Patsy quickly asked which organisation that was. "I only know she went to meet someone called F Crick," she replied. "I know it was somewhere in Bloomsbury because that's what was written in Evie's diary on the day she went to take the samples to the Institute."

Patsy pretended it was unimportant and Beth gave her a little grin and wandered back to her desk. Patsy couldn't help pulling her fist backwards through the air and whispering RESULT! She was still on her lunch break, so she went out to the street and walked a distance before calling her Dad on her mobile phone. "Great news Dad," she told him, "I've managed to discover that the DNA test has been taken to the Francis Crick Institute in Bloomsbury, I don't have an address and that's all I could find out." "Patsy, you've done a great job," Alec told her, "I'm sure that will be enough."

Patsy was unaware of Alec's position in the service, but he was a department head with a great deal of clout. As soon as he finished speaking to Patsy, he called Greg Brown his number two into the office. "I have an interesting job for you that's a little out of the ordinary, but I know you are the best man to deal with it." Greg nodded and thanked him." I need you to collect, well actually seize, some DNA samples from the Francis Crick Institute and there must be no trace of who collected them or where they've gone," said Alec. "How will I identify them?" Greg asked. Alec told him they were delivered personally by Evie Thomlinson on behalf of University College Hospital Laboratories and time was of the essence.

Within an hour Greg and his colleague Roxanne were entering the building. Within the time it had taken them to prepare for the visit they'd done enough research to speak intelligently about the tests, to know who the head researchers were and check photographs of people working in the Institute. Including the security guards in the reception area. Both wore convincing identification badges linking them to The Royal Society. When they entered Roxanne waved to the security guard as they were waiting to speak to the receptionist. He nodded back and wondered who the incredibly attractive woman was and if she knew him. Greg spoke to the receptionist, "We need to speak privately with Professor Wilson, the Head of Research." The receptionist looked up as if surprised, "Do you have an appointment." Greg showed her a letter from The Royal Society addressed to the professor and detailing the collection of specific DNA samples. The receptionist asked if they would take a seat and was immediately more respectful of them. Instead, Roxanne walked over to the security guard, "Hello Michael, do you remember me," she asked? "I'm Den's little sister Roxy, I remember you coming over to collect my brother for your Saturday nights out."

He was completely charmed by all the attention from this beautiful woman and although he did have a friend called Den, he couldn't remember having met his sister. She asked for his mobile phone number and he willingly gave it to her with his tongue hanging out. Roxanne kissed her right index finger and placed it on his lips walking away smiling as she did so. She sat down next to Greg who was idly reading a magazine from the desk and looked back to smile at the guard every so often.

Eventually, they were called back to the reception desk and asked to complete security cards within the registration book. The sides were torn off and placed into plastic badges for them to wear. They were escorted over to the entrance to the lifts and Roxanne's friendly security guard rushed over to let them through the electronic turnstiles and call the lift for them. When they reached the eleventh floor a middle-aged woman in a tweed suit greeted them formally at the lift doors and escorted them through the various security points along the corridors using her pass key until they reached the Professor's office.

She escorted them in and introduced the Professor then backed out of the room politely and closed the door. They both shook his hand and introduced themselves, referring to their fictitious job titles as they did so. The Professor invited them to sit down and Greg handed him the official-looking letter ordering the tissue samples and all files and documentation referring to them to be handed to Greg immediately as a matter of national security. The Professor's eyebrows went up as he read the letter. "Might I be told what the security threat might be?" Greg told him, "I'm only the messenger but I have strict instructions not to leave the Institute without everything on the list." The Professor didn't like being told what to do and resented not being told what the problem was first-hand. He lifted the handset on his phone and dialled a number, turning to Greg. "Although I do not doubt that the letter is authentic, I'm sure you will understand if I verify everything and speak to Doctor Becker first."

Greg placed his hand on the phone and cut off the call telling the Professor, "I'm sorry but I cannot allow you to speak to anyone else about this. As I told you this is a top-level security matter and far too high risk to be discussed over the telephone, which is the reason for the direct approach and the hand-delivered letter." The Professor was outraged by this and shouted at them, "I will not tolerate being treated this way. I'm a senior Official, not a child." Roxanne very calmly and professionally touched the professor's hand and told him, "We are sorry and we're not here to upset or insult you, we're just doing our jobs. The plan is simply easier if we collect the files and specimens directly and quickly so that we can leave you in peace and avoid any security complications." Greg took a harder line repeating that they would not be leaving until they had collected everything on the list.

The professor pressed the intercom button on his desk asking the respondent to come through and the smart middle-aged women appeared in the doorway a minute later. The Professor addressed her as Caroline, and he wrote down details of the tests and papers that he needed collecting from the Laboratory on the fourth floor. At the bottom of the note he had written, "Tell security not to let these people leave the building without following them." Caroline read the note quickly and nodded that she understood, again backing out of the room and closing the door quietly behind her. The Professor tried probing Greg and Roxanne for information about their work, casually asking "Who do you work for at the Royal Society and which department." They looked at each other and said nothing more. The Professor pressed on until Greg held up a hand saying, "I have already told you, Professor, that we are dealing with a top-level security matter." He stopped trying and the three of them spent the rest of the time waiting in silence. After twenty minutes or more the door knocked, and Caroline appeared with a tall young man in a white lab coat carrying a file. The Professor addressed him directly asking, "Are you certain that all reports and any biological samples relating to these tests are contained in the file?" The young man said they were and was about to ask questions when the Professor simply said, "Dismissed." The young man's face went red with frustration and he didn't want to give up the file. Greg stood up and took a hold of the file gently removing it from the young man's grip. Roxanne stood and they both nodded to the Professor and the young man. They turned to Caroline and she led them back down the corridors and waited as they entered the lift.

Back in the reception area, the friendly security guard was looking for them when the doors opened and let them through the turnstiles. Roxanne grinned at him and although his face was serious at first, he eventually beamed a smile back. They handed in their badges and collected their coats and bags and Greg silently slid the file into his brown leather briefcase. They stepped out into the street and walked purposefully and steadily down the road idly chatting about nothing as they went.

Roxanne took her mobile phone from her pocket and sent a long and detailed text to someone as she was walking along. They quickened their pace but only gradually until eventually, they were walking quite fast. At the next corner, Greg suddenly turned left into a long alleyway and Roxanne turned a second after him. Greg broke into a run and Roxanne stopped and leaned against the wall at the beginning of the alley. Just as Greg reached the other end a familiar dark face turned into the alley. It was Roxanne's friendly security guard and she grabbed the lapels of his jacket with both hands swinging him around to face her. This distracted him enough to enable Greg to leave the alley and turn to the right without being seen.

She planted a kiss on his lips seductively, "I knew you would follow me, sweetie," she told him purring. He didn't answer and was blown over by her beautiful face but then he suddenly realised that Greg had gone. However, before he had a chance to protest his mobile phone rang and a voice said, "Michael get back to the Institute on the double, there is a security alert and possible fire detected, we need to evacuate the entire building." He was both frustrated and annoyed, he mumbled a few words about having to go and made the call me signal with his small finger and thumb on his right hand as he turned and darted off.

Roxanne turned and legged it down the alley as soon as he was out of sight, eventually catching up with her colleague sitting on a park bench as pre-arranged. Her phone rang and a familiar voice from her office asked, "Did you manage to escape from your amorous pursuer" and laughed? Greg asked how she knew he would fall for it. She just shrugged and told him that men are predictable. They both laughed and headed back to their rendezvous with Alec.

When he received the file, Alec read it from cover to cover in the privacy of his office. It revealed astounding information. The helix of Giin DNA, when mixed with human DNA, wraps around it, and eradicates any sick cells, even killing abnormal or cancerous cells but more importantly it restores them which has an anti-ageing effect. Alec knew immediately that this information was worth £Billions and the danger it posed to Adiim and his family trying to keep it from the rest of the world. The health benefits would be enough to create a frenzy let alone its anti-ageing or restorative qualities. Alec shuddered and hid the file in his safe then called and arranged to meet Patsy after work in a local pizza restaurant.

It was a noisy eatery and they could talk there without anyone even paying any attention to them, unfortunately, that included the waiters. Alec now had the sample taken from Adiim and all documents relating to the tests and any results, so he relayed what had been discovered about the DNA helix and Patsy was both impressed and surprised by the breadth of his knowledge.

She fully understood what this would mean to Adiim but the scientist in her was also thrilled by the possibility of curing some of the world's most terrible diseases. They both agreed that if they could find a way to help without any danger to Adiim or their family, they would be the first to try. However, Alec knew that there was about to be a full-on focus on Patsy, while they tried to get any information they could from her, relating to the DNA sample.

"There are people who would kill to get their hands on this," he warned, "That's how serious things are." Alec drove Patsy home and dropped her off. "We have to form a plan for dealing with this but in the meantime stick to your story, it's a good one," he told her.

Investigation - Chapter 6

The very next day at work there was a full team meeting that must have been hurriedly arranged because she heard Evie's assistant complaining about having to re-book everyone's appointments just to fit it in. During the meeting, the senior management team announced that Patsy had been selected to attend a special training day the next day in Shropshire. She was told it will be an overnight stay in a luxury hotel and spa. Several of her colleagues clapped and patted her on the back telling her well done and she agreed to attend. Although she was pretending to be excited, she knew in her heart she had been selected to get to her away from home so that they could get into her flat unnoticed.

The rest of the day at work was uneventful but Patsy was churning with anxiety until lunchtime when she managed to go outside to call her Dad. That evening after work she met Alec in a lovely French restaurant as arranged during their earlier phone call. It was a beautiful peaceful place and quite a change from the fast food outlets they had been meeting in lately. When he arrived, she told him more about having been selected for the training day. Alec had mulled it over since lunchtime. "I'm sorry Darling but you couldn't possibly go, it's so obviously been set up." Patsy agreed that they were probably setting her up, "I am certain they just want to get into my flat and have a poke around, so perhaps I should just let them," she suggested?

Alec could see her point and agreed it was probably better to appear as normal as possible for now while he decided how to protect Adiim and the rest of the family. They quickly finished their meal and went to Patsy's flat to purge it of anything that could be incriminating, especially the vase which although empty, may hold something that would trigger their interest. They also decided to pack for Patsy's training event and to store enough at Alec and Jean's place to enable her to be comfortable if it became impossible for her to return.

While they were packing and removing her things, there was a knock on the door. Alec told Patsy to stay quiet as he went to answer. It was a charming young woman, one of the neighbours, asking about Patsy's missing cat and enquiring if she was aware that several local cats have now gone missing in the neighbourhood and suggesting something should be done about it. Alec showed real concern and suggested they all needed to make a statement at the local police station.

After he had shut the door he turned to Patsy and told her, "It's started, they'll try anything to find more DNA because it's worth so much they'll be ruthless in their search. They'll be checking everything from your grocery list to your bank account information." Patsy shuddered, "They'll find out that I went to Edinburgh recently when I was meant to be sick." Alec nodded and agreed, "That could mean danger for the others and Adiim especially. The best plan is to carry on as agreed tomorrow with you attending the training session which will give me time to arrange everything else." As Alec was leaving, Patsy hugged him and asked point-blank, "Dad are you really just a Banker or have you been hiding things all these years?" Alec shrugged but said nothing and Patsy allowed herself to fantasise that he was an MI5 agent which was beginning to sound less incredible every day.

As he was leaving, Alec suddenly remembered something and reached into his pocket. He gave Patsy a brand new, unregistered mobile phone on pay as you go and told her, "In future use only this phone to contact me, I have the same phone and I've programmed my number in as Darling." Patsy giggled but Alec pointed out the reason, "In future, answer my calls on this phone with the word Darling if you are unable to speak easily and I will do the same. If that happens, say whatever seems suitable and get off the phone as quickly as possible. We'll wait for a call back when the other has moved to somewhere private so that we can speak privately." Alec also suggested that Patsy should only call him from an outside location where possible in case her car and flat were bugged at any stage. Patsy's head was reeling at the thought of that, but she agreed and said she would follow his instructions to the letter.

The following morning, she rose early and set off in her car to Shropshire. She arrived at the beautiful countryside hotel at nine forty-five and immediately checked in as registration for the training was at ten-fifteen. Fortunately, the Science and Technology training centre was only a short two-minute walk from the hotel down a leafy lane. The main part of the day was quite normal, and Patsy learned some exciting and innovative research techniques.

Lunch was served in a lovely dining room and everyone was invited to have a drink at the small bar beforehand. Patsy didn't like drinking alcohol during the day and had a large orange juice with ice. In the afternoon after the final session, a young woman came into the room and handed all the candidates an envelope. Patsy opened hers immediately and found a certificate of attendance and an invitation to join the college principal for dinner that evening. As everyone in the room had received the same envelope, Patsy assumed they had all been invited for dinner. She went back to her hotel and lay in a bubble bath before dressing and putting on makeup ready for dinner. She re-read the invitation and realised it didn't give a time. Not knowing what to do she grabbed her bag and strolled back down the lane to the Training Centre. When she reached the reception desk the same young girl who'd handed out the envelopes was on duty. Patsy asked her if she knew what time she was expected for dinner with the principal and the young girl said she didn't but to wait in the bar where someone would collect her and in the meantime drinks were on the house.

There was no one else in the bar when she walked in, but the barman smiled, "Good evening Madam, what you would like to drink while you are wait for dinner?" He had a strong accent, but Patsy was unable to place it and didn't care to make small talk with him either. "A gin and tonic with lots of ice and lemon please," she requested. "Certainly, Madam, " he answered, "Please to find table and I would bring over drink to you." By now it was ten past six and as lunch had been at one o'clock, she was hungry. Not only that but she went for the salmon at lunch which turned out to be a tiny portion and not very filling. The drink was lovely and after only two big sips she could feel herself relaxing more. She'd brought a few of her notes from the training session so that she could refer to them in her conversation with the Principal and her fellow candidates from the training course.

As she went through them again, she snuggled down into the deep sofa with her G&T and felt surprisingly more relaxed than she had for a while. Without noticing she finished her first drink quite quickly and the barman came over with another immediately. She thanked him and was impressed by his efficiency, thinking she may have misjudged him and taking a long sip of her second drink which tasted even better than the first. She became lost in her own world thinking partly about the events of the last few weeks, Adiim and her surprisingly resourceful father. When the barman came over with a third drink for her she was feeling completely relaxed and enjoying that feeling. She asked him, "Do you happen to know what time dinner is being served?" "I'm sorry," he replied, "I not know Madam."

Patsy almost gulped down the third dink but gradually it dawned on her that she was still the only person in the bar, it was twenty-two minutes past eight and getting rather late for dinner. She realised she was feeling a little drunk and decided to go to the loo to freshen up. She walked as steadily as she could out of the bar and went over to the girl on reception, "Scuse me but can you tell me where the nearest loo is and what time dinner is going to be served," she slurred. The girl was surprised to see her and responded quite abruptly, "As I have already told you, you should wait in the bar until the Principal is ready." Patsy noticed the place was almost in total darkness and there certainly weren't any of her fellow candidates around. She turned back to the girl, "Aren't any of the other candidates invited?" Without looking up the girl mumbled, "No Miss you are the only one invited."

Patsy turned around and headed back in the other direction noticing a sign for the female toilet as she did so. She walked into a cubicle and locked the door behind her. Her anxiety levels were climbing as she realised, she had not only been set up but that her drinks were probably laced with something, no wonder she felt so relaxed. In a kind of panic, she reached into her handbag and grabbed a handful of caffeine pills she'd bought to take at work during her period without sleep. She gulped them down then went out and stuck her mouth under a tap and drank as much water as she could then locked herself back into the cubicle to try and pull herself together.

Just then Adiim appeared in front of her in cloud form that slowly solidified. "Are you alright Patsy?" he said in a concerned voice. He'd sensed that something was wrong and came to help her. Patsy quickly told him what was happening and that she knew she'd been drugged. Adiim made himself into the smoky image and softly melted into her body. He soon found the drugs which he cleared from her system along with effects of the alcohol and for good measure temporarily prevented any other drugs from affecting her. "Okay that is done, now I will take you home," said Adiim. "No wait," said Patsy. "I'm going to pretend to be drugged to see what happens and hopefully they won't be suspicious, which should give me the upper hand." She promised Adiim that if she thought there was any danger, she'd call his name immediately. He said he'd call back periodically to check she was alright but would stay hidden.

After a few minutes, she left the cubicle, checked her hair and makeup in the mirror then realised she probably looked a bit more together than someone drugged. She scuffled her hair slightly and remembered to stagger slightly as she made her way back to the bar. The same barman carried over another gin and tonic for her, but she pretended she was about to pass out. "Are you alright Madam," he asked her and patted her face gently. Patsy pretended to murmur something, and he tried to lift one of her eyelids. He seemed satisfied and leaned her gently against the chair back and went back behind the bar, picked up the phone and called someone. Patsy tried to keep both eyes closed as much as possible but opened them every so often to get her bearings.

There were three men including the barman, carrying her down one of the darkened corridors. Eventually, they reached a door and she felt one of them trying to balance her weight in one hand as he opened the lock. Once inside she took a quick peek and saw a consulting room like the ones found in Doctors surgeries or hospitals with a bed on one wall, a hand wash basin, a desk and three chairs. An older man came into the room and asked the others to leave. He was eventually joined by the young woman from the reception desk although Patsy pretended not to notice.

The man asked her what her name was and where she was. She told him she was Patsy and asked him if he knew where she was. He told her she must answer all his questions and she agreed. He began by asking her where she worked, which department and what she did at work. Then he asked her what the special test contained, the one that Evie had found on her desk without a label. She said she couldn't tell him because she shouldn't have taken it. He asked her what she'd taken, and she told him it was a test kit from the Lab, so she'd be sacked for stealing. The young woman laughed lightly at this and Patsy decided then and there that she didn't like her. The man told her she wouldn't be in trouble; he was the senior consultant and she had permission to take test kits home anytime she found something interesting. She smiled sleepily and said she felt better. He again asked what was in the test that she'd been working on at the lab.

Patsy churned out the same old story about the cat bringing something odd-looking into her flat. She tried to get it from him, but he ate most of it leaving just a few cells and blood on the floor. She'd opened a pack of disposable cloths, and picked up the remaining cells, placing them into an airtight container to examine them later. The man asked her why she didn't take the container to work the next day and she said she had forgotten about it until sometime during the next working day and decided to take the kit home to collect the sample in. He asked her what she'd noticed about the cells when she examined them, and she told him she knew they were unusual, but she hadn't had time to check again as the lab was busy. He asked her if she thought they were at all special, but she lied and said no.

He asked a few more mundane questions and Patsy told him she was upset because her cat disappeared, and last time she'd seen him he looked unwell. He seemed satisfied with what she had said. He called a colleague on his phone. "She's said nothing different from her previous statement about her cat catching a strange creature, she has no idea what it was or where the cat found it." He continued, "Yes, of course, it must be true, there is no way she would be able to fight against the drugs we have given to her." She couldn't hear the other side of the conversation but the old guy also told the other party, "Make sure they check for the cat alive or dead, any other cats in that block, bins, roads, fields, gardens, drains, communal areas, gutters and along the river bank and anywhere at all that a cat would go hunting." Her plan had worked, and they believed her so Adiim was safe again.

The girl lifted her head and gave Patsy a drink of water, "Here you are Miss, she said sounding disgusted," I'm afraid you have drunk too much gin and passed out." Patsy knew there was antidote in the glass and that it would do her no harm as Adiim had seen to that. The girl and one of the other men escorted her back to the hotel and she was left to find her way to her room. She told them she was a bit groggy but feeling a bit better and thanked them several times through her teeth for taking care of her.

To play safe she stayed in her room and tried to get some sleep, checking out of the hotel the next morning as expected. She drove a few miles down the road and stopped at a petrol station to fill up and call Alec. Alec already knew everything that had happened because Jean updated him. He told her Adiim had been back a few times to check she was alright without anyone being aware. She was right and they believed her although there had been forensic people all over her flat day and night and the neighbours were being pestered by them. The story they'd given to neighbours was that they feared there may be a rabid cat in the neighbourhood, and they were not to be alarmed as they would find it if the report was true. The neighbourhood was told to report any cat and submit them for testing but also to watch out for any other animals displaying unusual character traits. Alec knew they'd covered everything with a fine-tooth comb, but they had found absolutely nothing and were furious.

It was just after lunch when Patsy arrived home and although her flat appeared untouched, she felt violated and highly unsettled. She unpacked her things and threw some laundry into the machine, wishing that Adiim was there to do his trick and save her washing and drying it. She was not due back in the Lab until tomorrow morning, but she had to prepare a feedback report to present to the team and she may as well get on with it. She sat at her small desk and began typing up her notes and her mind wandered to Willam and how he would usually jump on the desk and walk between her face and the paper she was holding just to get attention. Although she missed him, she was so glad that he was safe and dreaded to think what they would have done to him if he was still in the flat. Margaret told her he was genuinely happy running around the big walled garden and chatting away to Adiim. Later, Alec called and asked her out for dinner that evening. Patsy agreed knowing he wanted to talk to her in private.

It was Mexican food tonight, Alec's choice although Patsy had never been keen on too much chilli sauce. They were pleased to see each other although it had only been a couple of days. Alec had worried for her safety and he hugged her tightly. They had a glass of wine and relaxed and as they waited for their first course, Alec took her hand. She knew this was something important and looked at him in a concerned way. "Patsy, the problem hasn't gone away, they will never let go because the potential for manufacturing drugs and treatments from Adiim's DNA is worth billions of pounds." He could see a forlorn and crestfallen look on Patsy's face as he told her, "Darling, your life will have to change dramatically and very soon." Patsy answered sincerely, "Dad, I think I already knew, I feel unhappy with my job and how they treat me and now my home has been violated, it won't be too much of a problem it's just what to do next."

Alec had a plan and explained, "First you have to get sacked from your job, then we'll sell or rent out your flat and leave London for a while." "In the meantime, I've been working on a new place for all of us to go where we can be safe. Patsy agreed and said, "I'm looking forward to giving out a few home truths at work and if I say what I feel like saying, that should give them grounds enough to fire me on the spot." They both chuckled at the idea although there was a hot stone in the pit of Patsy's stomach when she thought about it.

It had been several weeks now since Margaret and Jean had taken Adiim and Willam to live in Edinburgh. No one had come near the house and Margaret returned to her normal social calendar to avoid further suspicion. She didn't find it necessary to tell anyone that Jean and Adiim were staying with her unless the issue came up and then she would keep to the story they'd, that Adiim was the grandson of an old friend. In the meantime, Adiim was being taught to read and write by Jean and Margaret and was also self-learning IT skills in the process. Both women are remarkably good and natural teachers and Adiim was an amazingly fast learner and a keen scholar. It was difficult at times to think of Adiim as centuries-old because he looked and behaved like a young man. He was amazed by the internet and soon couldn't leave it alone, studying all kinds of things exactly like a young person of his assumed age would. He began to understand the modern world more but still baffled Jean by saying odd things that she was unable to relate to.

During a geography lesson with Margaret, Adiim stood upright from his desk with a strange look on his face. He began babbling something in another language and Margaret had to shout at him to stop. Jean rushed in from the kitchen where she'd been preparing lunch. She shook him, "Stop this Adiim, you are not making any sense." He blurted out, "Patsy is in trouble and I have to go to her immediately." They asked him to explain but he said he couldn't he just knew because he was joined to her and he didn't have time now. He promised to explain everything when he came back then faded into a smoky cloud and disappeared altogether.

Jean immediately tried to call Patsy, but her phone was switched off, so she called Alec. He answered immediately, he knew it had to be one of three people calling on that phone. He brought them up to date on where Patsy was and told them not to worry as Adiim would know what to do. Not too much later Adiim re-appeared in the kitchen as they were drinking tea. He told them what was happening, but he had to return to Patsy to make sure she was safe. He'd be staying invisible so he wouldn't spoil Patsy's plan to convince them that Willam caught the creature. After what seemed like an eternity he returned with a big smile on his face, told them everything went to plan, and Patsy was safely in bed asleep, exhausted and calmer now. They all heaved a sigh of relief and Jean rang her husband to let him know. It felt like the pressure was off although they knew someone somewhere would still be looking for the cat and the origin of the creature it had eaten.

The next morning Patsy set off for work at the usual time and stormed into the lab as though she was in a bad mood. Everyone tried to say good morning, but she just glared at them as if to say don't even speak to me. Eventually, word of her foul mood got through to Evie and she made her way over to Patsy's workstation to see what was wrong. She made sure not to give too much away but showed a new side of herself that Evie was almost afraid of. In many ways, Evie felt guilty that Patsy had been treated awfully by the organisation. Until very recently she'd been the ideal employee, dedicated to her work, resourceful and very enthusiastic. Evie knew she'd done nothing wrong but was powerless to stop the sponsors who were poking and probing her, determined to find the source of DNA that performed miracles. Her boss told her Patsy was given a truth serum during her time in Shropshire which Evie found extremely distasteful and unnecessary. She was also fully aware of the forensic science work that took place in Patsy's flat and the neighbourhood while she was away. She felt a pang of guilt for sending her to Shropshire and not being more upfront with her. She wondered if Patsy was annoyed about the intrusion on her home, or did she have some vague recollection of being drugged. Evie would never know the real reason for Patsy's anger, but she tried to talk to her.

"Patsy if there's anything wrong you can tell me, I'm your friend." Patsy thought how much of a hypocrite Evie was and suddenly launched into a tirade of bad language and shouted, "Why am I being persecuted?" She said it loudly enough so that the entire floor could hear. She followed this by shouting as loudly as she could, "what exactly was in that DNA sample that the sponsors are so bothered about?" She smashed a few things and pretended to be drunk at the same time drawing more and more attention to herself and embarrassing Evie in the process. Evie tried her best to calm her anger, but she just fed the flames and things escalated to a level where Patsy began to smash more things up and swear like a sailor. Others came over to try to calm things including Phil who thought he had a chance of getting through to her.

She pretended to be drunk and addressed the whole team," You lot need to wake up like I have and realise you are working for a rubbish organisation that persecutes staff for being innovative." Evie can take no more and tells her, "that's enough you are suspended with immediate notice and must go home." Patsy pushed on because her plan was coming together and pretended to be falling over drunk which she knew for certain is a sacking offence.

Evie was left with no option, "Okay you've gone too far now, you're fired, collect your things together and go." Patsy then smiled and turned to Evie saying, "You know what, you can stick the job up your jacksie." She grabbed her bag and wandered drunkenly out of the door smiling to herself. The faces of her old colleagues were a picture, they were shocked and couldn't believe what had happened. As Patsy walked past Phil, she realised there could be a loose end that needed closing. She stopped and looked him in the eye, telling him, "Phil, you are a boring nerd who bored the life out of me, please don't bother calling around anymore I can't stand the boredom." He grabbed her hand hurt by what she said, and Patsy felt a pang of guilt as Phil had been a great friend to her. She shook him away and told him, "Don't touch me, you make my skin creep, you're so slimy and awful." His pained look turned to an angry one and she knew the message had gone in. She turned on her heels and staggered the rest of the way out of the building and down the street, just far enough to be sure no one could see her, then broke into a run and burst out laughing.

While she waited for her bus home she called Alec and told him what had happened and he was pleased with what she had done, particularly pretending to be drunk in the Lab which was enough to make sure she didn't get asked back. He laughed when she told him what she had said although he sympathised with her regarding the loss of Phil as a friend. Arriving home, she immediately felt sad about her job and Phil, but she was unsettled in the flat now that the sponsors had poked into every nook and cranny. The neighbours were furious with her, they knew she was the cause of all their grief, although none of them knew exactly why. All Patsy knew now was that she felt unwelcome, in her own home, at the Lab and in fact in London. She lolled about the place all day and couldn't settle. Alec called her during the afternoon and said he'd be calling over and to maybe cook something for a late lunch as he had plans for the evening that could mean they wouldn't eat again until supper time.

Retreat - Chapter 7

When he arrived, they sat and ate the spaghetti Bolognese that Patsy had been cooking on a low heat and drank almost an entire bottle of sparkling water between them. Alec passed her a note that said he was almost certain that the flat was bugged and to be careful what she said. He told her she would have to leave because she would find it hard to get another job that would pay enough to stay there. His suggestion was to let the flat and for Patsy to move back to stay with her parents. Alec wrote another note saying he was going to move them all to a secret location with Adiim while they tried to decide what to do next. Patsy nodded and agreed, mainly because she didn't want to be at the flat any longer than she had to and partly because she wanted to be with the others.

Alec arranged things with his PA Diana earlier and booked an appointment with an agent who would let the flat. Diana would deal with the letting on Patsy's behalf so all they had to do was move Patsy's personal stuff out and drop off the keys. The first move was to get her things into a van and take them to Alec and Jean's house. Alec had arranged for a removals van to come over at 4:30 pm to help them pack and move. They moved swiftly and with the help of the two removals men packed everything in just over two hours. Most of it went in the van but Patsy put a few personal items in her car and the most delicate glass and china in the back of Alec's car. Back in

Wimbledon Patsy felt like she was coming home although she knew it would be short-lived. The removals guys finished unloading her things into her room and Alec called for a Chinese takeaway. "I've booked a couple of weeks off work to give me time to arrange everything so try not to worry." "My plan," he continued, "is that we take only our most essential items and enough clothing for a couple of weeks. In the morning we're heading for a remote place in East Yorkshire, very close to an abandoned village called Wharram Percy." "There's a safe house there that's used sometimes by the organisation I work for, although only my Diana knows we will be going there."

The next morning, they had a leisurely breakfast and waited for the rush hour traffic to die down then packed their things into the back of the car. They included a few other items that Jean wanted, including the vase that Adiim had been contained in. They'd discussed leaving it behind but were afraid it may contain more of Adiim's DNA which would create even more problems if it fell into the wrong hands. They set off for Yorkshire at around nine o'clock and arrived in the village in the early afternoon after an event-free journey. The house was more of a cottage which was very well hidden and extremely difficult to find but ideal for them to hide away in.

They unpacked the car and then went off to Driffield the nearest small town to buy groceries and other provisions to keep them going. Alec called Jean and told them to be packed and ready the next day, they would drive up to collect them. They would set out tomorrow morning, stay overnight in Edinburgh and then all return to Yorkshire early the following morning. Later that afternoon Alec asked Patsy, "Darling would you mind sorting out something for dinner while I go and arrange to hire a bigger car that we can all fit into comfortably?" Patsy was glad to have something to do and soon set to it. Alec drove to York which was the nearest large town and called Diana while on the way. She sounded concerned, "I hope you're alright Alec, I've arranged for a courier to drop off the documents you needed at a kiosk on the High Street that arranges money transfers." He thanked her both as her boss and as a friend.

He collected the documents without a hitch and was pleased to see new driving licences, credit card, a phone bill and electricity bill and passports for James Parsons and his daughter Anne. Although there were none of the standard background histories to go with the names, they would be fine for renting a car without using their ID.

He went and booked a people carrier from the hiring company that was big enough to carry two men, three women, a cat and all their luggage and arranged to collect it the next day. He then went to the other side of town and purchased a small motorcycle which was just small enough to fit into the back of his car with the seats down then he drove back to the cottage. When he arrived, he could hear Patsy banging about with pots and pans and if his ears weren't deceiving him, she was singing to herself. The cottage was lovely, well equipped, smartly furnished, clean as a new pin and comfortable to be in. Even the garden was beautifully kept with roses and taller flowering plants like delphiniums growing in neatly tended borders. Patsy was feeling at home and free from the recent stresses of London. They had a lovely supper then sat out in the garden with a glass of wine until the air grew too chilly. They both slept peacefully in the quiet little cottage and woke refreshed the next morning.

They climbed into Alec's car and set off to collect the people carrier, arriving just as it was time for the hire company's offices to open. On the way, Alec explained they had a new ID for the car hire. "Oh Dad, was that necessary?" she asked. "Oh yes indeed," he responded, "I think it's very necessary for now not to leave a trail just in case the sponsors are still trying to find out where you are." "How on earth did you manage to arrange that," she asked? Alec just shrugged and smiled but said nothing and Patsy let it go, at least for now. Patsy was nervous but Alec handled the contract and the payment made on the credit card under the new name went through without a hitch. He fully trusted Diana, they'd worked together for many years and he knew she was on his side no matter what.

Patsy drove the people carrier back to the cottage and Alec went off and parked his car in the barn that was attached to the back of the cottage a short way down the lane. "I think it's best if we keep my car hidden for the time being until we can be sure we're safe," he told her when he was back in the cottage. They were ready to leave so they put their overnight bags, food and drinks into the people carrier and set off for Edinburgh, taking it in turns to share the four and a half-hour drive.

When they arrived Adiim was so excited to see Patsy and couldn't wait to tell her everything he'd learned. Willam also heard Patsy's voice and came running in from the garden where he'd been sunning himself on top of the potting shed as usual. She hugged them both and eventually managed to break away and give her mother and grandmother a hug too.

They had a marvellous dinner that evening out in the garden and used up as much of the fresh food from the fridge and larder as possible. Adiim made delicious bread, pastries and small cakes, some of them to be used for the journey back to Yorkshire.

Willam was lucky enough to get sardines and some liver pate that needed eating up. He believed he was having a special feast because Patsy had arrived. When Adiim relayed this everyone had a good laugh and Margaret who was nearest picked him up and hugged him.

The next morning, they had a light breakfast and while Adiim and Alec packed everything into the car the three women went around the house tidying up and making sure nothing incriminating was left around. To be on the safe side Margaret decided to take any books and papers from her library that referred to the family and their ancestry. As she was doing it, she felt a sudden pang in her chest that she put down to anxiety and fear that she may never be able to come back to the house that she loved so much.

As she was about to close the door to the library, she saw a lovely framed photograph of her beloved husband Andrew which she tucked into her bag with the books and papers. Despite the size of the hired vehicle, their bags took up an enormous amount of space, so they had to slot things between seats. It was suggested that for the first leg of the journey Alec would drive and Adiim would take the front passenger seat. Not far down the road, Margaret burst into song and to Alec and Adiim's astonishment, Patsy and Jean joined in. Some of the songs were a little risqué and included putting a finger in a woodpecker hole and an old woman of ninety-two. Alec was quite surprised and delighted to hear Jean loosening up and pretended to be disgusted at first but eventually, he couldn't help but laugh and join in with them. Even Adiim who'd never heard the songs before quickly caught on and joined in which caused Patsy to go into a great fit of laughter that hurt her sides. Poor Willam was in a basket in the back trying to get some sleep but he knew everyone was happy and feeling far less tension, so he didn't mind the noise at all.

They arrived at the cottage, unpacked and Patsy took them on a grand tour of the house and garden. Everyone had to agree that the cottage was very lovely. Willam was slightly nervous of new, unexplored territory and he would have to check it out thoroughly with his nose before he could feel comfortable. He told Adiim he was excited by their new garden with lovely tall plants that he could hide in and a large variety of birds visiting.

They made a nice lunch after which Margaret yawned saying, "I hope no one minds but I'm going for an afternoon nap because getting up early and the long journey has quite worn me out." Everyone smiled and said it was a good idea so off she went up to her neat and bright little room at the front of the house and fell asleep as soon as her head touched the downy pillow. In the meantime, Alec decided to sweep out the hire car and check his car over in the barn. Jean was washing all the crockery and glass-wear from all the cupboards. "I just want to be certain that everything is as clean as we want it to be," she said, even though everyone else knew it was.

Adiim and Patsy were setting up the laptop computers as there was no IT connection at the cottage so they would have to use pay as you go modems that Patsy referred to as dongles, much to Adiim's amusement. She was impressed by his understanding of technology after such a short time of being exposed to it. He seemed to have learned it like a young child and was already finding his way around things that Patsy hadn't managed to get around to yet. Once they managed to get three laptops "online" they began researching the local area. Willam decided he would try venturing a short way along the garden path to check things out but not so far that he couldn't dash back into the cottage if danger threatened him. Before long, the sun was setting, and Jean went to wake Margaret with a cup of tea. When she tried to rouse her from her sleep, she was dismayed to find that her mother was extremely sick and couldn't answer. Jean had a feeling she'd had a stroke and she could see the fear in her eyes as she tried desperately to speak. "Mother please try not to get stressed and lie still while I go and fetch Alec and Patricia," said Jean. Margaret knew exactly what had happened to her and was very afraid. She'd laid in bed for about two hours like this and hadn't been able to speak or move enough to let the others know. Most of all she was afraid she was going to be a burden to them and would need medical help that would draw attention to the family that was trying so hard to be private.

When Jean returned with Alec a frightened-looking Patsy was close on his heels. Alec quickly established that Margaret could both hear and understand what they were saying. "Margaret dear," he told her, "I know you can understand us so don't try to speak, for now, just blink once for yes, twice for no and I'll ask questions." As they were fussing over Margaret and trying to decide how to call a doctor, Margaret noticed Adiim peeking into the room with a concerned look on his face. He knew what had happened and used his thoughts to speak directly to Margaret and she answered his questions. She told him she had a blood clot that had starved her brain of oxygen and had caused it to stop working. This was the part of her brain that enabled her to talk and to control most of her body. He let her know that he could heal her and repair anything that was broken or worn out inside her, but he would have to pass into her like smoke.

Margaret immediately agreed to this but asked Adiim to explain to the family what they had discussed. When Adiim spoke, the others were so frantic with worry that at first, they didn't hear him, but he quietly repeated himself until Alec realised what he'd said and shushed the others. All three of them agreed and Alec confirmed with Margaret through blinking that she both consented and wanted Adiim to try and help her.

Within seconds Adiim had melted into a smoky image of himself and then disappeared. They watched in awe, particularly at Margaret's face as she visibly relaxed and her eyes closed. Then something remarkable happened, her face began to look younger, her skin looked bright and new and even her hair which was grey but thick and curly began to regain its colour and turned back to the luscious shiny black of her younger days. When Adiim reappeared, the others were startled but then Margaret opened her bright younger-looking eyes and a big grin appeared on her face. She stretched as though she'd just woken from a long sleep and announced, "I feel wonderful and better than I have in years."

Patsy couldn't believe the transformation, she looked twenty years old and even her voice sounded young again. Adiim was delighted with everyone's reaction and not at all affected by the process. Margaret threw back the bedclothes and dashed over to the mirror to have a good look at herself. "Oh, my goodness, I look beautiful and just as I did when I was twenty years old," she trilled. She burst into tears and hugged Adiim tightly which disturbed him slightly. "Margaret, why are you crying, did I do something bad," he asked? He just couldn't understand the tears. "Don't be silly Adiim," Margaret explained, "I'm crying because I feel so happy." He leaned back and looked at her face saying, "what a crazy woman you are," and then laughed out loud hugging her tightly.

Patsy tapped Adiim on the arm and asked, "Just one thing before we all get too excited, how long will these effects last?" Adiim explained, "She is well and returned to her best condition, but she will still begin to age again in the normal way." Everyone agreed that was fantastic and hugged Margaret. Later while they were eating dinner and trying to get used to a Grandmother who looked younger than any of them, Alec had an idea. While the others chatted away excitedly, he ran through different scenarios in his mind. Eventually Jean noticed that he hadn't spoken for a while. "Alec Dear, is there anything wrong," she asked, perhaps slightly worried?

They were all suddenly concerned about him and turned and waited to hear what it was. Alec explained, "I'm still concerned that the sponsors from Patsy's lab will be searching for us, so we need to stay hidden for a long time to avoid Adiim being caught and abused by them." "Margaret's transformation has made me realise that if Adiim could do that same with all of us and make us younger, no one would be looking for a group of young people and it would help us to stay hidden." Everyone thought it was a great idea although Patsy flatly refused to do it herself. She had concerns and asked, "How would we be able to manage finances and driving licences or passports and anything else that requires photo ID?" Alec told them, "Look, it may be hard to believe but I have a contact who could arrange new ID's for all of us and I have a secure bank account that we can draw money from and pay for what we need." Margaret, smiled and stroked his face saying, "You are almost as mysterious as my dear husband, did he teach you?" Alec said nothing as was his way, but he smiled sweetly, and Patsy nudged him in the ribs playfully. The two women secretly winked at each other knowingly, but Jean remained oblivious to the whole thing.

So, it was agreed that Jean and Alec would allow Adiim to change their appearance back to twenty-year-olds, Patsy would stay as she was and she and Adiim would use hair bleach and makeup to change their appearances. Within half an hour Jean and Alec stood in front of the large mirror in the hall staring at their new look. Jean's hair was even more lustrous than Margaret's and both women could have been easily taken for sisters, even twins. Most surprising of all was Alec, his balding head and thinning hair returned to a thick glossy brown that needed cutting. He'd regained his muscular body and although he'd tried his best to stay in shape throughout the years, he now looked fit.

None of them had the right clothing for that generation and so that evening Patsy shared some of her limited wardrobe with the two women and they decided to drive to Hull the next day to buy clothes and get Alec's haircut. They needed makeup and hair dye, glasses and a few other props that would help to disguise Patsy and Adiim. The whole idea of it seemed to be getting more like an adventure every day. Alec couldn't drive the hire car without the correct ID and for now, it had to stay that way, which made Patsy feel like the only responsible adult. She realised her family now looked like a group of young people on holiday and although she was only twenty-five, she suddenly looked and almost felt like the oldest.

The next day they went shopping in stores and boutiques around the city centre while Alec and Adiim were at the barbershop. They agreed to pretend to be sisters and they also went to have their hair styled. Margaret and Jean received advice on modern makeup techniques which Patsy couldn't help sniggering about.

When they met up with the men at lunchtime all five of them looked amazing including Alec and Adiim who both sported a modern hairstyle that was noticeably short at the sides, longer on top and flicked over to the side. Jean and Margaret had their curly hair cut, straightened and styled and looked like glamorous fashion models.

Patsy kept to her normal style but had a trim then lots of blonde highlights and a spray tan which went against the grain, but she knew she had to change her look. Margaret tried to tell her she looked great, but Jean said nothing about it and that told Patsy she didn't approve. She tried to explain the reason for her extreme style, but it was falling on deaf ears. Adiim grabbed her hand and told her he loved it and that she looked like a lady from the TV. They all had a good laugh and went to have coffee before continuing the big shopping spree.   They ended the day with a large assortment of T-shirts, jeans, trainers, coats, jackets, shoes, dresses, skirts, sunglasses, handbags, sweaters and a collection of sportswear.   When they arrived back at the cottage, they systematically gathered up all their old clothes ready to go to a charity shop.

Adiim and Patsy kept most of theirs because they hadn't changed their appearance or age and the clothes were entirely appropriate. Margaret's only salute to her old style was a series of garish hats that she insisted on buying, although they were modern and none of them looked at all like cushions. Willam returned from the garden and was curious but they all smelled like themselves, so he wasn't perturbed. He knew he had a lovely marmalade coat and didn't understand why anyone would want to change themself.

It was already evening so they had a few drinks and there was a party atmosphere. Patsy played music from her iPod and everyone danced, including Jean after they told her she had to behave like a twenty-year-old not a seventy-year-old. She was furious with this suggestion so she decided to show them all what she could do. After a while, she enjoyed herself more than ever before and crashed into Alec's lap laughing and giggling more like a teenager. Margaret was leaping around like a lunatic, but she looked so grateful to have a second chance at youth she wasn't going to waste it. Patsy had to pinch herself from time to time when she realised she was having a party with her family and she felt like the responsible adult; how ironic she thought. Eventually, they wore themselves out and everyone went to bed when it was getting light. Adiim was beginning to look at Patsy differently and could feel things that made him afraid of himself, but for now, he said nothing, and he knew he would cope.

The next morning after breakfast Alec told them all to get dressed in their best clothes because they all needed photographs taken for their new ID. Alec asked them to sit down at the kitchen table while they worked out what to do next. "We need to decide what our temporary identities will be, how we're related and where we come from." Margaret immediately insisted, "I want to be Sarah after my grandmother." Alec explained he would become

Alexander because he knew Jean wouldn't be able to stop calling him Alec in an absent-minded way. At least that way everyone would think she was saying Alex. After a bit of thought, Jean decided she rather liked the name, Julia. "We should choose a fairly common surname such as Smith," suggested Alec. Jean thought Evans was less common and more acceptable. So, it was decided they would be Mr and Mrs Evans and the three women would be sisters named Julia Evans (nee Jones) Sarah and Patricia Jones. Now they only had to decide what name to give to Adiim. With his Middle Eastern looks, he needed a name that reflected those origins. An amazing linguist, he'd become so expert in speaking English that he could have been born in London. Alec suggested he's from a Turkish family who've been living in London for several generations and has an English mother who named him Adam.

It was agreed that he'd be Adam Osman. In all the years he'd lived, Adiim had never had any other name. "I like it," he announced, "most of the time I am certain British people will call me Adam anyhow, so I won't have to correct them." Everyone agreed and Alec was pleased with what was decided. "I think you should pretend to be Patsy's boyfriend too, said Alec. Both Patsy and Adiim nodded to each other in complete agreement and the matter was settled.

Alec then spent the rest of the afternoon on the laptop sending the photographs and names to his PA Diana using a top security email address. The arrangement as before, with him collecting them from the money transfer kiosk in

York. Diana persuaded him against that and instead set up a PO Box in Hull and arranged for the keys to be sent to Alec so that he could then pick up the documents. Diana was confused by the edited pictures Alec sent to her. They made everyone look younger and she wondered how that could work but she trusted him. Alec sensed stress in her voice when he spoke to her, but they had a specific protocol, a practised coding system used to let the other know there was a problem. She hadn't used any of the coded references, so he just asked her outright if she was okay. She told him there were no problems, but she had a vague niggling feeling at the back of her mind. He told her to try not to worry and thanked her several times for everything she'd done for him and his family. She just told him to take care and said a gentle bye.

The next afternoon Alec received a call from Diana. "Hello young Alex," she said and chuckled lightly, "If you go to your favourite kiosk there will be a package waiting for you that will include a key and a coded address for you to pick up your items!. "Thank you so much flower," he replied, "I owe you an excessively big favour." "Your bank account will be ready on Friday," she continued," "after that, you'll be on your own for a while, so please take care of yourself and the others." They said a quick bye and hung up. Alec couldn't help thinking he may have also put Diana in the firing line, but he had little choice and she knew he'd do the same for her anytime.

The next morning Patsy drove Alec to the kiosk to collect the package containing the key. For one tiny moment, he almost signed himself Alec Miller until he realised he already had an earlier temporary set of ID documents. He opened the package in the hire car, and they drove to the Mailbox shop where his PO Box had been set up. He didn't acknowledge the guy behind the counter and went directly to the box to collect his items. Patsy was waiting in the car and they drove back to the cottage without opening them.

They left the city and a few miles on turned onto one of the side roads back to the village. Patsy was surprised when a sporty looking Mercedes turned after them. She didn't say anything to Alec at first, but she made sure to have a good look at the driver and his passenger. It was a dark-haired man in his thirties and a blonde woman who looked about forty-five. She slowed down slightly, and Alec looked at her suddenly. "What's wrong Patsy," he asked? "I think we are being followed, Dad," she told him. "Okay don't go back to the cottage, at the junction where we normally turn left, go straight on, it will take us to Driffield." As they were driving along, Alec opened the package and started pushing the passports and other documents into the pockets in the back of his seat. He told Patsy, "When we get to the newsagent in the town, I want you to pull into the car park next to it. I'll jump out and I want you to turn around and drive back towards the cottage but stop at the pub called the Dog and Fox and wait there until I come to you." "But what if" Patsy started to say when Alec cut her off. "I told you," he said firmly, "I'll meet you there in less than an hour now off you go, and don't forget to lock the car when you go inside."

Patsy stopped as agreed, Alec leapt out in one action and Patsy turned the car sharply and headed back down the lane. Looking in the mirror she saw the woman jump out and the guy turned and followed her back down the lane but at a slower pace. Patsy rammed her foot down and sped off down the country lanes praying nothing was coming in the other direction. Lucky for her, a tractor, pulled out from a nearby field just as she sped past. The farmer shook his fist and swore at her as he parked up to close the gate to his field. The swish Mercedes pulled up behind his tractor, the driver tooting his horn impatiently. This only served to annoy the farmer, he glared at the driver and made sure to take even longer to close the gate, checking each wheel on the tractor before he climbed back into the seat and resumed driving slowly along the lane. Patsy was delighted with her luck and drove into the pub car park, making sure to park right around the rear of the building. Luckily, she had money with her to buy a drink and she needed it too.

In the meantime, after Alec leapt from the car, he deliberately wafted the empty package around. He went into the newsagent and walked to the tiny post office counter at the rear. He was aware of the blonde woman who followed him in. He leaned on a shelf to the side, peeled the labels off the package and wrote a new name and address on the empty package, went over to the counter and asked to post it for special delivery. He knew they'd have a hard time finding the old house he was born in as it was knocked down more than thirty-five years ago, but he still remembered the full address and postcode. He was aware of the woman watching him the whole time as she pretended to select a birthday card with "Mother" on the front.

When Alec had finished at the post office counter, he pretended to be shopping until the woman had no choice but to pay for the birthday card. As soon as she went to the front counter, Alec rushed out of the front door and ran at great speed down the lane in the opposite direction to Patsy. However, he knew Driffield town quite well by now and he swiftly turned down an alley at the side of a row of terraced houses. He was as fit as when he was at University and could run at quite a speed. He knew the woman was much older than him and would never be able to catch him. He climbed a gate into a field and ran around two sides keeping near to the hedge so he couldn't be spotted.

Eventually, he could see the pub just a short way down the hill and allowed himself to slow to a trot. When he was near, he carefully looked up and down the lane and then nipped over the road and round the back to the car park. He soon found the car, so he knew Patsy had arrived and there was no sign of the Mercedes. "Good girl," he said to himself as he walked through to the bar, only then realising, he was soaked with sweat. Patsy was relieved to see him and quickly ordered him a double scotch and soda on the rocks, just the way he liked it. Patsy told him about the tractor and Alec filled her in about the Post Office and his marathon. They both laughed but knew they'd had a lucky escape. Patsy asked why he bothered to post the package. "They are going to waste precious time trying to find out what was in it and where I sent it," he told her. "We won't be able to stay at the cottage but at least we have our ID sorted so it's just a question of where to go next," he told her trying to stay positive. "In the meantime," said Patsy, "I think it's best if we don't mention any of this to the others because they'll be worried." Alec agreed and they drank the rest of their drinks in silence.

No one was around when they left the pub, but Patsy took them on a detour all around the village in case they were being watched before finally heading back to the cottage. "We have to get rid of this hire car" Alec pointed out as they turned into the driveway. Patsy agreed, "We'll take it back first thing tomorrow and sort out an alternative at the same time in both our new names."

The next morning while everyone was examining their new passports to see where they were born, Adiim was smiling happily because he'd never had an ID before. Alec explained about exchanging the hire car as it wasn't fair to leave Patsy to do all the driving and it was booked under the previous alias. They had to lose that hire car contract before they could get rid of that ID. No one thought anything of it and Alec and Patsy set off just after eight-thirty, driving a long-winded route back to York to avoid the area where they were followed the day before. They dropped off the car without a hitch and then walked across the town trying to find another hire company where they could use their new ID.

When they reached the town centre Alec went to a cash machine to check the balance of his account. He was shocked to see that the balance was zero. Then he remembered that Diana had set up a new bank account in his new name Alex Evans, so he tried his new bank card in the machine. The balance in that account was also zero. He told himself to calm down, that money was between accounts and Diana had said it wouldn't be ready for him until Friday.

The problem with that was it was Friday today. Maybe the money won't go in until close of play or something he argued with himself. Patsy had been waiting on the corner for him and when she looked over, she could see by his face that no money was ever coming out of that machine. "Hey Dad," what about that credit card you gave to me recently in the name of Anne Parsons," she asked? "Okay let's try it," he said and beckoned to her.

Luckily, it worked, and Patsy drew out the daily maximum which was three hundred pounds. They carried on walking and eventually found another hire company. This time Patsy took the lead and sorted out the contract on her credit card in her old Alias but she was also able to add Alex Evans as a named driver and he showed his new driving licence and passport which went through without a hitch. They drove back to the cottage wondering what to do next, especially if Alec had no money.

During the last few weeks, Margaret and Patsy had both offered to pay for things but Alec asked them not to use their bank cards as it would leave a clear trail of where they'd been. Alec dropped Patsy off and then drove off towards the village pretending to go to the shop for something he'd forgotten.

He pulled into a layby about two miles from the cottage and called Diana. She answered the call with "Good day to you sir." Immediately Alec knew she was being watched or listened to, so he pretended to be Professor Edwards which was part of their agreed code. Diana asked, "Is this about my son, is everything alright?" "I'm afraid it is," said Alec in a stuffy old man's voice, his fees have not been paid again and we have checked a couple of times to make sure we have the correct information." "Well," said Diana in an indignant tone, "I arranged for the normal transfer of funds into his bank so I can only assume that the problem has occurred since then at my son's bank." "In that case," said Alec in the old professor voice, "I apologise for disturbing you and I will speak directly to your son, Good day." "It was about my son's school, what a rude man," said Diana to the male colleague sitting directly next to her as he was systematically going through her computer files. "As I was saying," said the man, "This is just a routine audit of systems and nothing to worry about." Diana knew only too well what it was, but they'd have to get up early to catch out a couple of old pros like Alec and herself.

Cash shortage - Chapter 8

Alec was shocked to find his bank account had been frozen because there was no other way for any of them to get hold of money. From the coded conversation he knew that Diana had done her part and transferred the money so someone must have been watching the account and had the transfer stopped. He had no idea what to do next and he was also worried about Diana.

While he drove along, he wondered if he'd caused any problems for her, he knew from that call that he couldn't call her again and she was being closely watched. He drove around aimlessly for almost an hour until he realised the same Mercedes was behind him following from enough distance that he couldn't see the driver. "That's all I need," he said out loud and planned his next move.

He reached a T junction at the end of the lane and indicated left. At the last minute, he swerved right and sped off as fast as he could. The other driver had seen him indicate left, but he turned sharply right so they knew he'd spotted them following him. Alec was driving blindly and couldn't lose them, so he tried to calm himself down and pulled into yet another country pub car park.

The Labour in Vain, was busy, serving lunchtime drinks and food. Alec ordered a pint of beer and was paying for it when the young dark-haired man and his blonde female friend arrived at the bar across from him. He pretended not to notice and asked the barman where the loo was. Leaving his beer on the counter he nipped out to the loo at the side of the bar. He was glad to see a large window at ground level, so he pulled one of the cubicle doors closed and quickly jumped out of the window taking care to close it behind him as he dropped off the ledge. As soon as his feet hit the floor, he ran at full speed down the garden at the back of the pub. He went over the fence at the bottom, through another garden where an old lady was bedding out wallflowers, over her fence and away across a field of rapeseed. He continued to run for a good twenty minutes until he reached a lane that looked familiar.

He carried on down the lane until he reached a telephone box. Dashing inside he was relieved to find it working and he quickly called Patsy's mobile phone. Although he was out of breath, he managed to tell her what happened and read the address of the phone box out to her. "Get the keys to my car and come and meet me, Darling," he told her. To add to the address he'd given to her, he also told her he could see a windmill near him on the hill. "Don't worry Dad," she told him, "I'm on my way." She grabbed a laptop from the sitting room and told Adiim to follow her quickly as it was an emergency.

They opened the doors to the barn and Patsy reversed out, waiting for Adiim to close them again before jumping in. "I want you to look at local maps on the internet and see if you can find a windmill," she said to Adiim. "Do you mean they still use windmills," he asked in astonishment? "No, it's more like a museum or sometimes people convert them into houses and live there" she responded. It took Adiim no time at all to find the right place on the map and he began to try and describe it to her. It just didn't work, and they were becoming more confused than anything else. "Well, said Adiim, "If you let me use Giin magic I can find Alec easily." Patsy smacked herself on the forehead for being so dumb. "Yes, let's go!

Adiim quickly began giving her directions and after only a few minutes they were driving towards the telephone box and a wildly waving Alec. During the drive back to the cottage, they discussed the situation and agreed they had to get away from this area. Patsy suggested they shouldn't worry the others, but Alec said they had a right to know. While they all sat together and ate lunch, Alec went through the current problems they were facing and held nothing back. Jean was most worried about having no access to money and became almost hysterical.

Fortunately, Margaret had a more pragmatic approach, " I think the easiest thing to do by far would be to access my savings account and the safety deposit box that Andrew had set up for me, it contains at least two thousand pounds and is there for exactly this type of emergency," she suggested. "Thank you for your very kind offer," said Alec, "but how would a young person named Sarah Jones gain access to the box or the bank account without drawing attention? Not to be outsmarted Margaret responded, "what about all my jewellery, it must be worth quite a bit?" "We all have things that we could sell," chipped in Jean. Alec had to agree that it was a possible short-term solution, but it wouldn't keep them all going for long. Adiim suddenly stood up and asked Alec if he would come out to the garden as he had something he wanted to talk about. The three women looked at each other wondering what it could be. Once they were halfway down the garden, Adiim stopped so that they could talk. "As you know, Patsy has asked me not to use Giin magic unless she has agreed to it," he began. Since then I have tried to keep to this because it was her wish, but I am also sworn to protect her, and I will always use any power I can to do this if I need to." "I understand that," Alec responded, "but what are you trying to say?" Adiim glanced towards the house to make sure no one could hear. "I know Patsy would never let me produce money by magic but in years past the Giin were used to help find lost things, including treasure and lost jewels that are often buried under the ground." "This is something I can do, and we can sell the treasure" Alec was heartened by the idea and he could, at last, see a way out of their current predicament. "Okay, we can begin this afternoon while the weather is good. I'll go and explain to the others, fetch a spade from the barn and we'll see what we can find."

Adiim walked purposefully across a field opposite the cottage and stopped when he reached the right spot. Alec began digging and up came a rotted leather pouch with fifteen old Roman coins inside it. Alec was delighted with their first haul. "This way," said Adiim and set off again through a five-bar gate and diagonally across another field. He stopped again and told Alec this one was nearer the surface.

He was right and up came three gold bangles with intricate designs wound around them. Alec scooped them up and popped them into his jacket pocket and as he did so Adiim set off again towards the back of the field. He pointed to a spot under the hedge and again Alec dug out the treasure which this time looked like a Victorian engagement ring that had been lost many years before. "I think that's enough for today," declared Alec, "if we have too many things it will be hard to sell them." They walked back to the cottage which was only a stone's throw away and Alec wondered how many people had been past these things without knowing they were there.

Back at the cottage, Patsy cleaned the items under the tap at the kitchen sink and everyone gathered around to have a good look at them. "Now we have to decide where and how to sell them," she noted? Adiim was ahead of her and he brought over the laptop to show a website with a slogan, "We pay top rates for your gold" and located in Driffield, the nearby market town. Alec was looking at his laptop and suddenly announced, "Unfortunately some of these things are rare items and must be declared as treasure." "In other words, they are worth nothing to us and unfortunately we have fifteen days to declare them by law after which we may be offered a reward, but it has to be agreed by the landowner first." Adiim didn't understand and was almost angered by what Alec said.

In the end, Jean decided she would take them into York and hand them in at the museum. "I could just tell them I found them while out walking across the Dales with my metal detector and that way the local owners of these fields would not need to be contacted." Alec agreed that was a good idea although he felt guilty that from the view of an archaeologist, they would be corrupting the history of those items, but they had little choice. "There will almost certainly be a reward and a big fuss made so you will have to be careful. They will also want to know where you found them, so we need to buy a map and mark it for them," said Alec almost bitterly. "At least the ring looks Victorian," said Jean, "so perhaps we can sell that." Adiim had become noticeably quiet and Patsy knew he was seething with anger, so she took him into the kitchen to talk to him. "I don't understand why we can't sell the gold," he blurted out. Patsy sat him down and explained the whole thing about treasure and hallmarks and the reason for them. Although he better understood he was still upset that he hadn't been able to help as much as he'd wanted.

He said he was okay then went through to the study and began researching British hallmarks on one of the laptops. When he'd finished his research, Adiim found Alec and Patsy sitting together discussing how to sell the ring. "I know where there is more gold and it has the hallmarks of England so we could sell it," he announced. "Is it legitimate though?" asked Alec. "It has been left behind or lost in time, not stolen if this is what you mean," replied Adiim indignantly. "I'm sorry," said Alec, "I wasn't suggesting you would steal, only that you knew where it came from." "There is only one problem," he replied, "It is in a place quite far from here." "How far away," asked Patsy? "That does not matter, if you allow me to go there with GIIN magic, it will take only minutes," answered

Adiim. Patsy could see the look on Alec's face and knew she would have a big argument on her hands if she didn't agree to it, so she just nodded. In seconds, a grinning Adiim folded his arms against himself holding the front of his shoulders as he faded into a cloud of swirling sand or smoke. "I just hope he knows what he's doing," said Patsy. "Give the lad credit for some intelligence," said Alec then he began to laugh, "Lad, he's thousands of years old." They both had a chuckle about it because they knew they sometimes treated him like a young teenage boy.

Adiim was already soaring over the Mediterranean and over the land that is now named Israel until he dropped down onto the top of a craggy mountain in the desert next to the Dead Sea. There was a small hole in the top of the mountain and Adiim had no difficulty squeezing through it as a cloud of smoke. He dropped down into an enormous cavern and his image began to solidify again. Although the cave was enormous, the walls and ceiling were coated with crystals that bounced around and shared out the light that came in from the hole that Adiim entered through. The entire place was stacked with gold and jewels, some of the items were huge, including statues and chests made entirely from gold, there were stacks of coins and sparkling diamonds, rubies, sapphires, emeralds and lapis lazuli everywhere.

The scene to any human would have been breath-taking but Adiim had been here many times in the past and he was glad that everything was still there. The cave, a holy place to the Giin in centuries gone by, where their treasures were stored. According to their folk law, the treasures stored are for the day when the Giin are released from slavery so that there will be enough to begin their lives of freedom. There is also a gateway to Deo Jagah, the Giin world, inside the cave but Adiim had never found any sign of it.

He had been born in the human world as his father was human and was a great Pharaoh, but his mother was a female Giin or rather Giiniri. It was considered a terrible sin from both tribes and his mother's tribe had decreed that neither of them was permitted to enter the Giin world. Both had been sold as slaves when he was only a small boy and he had never seen his mother again since that time. After many years Adiim discovered that his father had been struck from power and stoned to death. His mother had always told him that they couldn't help their great love for each other and that he should never be ashamed of who he was because he was the result of deep and pure love. They were two people who sacrificed everything to be together, even for a short time. Although he was saddened by the long-ago memories, he decided he was lucky, and he now had a new life in the modern world with people who he knew loved him. They'd put themselves into danger and disrupted their entire lives just to keep him safe and now he'd make sure they could have what they needed.

He began searching through the treasure, collecting rings and bangles, bracelets and items that would be easier to sell. He laid them all out on one of the flat rocks and using Giin magic embossed them all with English hallmarks, making sure to vary them so that they would not cause anyone to suspect or doubt them. He found a small basket made from rushes, perfectly preserved in the cave's atmosphere, and put all the items into it. Although the hallmarks were completely new, Adiim was careful to ensure they looked at least a hundred years old. The items he had selected wouldn't look out of place in the modern world and he was delighted with them. He tied the basket to his belt, folded his arms up with his hands on his shoulders as before and faded into dust and smoke finding his way through the hole in the mountain and back over the sea.

When he arrived back at the cottage, Patsy was still waiting for him, but Alec had gone to get his car out of the barn as he was plotting another idea. Adiim gave the basket to Patsy and she counted out two diamond rings, one sapphire ring, two ruby rings with beautiful stones and six bangles made from solid gold. All of them were hallmarked and everything looked right except for the reed basket that looked as though it had been made by a skilled tribesman from the Kalahari Desert or something. "Don't worry, these things were hidden by someone more than a lifetime ago, they have been forgotten in time and we won't have any problems if we try to sell them," he assured her.

Just then Alec came back into the cottage and was pleased to see all the items spread out on the kitchen table. He picked each one up and checked it for hallmarks and was delighted with them. "I've already asked if they're hot, Adiim says they were hidden by someone long ago to avoid them being stolen, so no one will be looking for them." "Fantastic," declared Alec, "now all we have to do is sell them for the right price." "I'm going to sell the first lot," said Patsy, "I've even planned how to do it."

Patsy ran through her idea speaking in an Essex accent as she did so. "Look, Babe," she said wearing her designer sunglasses. "I'm only here on my hols from Essex," she announced. She lifted her sunglasses to tell them, "I'll be wearing the right clothes and loads of jewellery, and I go to a goldsmith to sell a few things because my car has broken down." "Babes," she continued, "You've gotta help me, my credit cards are maxed out and I need some cash to get my BM fixed; will you buy some of my bling?" She lifted her sunglasses again saying, "I'll pretend to be stressed and worried about how I'll get home and what my boyfriend Darren will say when he finds out. Alec burst out laughing for a while before Patsy realised Jean had been standing behind her the whole time with a stern look on her face. "What an awful accent," said Jean, "It's perfect and I'm sure they will be completely convinced by it." She cupped Patsy's face in her hands and kissed her then laughed. Both Patsy and Alec thought how much Jean had mellowed recently, was it because she felt younger?

When they were happy that Patsy would be able to sell at least some of the gold, Alec told them he had another plan that would help them. He took Adiim outside and the others followed. "This car is a boring standard edition Volvo with grey paint and black leather and grey interior." "Yes, I see that," said Adiim puzzled. Well, I want it to be black paint and have a red leather interior, can you do that with Giin magic?" "It is done," announced Adiim and in a split second the car had changed. Alec could hardly believe it and opened one of the doors to look inside. Everything looked fantastic except that absolutely everything inside the car was now covered in bright red leather, including the carpets and the whole dashboard, buttons, steering wheel, everything. "Oh! Can you put the inside back how it was," said Alec dismayed? Adiim nodded and the familiar black and grey interior returned. "This time," said Alec trying to be more precise," the colour red should be like red wine and only the parts that are black leather should be changed to the red leather." That looked so much better, but the carpet didn't look quite right, and it was slightly worn and grubby. "Can you make the carpet the same colour red but not leather, just change the colour and if you can, make it like new again," Alec asked in a more enquiring tone? Now the whole car looked amazing as though it just came off the production line and it even had that new smell. By now the whole family was outside pawing over the new looking car and complimenting Adiim on how wonderful it looked. At least we can use it for now, but the registered owner will still be Alec Miller if the police check the registration. "I'm still working on that one," said Alec.

Eventually, the women went back inside so Alec took advantage of the situation to talk to Adiim about logbooks and how they worked. He explained about the driver and vehicle licencing agency DVLA, in Swansea, South Wales and how it holds all the information on all cars and their drivers, including the make and colour of the car. He explained the special numbers on the engine and in other places around the car that Alec showed to him. "So, this is like hallmarks for cars," he asked? "Well," said Alec, "I suppose in a way it is." "So, all of this is to help the police to stop anyone stealing cars," said Adiim? "It's also to make sure everyone is safe and that the car they own has been made correctly and has insurance and that the person driving has a licence that shows they are allowed to drive in case of an accident." "Adiim I want to ask you something," said Alec, turning him and himself away from the house so they couldn't be heard. "What I want to discuss is not strictly legal and we could get into trouble if anyone found out. Also, Patsy and Jean would be very against this idea." Adiim looked concerned but he just nodded. "Do you think you would be able to go to the DVLA and change all the records to show that the legal owner of the car is Alex Evans and that the car is black outside with a red leather interior and also give it a new registration?" Adiim said he was sure he could do most of those things, but he didn't know what the registration was. Alec showed him the number plate and explained that every car had a unique number.

Adiim thought about it for a while and then asked Alec, "Why do you want me to go to this Swansea when we have computers here with information available on them?" "Well," he answered, "That is called hacking. It takes a great deal of knowledge and skill to be able to break into the computer systems of an organisation like DVLA by using your laptop computer at home and hackers when they are caught get sent to prison." "Alec," he responded, `` we already are breaking laws, we have a false identity and false credit cards, we have false addresses on driving licences and I haven't been taught to drive a car so I shouldn't have a licence at all." Alec couldn't argue with him on this one and he looked down at the floor with frustration and slight despair. Adiim could feel his tension.

Saddened by it he put one arm over Alec's shoulder and said, "I owe you and your family everything and you've all done so many things to try to keep me safe. You've had to leave your homes and jobs and now you've lost your identities and are worried about money, but I have powers and skills that can easily help you if you let me." "My purpose is to serve Patsy and her family, I may be new to modern technology but I have been here for thousands of years and I have other knowledge that will allow me to do everything you ask if you will trust me." For once Alec felt like the youngster and Adiim took charge of the situation without creating any dividing line between them and he was impressed. Over the next few days, Alec spent a great deal of time with Adiim to teach him about all the agencies in the UK that would be holding records on the family so that he could change them all and at the same time create records for his own identity. After the second day when they went to the Po Box they had set up, they'd already received the replacement logbook for the car with the private registration of JUI 14, Adiim's birth certificate showing him as Adam Osman, born in Wood Green, London, to an English mother and Turkish father. It used the date he was released from the vase as his birth date and his year of birth as 1995 making him twenty-five years old. The marriage certificate for Alex and Julia also turned up in the same batch. Adiim had already changed the number plate on the car, confident in the knowledge that the records already existed.

After checking the PO Box, Margaret was able to take the Victorian engagement ring to a goldsmith in the town and sell it saying it had been left to her by her grandmother. She produced several documents with her name and address on them that satisfied the jeweller and produced a reward of almost three thousand pounds. The jeweller had raved about the clarity and quality of the diamond so Margret being much older than she looked, bartered like a professional. "Brilliant," said Alec when she showed them the cash, "That's just the start and it will help us to move but we need to keep going."

The next day it was Patsy's turn to sell the gold bangles. She spent around two hours doing her hair, applying fake tan, makeup tight-fitting clothes with a very heavily padded bra and shoes that she could barely stand upright in, let alone walk. She put her designer sunglasses on, placed all the gold bangles on her wrist, gum in her mouth and examined herself in the mirror quietly trying out her best Essex voice, "Hello Babes," then giggling to herself, even she wouldn't recognise herself. She clomped her way down the stairs in the ungainly shoes and was met with gasps of Patricia and Patsy, all in one go. "Do I look good Babes?" she asked them? Jean was so impressed she began clapping, Margret joined in and she took a bow giggling.

She set off to York in the car with Adiim in the back seat and Alec driving, she was looking forward to having a bit of fun. All her documents were in place and Adiim had produced a receipt based on one that Jean had in her jewellery box from London about seven years ago. Patsy had researched the bangles and knew they were worth in the region of six thousand pounds if only by their weight.

The shop was empty when she entered it and she went through her entire routine about her car breaking down and needing to sell some bling to get it fixed. The middle-aged woman behind the counter was not impressed or vaguely amused by this stupid rich girl from Essex who was probably spoiled rotten by her footballer boyfriend. However, when she felt the weight of the bangles and tested their gold content her attitude changed, and she became suddenly warmer and smiled. "There is a great deal of gold in these," she told Patsy, and "So I will have to get my husband to have a look at them before I can give you a price." "No probs Babes," replied Patsy smiling sweetly. "I'm afraid the door will be locked," continued the woman, "but I should only be a minute."

In literally one minute the woman appeared with a grey-haired man who looked at least ten years her senior. Unlike his wife, he had a kind face and smiled saying hello softly to Patsy. No one spoke for a while as the man examined the gold, weighed it and examined the hallmarks with his magnifying glass. "This is a beautiful gold and has an extraordinarily rich colour to it. Do you have any paperwork to show where these items were purchased," he asked gently? "Only one of them Babes," responded Patsy, "that's the last one that Darren bought me." I've still got the receipt for that one in me purse," she declared pointing at one of the bangles. "We got them all at the same place though Babes," she said nonchalantly. Patsy rooted through her handbag, pulled out her driving licence, a crumpled receipt, her birth certificate and a phone bill with her address on it and handed them over to the man.

He seemed satisfied with what she had shown him and took copies of them on a copier next him then laid everything out before him on the counter in front of Patsy. "Well Madam, we have everything we need to continue our business except a price, do you know what you want for them," said the man. "Darren bought me one of them for every year we was together so there's seven of them and we paid one thousand three hundred and fifty pounds for each one as you can see from the receipt Babes" She pretended to sob slightly as she said they were together for seven years. "Will he be annoyed if you sell them though," asked the man? Patsy pretended to cry and told him," My Darren don't want me no more Babes, he dumped me last month, he said I was mugging him off." I've had to move out and now I'm finding it hard to get by and he's stopped all me cards, so you see, that's why I need to sell some off me bling Babes."

It worked a treat and the man fell for it hook line and sinker, much to his wife's total disgust. "Don't worry my dear," he told her, "I'm going to give you a good price and when he realises he's lost such a beautiful girl and comes running back, he'll have to buy them back from me if I haven't already sold them on." "I can give you six thousand five hundred and fifty pounds for them, which is a really good offer." Patsy knew only too well that it was a good offer, so she shook the man's hand camply. His wife went redder and redder as he counted out the cash from the safe. Patsy thanked him and stuffed her documents and the stacks of fifty and twenty-pound notes into her handbag, the woman led her to the door and unlocked it as she walked out saying "Bye Babes and thank you." The woman slammed the door closed behind her and Patsy heard raised voices as she walked away but she didn't look back and then clomped as fast as she could back to the car in her monster heels. Back at the car they all whooped and celebrated having made more than eight thousand pounds in two days. "At this rate," said Alec," by the end of the month we should have over a hundred thousand." They laughed but Adiim didn't, he knew it could be a reality.

The next day Alec and Jean went back into York, this time it was to drop off the coins and ancient bracelets at the museum. As agreed, Jean told them her husband had given her a metal detector and as they had been walking in the Dales, they had discovered these two finds right next to each other within a few feet. She handed over the ordnance-survey map used by ramblers, showing a point marked with a cross. The museum was thrilled with the find, especially as the ground they were found on was already owned by the state. They took a photocopy of Julia Evan's passport, her email address and other contact information and told her she may not get anything more than a thank you letter, although there may be a small reward. She told them she was not expecting anything and was happy that the museum could benefit, she sounded genuine because she was being genuine and as she walked away, she was glad they would be put on display for everyone to enjoy.

While they were in town, they went to a local bank and asked about opening a new account. "We will need you to complete an application form giving details of your address and current banking arrangement, employer etc.," said the chatty girl at the desk. It was the word employer that did it for Alec, it sort of made him feel depressed to think he could no longer go back to his office. He was very worried about Diana too and he just wanted to know that she was alright, but most of all he'd lost that security that comes with having a job, especially one where the right people could arrange anything for you. He collected an application pack for each of them and Jean linked his arm chatting peacefully about nothing as they headed back to the car.

A few days later it was clear that Alec was not his normal positive self and although Jean tried to talk to him, he couldn't tell her what was wrong. It would mean opening-up about a job he'd kept secret for all the years he'd known her. In the end, Patsy thought she'd worked it out and asked him to come with her for a ride into Driffield to get some magazines, milk and a few other groceries. Adiim stood up intending to go along but Patsy whispered in his ear that she needed to talk to her Dad alone. Adiim understood and nodded whispering back, "Let me know if I can do something."

When they were on the way and well out of earshot, Patsy told him that she knew the type of job he'd been doing, and she knew he was missing it. Alec couldn't answer but his face said it all. "Look, Dad, we're going through the toughest time of our lives but we're coping, if you can't trust me now you can't trust anyone." He thought about it for a while and then began to tell her everything he was able to and that was just enough to make her realise how much Diana had put her neck on the line for them. Patsy had met Diana a few times over the years and liked her very much. More to the point, Jean had become particularly good friends with her, and they looked forward to seeing each other at any social event arranged by Alec's company. "You have to go and check that's she's alright Dad," Patsy urged him, "We owe that much to her at least." "I want to go but I'm afraid it could draw attention to us and if anyone saw me." "That's just it" Patsy jumped in, "even if they did see you now you just look like your own son or something, you're twenty years old." Alec was stunned that he hadn't realised, it was probably because he felt just the same apart from feeling fitter. "I know you hate Adiim using his powers but do you think he could take me to watch her without being seen by anyone and then I could try to talk to her when I know she's on her own," Alec asked? "Well we could try asking him what he thinks," said Patsy, "I've started to realise that he knows far more about everything than we've been giving him credit for." "I know, I feel bad sometimes for treating him like he's a child but look how amazingly well he has learned to use the internet. He can hack into any computer in the world by using intuition to pick up on passwords and codes." "Dad, I don't think we will ever truly understand what Adiim is capable of, but I trust him, and I love him dearly." "So, do I," said Alec.

The rest of the day passed without too much fuss except that this time Margaret and Jean went to another shop in

York and sold one of the rings with a ruby stone for almost four thousand pounds. It was such a rare and finely cut stone that they didn't have to barter that much to get the price up because the jeweller wanted it badly. During the afternoon Patsy had been researching things on one of the laptops again and had come up with an idea of what they could do to get away from the cottage, still have a home, and be able to move easily if they had to.

When Margaret and Jean arrived home with their spoils from selling the ring, everyone was pleased as they now had more than twelve thousand pounds already. Patsy had made a lovely cottage pie and carrots and cabbage to go with it and even a bread and butter pudding for dessert. Adiim wanted to help by using his powers to cook for her but she refused, she enjoyed doing it. They sat down to eat, and Patsy told them her idea. "I've been looking at RV's on the internet." "What on earth is an RV, Patricia dear," questioned Jean? It's one of those giant vehicles that are like a house on wheels," she responded. "Do you mean a caravan," asked Jean, startled? "No Mother they are completely luxurious with hot running water, bathroom, refrigerator, central heating and even satellite television," said Patsy. The ones I've been looking at have three quite large bedrooms with fitted wardrobes, they look fabulous."

Margaret and Alec thought it was a fantastic idea, but they wanted to know how much it would cost. We need to get about a hundred thousand together to buy one big enough and nice enough to call home for now. "Well actually we should get a fair bit for my car now that Adiim has made it look like it's brand new," began Alec. Then an idea struck him that he hadn't thought of before. "Hang on," he said, "what if we buy old cars, preferably old ones. We have cash and could get a great deal on them and then get Adiim to make them look like new. We could resell them for a massive profit." Realising it would be much easier than trying to sell lots of jewellery and could be done mostly using the internet, everyone had to agree it was a fantastic idea. Patsy suggested that the next day she could go out with Alec and Adiim and look around some of the local car lots to have a practice. Again, everyone agreed but Patsy had alternate plans for the two men.

After breakfast the next morning, they set off for a nearby car lot that Adiim found on the laptop. On the way there, Patsy talked to Adiim about the discussion she'd with her Dad. Adiim listened until she'd finished and agreed to it without question. "We can all go together but I'll have to make you into a cloud though first," he warned them. "If I remember correctly, it can make you feel very dizzy and disorientated the first few times, but you'll be able to get used to it." They agreed and parked the car in a car park used by ramblers, way out in the country. Adiim showed them how to cross their arms upwards and put their hands on their shoulders. The second they were in position, they both felt a strange sensation like the tingling when you get goose pimples, not unpleasant but surprising. Suddenly they felt Adiim's arms wrap around them and they lifted off the ground instantly. Soon they were soaring over trees and houses faster and faster until almost incomprehensibly the city of London came into sight beneath them and they slowed down. Adiim read

Alec's thoughts when he saw the City and used his knowledge to find the right building and down they went.

Inside the office, Alec couldn't believe they could be there without anyone even being aware of them in the room. Diana looked worn out and otherwise okay but there was no sign of Greg, Roxy or anyone else familiar. As they watched what was going on, a man he didn't recognise came over to Diana and began ordering her around. Diana jumped as though she'd been poked with a cattle prod and did as he said. Alec was furious, no one ever needed to treat Diana that way, she would do anything for anyone if they only asked her politely. Just then a woman came and sat in a seat right next to her. "Any calls while I was at lunch," she asked? Diana just shook her head. "Look," she said, "why don't you make it easy for yourself and tell us where Miller is, it's only a matter of time before he calls you again and we'll have him and his renegade family. Diana said nothing but he recognised that stoic look on her face and he knew she would never tell them anything. "Okay, said the woman, it's your turn to go for lunch but leave your phone here." Poor Diana stood and handed over her mobile phone with a worn-down look on her face and then made her way out. Adiim moved their cloud along with her and they followed her down in the lift out through the foyer and down through the gardens at the front of the building. I must speak to her, said Alec and without a word, Adiim landed behind an outbuilding and they became solid again. "I'll meet you outside the café on the corner of this street in an hour," he called to them as he jogged after Diana.

When he caught up with her, he called her name and walked alongside her. "Yes," she replied not recognising him in the slightest at first. "Diana, it's me, Alec," he said, and quickly continued, "I have very little time, so please listen." Diana stopped and just stared into his face. "My god it is you I recognise you from that photo you sent, how on earth did you manage to look so young, it's impossible?" "It's real but I don't have time to go through everything," said Alec. "I want you to know that I'm sorry for any problems my family and I have caused you. I can't do anything to help you at this precise moment, but I promise I'll make it up to you.

There are some strange and quite wonderful things happening. I can't tell you what they are, not because I don't trust you but because the less you know the better for you. All you need to know is that Patsy stumbled upon something that has amazing restorative properties and various powerful organisations want to get their hands on it. That would be fine but harvesting this substance would create terrible conditions for someone close to us." Diana looked into his eyes and said, "thank you for risking things to come and tell me, Alec, I love you like a brother and I would do anything for you." "Trust me for now," said Alec, "my family and I are going to generate a great deal of money and I'll make sure to always look after you and your family. If you decide to quit your job because of the pressure, we will make sure you're okay." He gave her a gentle kiss on the forehead and then went running off down the street.

Diana smiled to herself and turned towards the building. It had always been an important place to her but now it felt cold and horrible without Alec, never mind all the coldness she was having to endure as part of the investigation.

At least now she had some idea of what Alec was dealing with. She knew it was something incredible when they came that day and cut open Alec's safe. Fortunately, there was nothing in there except a few highly secret documents but nothing to say where Alec was. She resisted all attempts at questioning, saying Alec left the office, as usual, one evening and never came back, she never heard from him again and had no idea where he could be. She mourned his leaving almost as though he'd died, and it helped her get through the endless questions.

As she looked up at the building, she noticed that bloody woman staring at her from the office window. For an instant, she worried that she'd seen her talking to Alec but realised that the young twenty-year-old boy bore no resemblance. She decided it was a nephew she hadn't seen for a while who was in London on a trip and looked her up.

As she turned to go and buy lunch she waved to that bloody woman and smiled to herself. Whatever else happened she knew Alec wouldn't be coming back but she could cope. Adiim and Patsy were where they agreed, Alec had spent the last half an hour writing a message to his most trusted friend and colleague Douglas Marklew, delivering it by hand to his secretary without her realising who he was. It may not solve all her problems, but Doug would do anything he could to help Diana and may even ask her to come and work for him. Adiim asked them to fold their arms again and off they went, arriving back at the car in only a few short minutes.

Unknown to them a bird watcher was snuggled down in the grass nearby. When a cloud suddenly appeared and the three of them stepped out of it, he nearly choked on his tongue. They walked over to the car, climbed in and drove away but not before the birdwatcher had written down their number plate and taken photos.

New for old - Chapter 9

The next day Alec had them all completing their bank account application forms. When it came to employment references, they were all stuck. "I've formed a company called Classic Like New and we all work for it. We convert old cars, renovate them to make them look like new and then re-sell them. I've used the Barn next door as the address for the business so we will have to start making it look like a workshop in action. Once we get going, we need reception and office staff as well as collection and delivery people." Everyone thought it was a great idea except for the address. "We will have to move somewhere else as soon as we have enough money in the bank but for now it will have to do," Alec told them. They handed in the forms and were issued with new bank accounts and cards within a couple of days. They shared out the money between all five accounts and heaved a sigh of relief.

It took no time at all to start buying suitable older cars for little money as most of them were so tatty that hardly anyone wanted them. It took Adiim no time at all to correct any engine problems and make both their insides and outsides look brand new. Even the engines looked new when the bonnet was open, and their tyres were shiny new rubber. Alec went out and purchased tools, overalls and spraying equipment to make everything look authentic. They occasionally sprayed things against the wall of the barn to create the effect and make the right smell. Their first purchase was a Triumph which they obtained for three hundred pounds and sold for eight thousand pounds the same day.

As fast as Jean could locate the cars and Alec and Margaret could collect them, Adiim renovated them, Patsy photographed them, had them for sale on the internet, they were under offer, she delivered them, and they sold immediately. They were making several thousands of pounds from every car and sometimes sold three per day. Alec set up the company bank account and they were able to start negotiations on a house with a huge outbuilding in Staffordshire in a village called Haverwich. Although they all dreaded having to move again, they knew they would feel more confident living in a new place with new identities and with their new money-making idea they wouldn't have to worry for a while.

Alec arranged for everything they owned to be moved by a removals company and although they didn't have much it was easier than trying to transport it themselves. They sold the last car a few days before the move and went to Staffordshire to clean the new house and wait for the furniture to arrive. For once Patsy didn't worry about the cost, she chose exactly what she wanted for her bedroom. It was so modern and sleek that it looked slightly out of place in this massive arts and crafts style building that Jean and Margaret both loved so much. Alec didn't mind where they lived as long as they were safe and comfortable, so he left the women to organise the interior. Adiim found their fussing about amusing, he could have arranged all of it in a few minutes, but Patsy had refused to allow him to do it. He realised that Patsy enjoyed doing things herself and he respected and loved her for it. It worried him sometimes that he felt so much love for her, but he always made sure to keep his feelings secret.

They all had to change address with their bank and on their driving licence which reminded Patsy how much had happened since her new driving licence arrived in London only a few short months ago. Moving to Staffordshire was a strategic move on Alec's part. He felt that being in the middle of the country would make collecting and delivering cars much easier logistically.

Willam was having to get used to another new house but he already preferred the smell of it. The other garden had lots of fox visitors and he didn't like them. There were also lots of badgers and although they didn't have anything to do with him, he objected to them entering his domain. Not only that but a beautiful grey Persian princess lived right next door to the new house and she already had her eye on him.

Over the last couple of weeks, Adiim told him about people following the car and he'd seen for himself people spying on the house so he realised they wouldn't be staying at the cottage much longer. His whole world was the five people he lived with, he loved them all and was secure in the knowledge that they loved him too. All in all, everyone felt much more settled in the new house and the atmosphere reflected just that.

Back in Yorkshire, the bird watcher had taken down their vehicle registration and managed to get one good photo as they were getting into the car. Fortunately, the car had been altered and already had a new registered keeper and number plate, but Patsy's face could be seen quite clearly although both Alec and Adiim were looking the wrong way. No one quite believed him when he told them about three people appearing in a cloud, but he wouldn't give in and told everyone who would listen.

A few days later he was having a pint in the Dog and Fox and telling the barman for the thirteenth time about the two men and one woman walking out of a cloud. A dark-haired young man with a blonde female friend was sitting on the other side of the bar looking crestfallen when in an absent-minded way, they began to listen to his story. The blonde woman suddenly began paying closer attention to what was being said.

The barman heard enough and went through to the rear pretending to sort out the beer barrels, anything to get away from the nutty guy. "Hey," said the woman, "that's a remarkably interesting story, why don't you come over and tell us more." He couldn't wait to talk to a willing audience at last and picked up his beer moving over to them. He began from the start which unfortunately included telling them exactly which birds he'd seen that morning. When he came to the part about the cloud appearing they asked him to slow down and asked about the three people. He described the swirling cloud and the three young people who stepped out of it. She wanted to know what they were wearing, what type of car it was. He told her he'd taken a photo and held his digital camera up as they both smiled at each other knowingly. When he told them that he'd taken down the registration of the car, they were ecstatic.

For the next few weeks, the family were remarkably busy, and the business was highly lucrative but otherwise uneventful. Alec was still concerned about Diana and eventually asked Adiim if he would take him back to see her again. They left from inside the house, arriving at the city of London moments later. They went directly to Diana's office but there was no sign of her anywhere. A new woman was sitting at her desk looking confident and efficient. Alec had a good idea where she would be and let Adiim know with his thoughts so that he could take him there.

They swiftly moved to Doug's office hoping to see Diana but there was no sign of her there either. Alec became worried and asked Adiim to help find her. He was shocked when Adiim located her in Holloway women's prison, but he had no idea why. They waited until she was alone before Alec spoke to her. She still couldn't see him, and she jumped in fear but as soon as she recognised his voice she relaxed. "Diana, "said Alec, "what on earth has happened and why are you in here?" She burst into tears and told him she had snapped when the woman investigating his disappearance said things that upset her, so she beat her over the head with a coffee cup and was charged with assault.

She went on to tell him that her husband of thirty years had also left her for another woman he'd been having an affair with for the last seventeen years. Her son had left London and no one knew where he was, her daughter had run away with a Brazilian boy and she last heard they had married and were living in Rio with a baby granddaughter she thought she'd never meet. She was a lonely woman in trouble on her own and she needed help. He couldn't believe how low she was, and he promised he'd get her out. She told him she only had two days left of her sentence and she'd be free. Alec told her to stay calm and he'd come to collect her in two days. She was about to ask him how she could speak to him without seeing him when they heard someone coming and Alec just said bye and left.

When they arrived back in Staffordshire Alec told the family what had happened to Diana. None of them could believe how terrible things had become for her and when Alec asked if they would mind if she came to live with them, they agreed without another thought. There were spare rooms at the house so it wouldn't be difficult to fit her in. Jean called the prison to ask her release time and pretended a cab had been ordered to pick her up. They told her it was normally between ten and eleven o clock.

The next morning Alec got up early and drove down to London ready to collect Diana. They all agreed that being transported by Adiim would be too much, Alec would be able to tell her everything that had happened during the drive back. She was delighted to see him and hugged him tightly. Alec hugged her back, they were like family. He told her she was coming to live with him and his family in the Midlands. She couldn't think or a reason not to and agreed to go back to her house and pack anything she needed. Alec told her not to worry too much as they could come back for anything she needed later. Nonetheless, she stuffed two suitcases with clothing and filled another bag with papers and odds and ends that were important to her then tapped the doorcase as she walked out saying goodbye to the old house. During the drive back Alec told her everything from the beginning. As the story unfolded, she was able to fill in blanks in her knowledge and she finally understood the reason for all the subterfuge. By the end of the story, she was looking forward to meeting Adiim and to seeing what Jean and Margaret's new image looked like. "I've always had a thing for vintage cars," she told Alec. "I'd love to get involved in the business if you'll allow me to?" Jokingly Alec said, "You don't think you're coming to live with us rent-free do you?" They had a good laugh and she hugged his arm, feeling happier than she had in months.

When they reached the house, the whole family was pleased to see her and there were hugs and kisses all round. She felt very welcome and even felt like Adiim was an old friend after only a few minutes. The two men took her bags upstairs and showed her the bedroom they'd furnished for her. She loved it and tried the massive bed out for size. Later a bottle of vintage bubbly was opened to celebrate, and they had a lovely cordon bleu dinner cooked by Jean and Margaret. That evening they discussed how young everyone was and Adiim suggested he could make Diana younger and healthier in the same way he had for Jean. Alec said he thought it would be a good idea to do that and they should also arrange a new identity for her as she now has a criminal record. Within minutes Diana was a young girl giggling at herself in the mirror. "I look like my daughter" she declared. She suddenly looked sad and Jean asked her why. "I can never see my daughter again now I look like this," she responded. "Yes, you can," said Patsy, "Adiim can change you back if you ever need him to." "I don't think I will ever get to Brazil anyway," concluded Diana. "Stranger things have happened," said Alec winking at Adiim.

One morning while Adiim was preparing to do his thing on a beautiful old Jaguar XK120 from the year 1951, Willam appeared on the wall next to the workshop. "Those people are here again," he told Adiim. "Which people are they," he asked? "The ones who came to the other house and watched us," Willam said, wondering why Adiim didn't know them. Now he had Adiim's attention completely. "Can you tell me what they looked like," he asked. "The male has dark fur and the female, has very light fur, he is younger and tall and they both watch us through those extended eyes." Adiim walked into the workshop telling Willam to follow and closed the door.

Once inside, he folded his arms and turned into the swirling cloud of smoky sand, then disappeared. As he was doing this, he told Willam, "Stay in here until I come back, these people could be dangerous." He drifted upwards and sent his senses out until he could identify the two people sitting in a car just down the road. The man was holding up a pair of binoculars and the woman was using a mobile phone. He dropped into the car next to them silently and listened to their conversation. The woman was talking on her phone saying, "no we haven't seen the car yet but this morning the woman from the photo drove a newly renovated Triumph Spitfire out of the garage and headed towards Lichfield." "We're certain she's the Miller woman, there's no sign of the parents but we've just seen a ginger cat that could be the one we're looking for. We'll let you know more when we've captured it and will report back at midday." As she clicked off the phone, the young man asked, "What do you think the cloud thing was that nutty guy was talking about?" "I think he's loop-the-loop and there was probably a morning mist as they came over the hill, nothing more." "I don't care what he thought he saw," she continued," I was only amusing myself until he showed me that picture and then I couldn't believe our luck when I saw Miller's face staring out."

Adiim went directly back to the workshop. "We have to hide you somewhere safe," he told Willam. "Those people want to catch you and take you away." Willam was slightly scared but he knew Adiim would look after him, so he agreed to do whatever he wanted. Adiim gathered him up and they turned into the swirling cloud floating high up into the sky. Willam was scared to death and struggled stupidly in Adiim's arms but Adiim gently told him he was quite safe. He still didn't feel happy but tried to stay still and suddenly they were dropping out of the sky into Margaret's beautiful walled garden in Edinburg. "You should be safe here for now," Adiim told him, "you know this place very well." Willam was relieved to be there, he knew of at least six places to hide if he needed to. Adiim patted the ground and up came around thirty earthworms that he collected. Then with Giin magic, he changed them into rabbit meat which is Willam's favourite. "I'll come back for you later," he told him, "but for now have fun and catch some mice." With that, he was gone but Willam didn't notice the swirling cloud, he was busy eating.

Patsy was delivering a Triumph Spitfire to a man on Chester Road, just outside Birmingham and Margaret followed behind in a Honda Civic that another client had specifically requested be fully restored. Adiim arrived in the front seat next to her and she nearly jumped out of her skin when he appeared. "You'd think I'd be used to that by now," she said, mainly to herself. "There is a big problem, Patsy," he told her. "Somehow the same people who were following us in Yorkshire have found us and they are sitting outside the house watching now." "Oh, please no," said Patsy in a forlorn voice.

Adiim explained that he had listened to them and someone had taken a photo of them which they used to identify her face. He told her Willam was safe in the garden in Edinburgh and suggested Patsy should also go there for now. "I don't think it can be that safe to go to Grans," Patsy argued. He assured her that he'd been back several times to her gran's house, her flat, Diana's and her parents' house to see what was happening. There were people still watching her flat after all this time. They'd been through her parent's house and took Alec's computer and a few other things away, but they'd given up and no one has been near for several weeks. Margaret's house was more difficult because of the security system but eventually, they managed to get in, swarmed over it for a couple of weeks and now it was quiet. The long driveway and the security gates at the end meant anyone watching that house could only wait in the road near the entrance. Adiim had been in and re-set all the security systems with new codes so if they wanted to get in again it could take them some time.

Patsy pulled over as her gran had seen Adiim from her position in the car behind and was trying to call them on her mobile phone. They both went to sit in the Honda as the Spitfire had only two seats. Adiim quickly brought Margaret up to speed with what happened, and they agreed to drop off both cars and let Adiim take them back home the fast way. They were both anxious, they dropped off the Spitfire and then set off for Sutton Coldfield where the Honda Civic had to go. Both deliveries went well, and the Honda guy was so delighted when he saw the fully restored car that he screamed like a girl. He insisted on giving them a lift to the station where they told him a colleague had arranged to pick them up. Unfortunately, it meant they had to walk quite a distance out of the town to find a quiet enough place for Adiim to transport them.

They agreed to go back directly into the house in Haverwich and stay out of sight. The people watching them would be expecting Patsy to arrive in a car the way she left so they wouldn't know she'd returned. Just after they arrived and were telling Jean the whole story, Diana arrived, and Alec brought in a dilapidated Rover P6 that would need all Adiim's magic to fix it up. It was near the end of the working day and they decided to stop work when Patsy told them what had been happening. Adiim went out to scout invisibly and could see that the car had gone. It was nowhere to be seen and when he cast his feelings out to locate them, he discovered they were checking into a hotel several miles away. While he was already in spirit form, Adiim went back to Margaret's house to collect Willam. He didn't notice when Adiim arrived, he was sleeping on top of the potting shed. Adiim smiled to himself to see his dear friend looking so content and he noticed that all the food had been eaten. He called to him in his cat language and Willam tribbled in response. "Time to go home now," said Adiim. He collected Willam up in his arms and they were soon on the way back to the family.

As they were eating dinner that evening, they tried to decide what to do next. Adiim had a suggestion that none of them had considered. "I could either change Patsy and Willam so they can't be identified, or I could change all of the information those people have at their hotel so that it doesn't match Alec's car or Patsy's face. "I'd rather you change things than people," blurted out Patsy, "Especially when it's me you're talking about." So, it was decided and after eating, Adiim would go to the hotel and while invisible, change any photographs they had to look only slightly like Patsy.

When he arrived, he found they had several other photographs of Patsy in files and he changed them, but he left the most recent one that the young man had taken that morning. There was a police report from DVLA giving Alex Evans name and Staffordshire address as details of the owner of a car with registration JUI 14, so Adiim changed the original information they held to say JUL14. After that, he made sure that the records held by DVLA related to a similar car with an owner in Aberdeen.

While the woman was relaxing on the hotel bed, he whispered into her ear, are you sure that's the right car, check the number again, check the number again, and check again. She was startled by the whisper, but she couldn't help acting on it and soon discovered that the stupid idiot in the next room had brought them to the wrong house. Not only that but when she checked the picture of the woman taken this morning, it looked nothing like the picture on the file of Patsy Miller. "I must have been crazy to trust that idiot," she said out loud to herself. She picked up the room phone and dialled him. A sleepy sounding male voice answered "ullo." "I suggest you wake yourself up sharpish and get in here, you've messed things up big time," she snapped at him. In less than a minute, there was a knock on the door, and she let him in. "I was half asleep when something told me to check things and lo and behold! you've traced the wrong car owner, just look at the registration and then check the owner, they live in Aberdeen for heaven's sake. Not only that but look at this picture you took of that woman this morning and then check it against Patsy Miller's mugshot." She held up the pictures for him to look at and then threw them at him in her temper. "You'd better get a good night's sleep tonight. We have a lot of explaining to do tomorrow".

Adiim was almost rolling on the floor trying not to laugh out loud but he couldn't resist making more trouble. "Fat camel," he suddenly said out loud. "I beg your pardon," said the woman, "how dare you try to insult me, you brain dead piece of rubbish." The young man was shocked and couldn't work out who had said the camel thing but being called brain dead by that lazy good for nothing blonde had rattled his bars. "I'm sick of doing all the work, including all the driving and watching houses while you casually doze your dumb blonde head off, you're a lazy old cow," he fumed.

Almost at breaking point and ready to cry the woman told him, "Get out of my room." "Tomorrow I'm going back to London," she told him, "and if they insist on me working with you and travelling to Aberdeen, I'll quit." Adiim quietly left but not before whispering "fat camel," one more time. He materialised back in the dining room still laughing out loud. "Adiim Dear, what on earth has tickled you," asked Jean? He told them what he'd done and left the bit about the fat camel until the end and then burst into laughter again, this time joined by Diana, Patsy, Margaret and Jean.

Alec was in the kitchen feeding Willam with some leftover meat when he heard all the laughter. When he learned what had happened, he joined in but there was still doubt in his mind about their safety and he knew they'd be moving again soon.

Down to Rio - Chapter 10

They continued with Classic Like New and soon they amassed a decent fortune. Alec had made sure they were equal shareholders in the business and that included Diana. One day as they prepared the roster for pick-ups and drop-offs and Alec was hidden behind the morning newspaper, he suddenly announced, "It's time we closed the business and went on holiday." Although the weather had become much colder and the grey sky had long replaced the summer and autumn sunshine, no one had even considered taking a holiday; they enjoyed the work so much. "Where should we go," asked Margaret? "Anywhere we want" responded Patsy smiling. "Should we all go together Alec dear," asked Jean. "Well we don't have to and if anyone would prefer to go their own way, that's fine," said Alec hoping no one would. Diana suddenly blurted out, "more than anything I want to go to Rio to visit my daughter Grace and my granddaughter Valentina." "What a great idea," said Jean, "Copacabana beach in my bikini just what I've always longed to do and now I am young and have a fantastic figure again, I can." She walked up and down the living room like a catwalk model singing the Girl from Ipanema, to the absolute delight and clapping from Alec and Patsy in particular.

Sometimes Alec found it hard to believe that this lively and excitable young woman who laughed so much and clowned around was the same stuffy, frustrated and wooden, middle-aged woman she had become not too long ago. Margaret understood fully, she knew Jean regretted not having more fun when she was young the first time and she was not going to miss this second chance. They decided they'd close the business for three weeks during the Christmas period so that they could spend both Christmas and New Year away. The women wasted no time going out to select bikinis and other swim and sun-wear, hats and lotions. They also made sure to buy trendy shorts and T-shirts, hats and designer sunglasses for the boys and Jean purchased an enormous set of matching luggage with enough pieces for all of them.

Adiim took Alec to Brazil so that they could have a look around and find somewhere to stay for the entire family. He settled on a beautiful villa with high walls surrounding it and lush gardens and a swimming pool. It brought back memories of the king's palace long ago and although Adiim loved the place he was saddened when he thought of Princess Akilah and the poor kitten. Alec was astounded that Adiim spoke perfect Portuguese and was able to negotiate for them to stay at the villa for the three weeks they had decided upon.

While they were viewing the villa Adiim told him he was concerned that Grace was in a slum area and may feel embarrassed if Diana saw where she was living. Alec agreed and while they were dealing with the villa, he had formed a plan. When they'd agreed on the dates for their stay, they went to find Grace on the pretence of being Alec's son Alex who was in Rio with his friend Adam. She was disturbed at first, but they explained that Alec and

Diana were now in business together and had made a great deal of money. They told her they'd been sent to try and find her as Diana wanted to visit and meet her granddaughter.

Grace was horrified and panicked but young Alex had a plan. He took her to an upmarket district where he asked her to choose a house for sale that she wanted to live in. Grace couldn't believe what he was asking, and, in the end, the young Alex had more or less forced her to choose. They then asked her what furniture she wanted, and they dashed about the town buying up everything she needed to furnish the house. Her husband Edwardo was completely shocked to discover that his wife was the daughter of such a wealthy woman, and he couldn't stop thanking the young Alex and his friend Adam for everything. Finally, they set up a bank account for them and arranged for a regular income to be paid into it. By the time they returned from the bank with Edwardo, Grace had been out and bought beautiful new clothes and makeup, had her hair styled and baby Valentina was dressed in the most exquisite and modern baby gear. When they completed everything they could, Alex and Adam asked Grace if she was now okay to meet her mother. "Oh yes I am," she responded, "I've missed her so much." "Just one thing before we leave," said the young Alex, "this visit and everything we've done must be our secret." Grace and Edwardo hugged and thanked them and agreed never to tell Diana what had happened.

It was quite late in the evening when they appeared back in the living room in Staffordshire. There was a marked contrast between the lovely bright skies of the southern hemisphere and the dark cloudy evening in England. Alec had taken pictures of the lovely villa and he showed them to the four women seeking their approval. He needn't have worried because they were thrilled, and Diana asked if the villa was near to where Grace lived. Adiim and Alec smiled at each other and told her it was extremely near. Now all they had to do was pack their bags and fly over.

They'd already decided Adiim would travel separately and the rest of them would share his luggage between them to enable him to bring Willam the fast way. Adiim offered to take them all over two at a time but Patsy insisted it was his holiday too and flying in an aeroplane was part of the holiday. They all had current passports in their new names including Dianna who had simply become Diane Jones, a cousin of the Jones girls from Essex. Adiim checked every computer record and anywhere that information should be stored, including their national health records and everything was in perfect order. They were leaving on Saturday 21st December and wouldn't be back until Saturday 11th January.

They'd long ago stopped advertising Classic Like New and now relied only on word of mouth. To close things down, they put a message on the website and an answering service on the phone telling any would-be customers that no more orders would be taken until the thirteenth of January. There were large gates on the front of the house that stopped anyone coming to the workshop uninvited and no one was ever allowed to see their car until the full transformation had been completed, for obvious reasons.

The business was Popular there had never been any complaints, only massive compliments, they could call the shots and had waiting lists of several weeks. Over some time, they began to ask their clients to identify exactly what shade of colour they wanted, what type of upholstery they wanted from a book of samples and any additions from pictures of classical motors. Adiim was able to make any car look like anything if he could interpret what the customer wanted and the best way to do that was by examples.

The few weeks before their holiday soon went by and the women had been packed ready for days. The workload slowed down and Adiim was able to spend time in the house learning more on the internet. He was looking forward to being on holiday and although he felt it was wrong, he secretly hoped he would get some time on his own with Patsy. She also caught herself looking at Adiim more than usual. She told herself not to be stupid, that he'd be horrified if he knew what she was thinking. Margaret, on the other hand, was a young girl with a wise old woman's mind and she could see things that passed others by. Adiim told Willam all about the holiday but it confused him. Why would they want to go to a completely strange territory? How could it be relaxing to do that instead of staying where everything was familiar? Adiim tried to explain the concept of working but a cat didn't need such a thing so the idea of needing to rest after work passed him by. When he explained that Diana's daughter and baby granddaughter lived there and she wanted to see them, he could understand the reason for that. He told Adiim his real family were those he lived with and if they wanted to go to a strange place for relaxing, he would go with them and try to enjoy it.

The day of departure arrived and everyone except Adiim and Willam left in an extra-large taxi for Heathrow airport. Adiim knew he had more than a full day to go before the others would arrive at the villa. They had an hour and a half ride to the airport and the flight alone was twelve hours then allowing for checking in times on the way out and passport and baggage on arrival, then the taxi to the villa, it would be around eighteen hours in total. Adiim settled down to watch TV, still one of his favourite things to do. Willam settled on his lap trying to relax although nervous about going to the new place. Adiim ate the food that Jean left for him and washed and dried the dishes as instructed. He gave Willam the remaining cat food and after he had finished, he washed Willam's dish also.

He went through the various rooms of the house and switched on the various timers that Patsy had set up. They included lights and lamps, a radio and an upstairs TV. There were electric gates on the front of the house and a state-of-the-art security system that included cameras, alarms and even anti-burglar paint and spikes on the tops of all the garden walls. The best security of all though was Adiim's own ability to go back and check without being seen and he' regularly checked Patsy's flat, Alec and Jeans, Margaret and Diana's houses. He went around one more time, checked all the windows, made sure all doors were locked including the front and back of the workshop. The only car left was Alec's original Volvo and that was safely locked too. With everything done, Adiim called Willam, picked him up and smiled as he grumbled about being taken from his home to go to another strange place.

When they arrived, the others were already unpacking and there was lots of excited chattering between the four women. Willam began to purr as he looked about and Adiim asked him if he'd changed his mind about being there. "The sun is shining and it's warm here, of course, I like it," he answered. He had no concept of being on the other side of the earth and didn't realise that the sun was always shining somewhere in the world. He always thought winter lasted if it did and there was no escape from it. Adiim put him down and he wandered through the villa saying hello to everyone by rubbing against their legs. They were all delighted to be there, but Diana was especially excited because she'd be seeing her family soon.

That evening they discussed how to handle the meeting. Should Adiim change her appearance again so that Grace wouldn't be too shocked and ask questions? Should the others go to meet her too and if they did, how would they explain their new younger looks? In the end, it was decided that Alec posing as his own son, Adiim as Adam, Patsy who had not been changed and Diana made to look older with makeup, would go to visit Grace. Patsy suggested they could pretend Margaret and Jean were her cousins Sarah and Julia and so it was agreed.

The following morning, they had breakfast next to the pool and Alec and Patsy gave Adiim his first swimming lessons. It was hard to believe that he had never learned but most of his life had been spent inside a vase. He loved the water and splashed about like a child, but he was serious about learning to swim properly. Willam thought they were crazy, he still preferred sitting under a sun lounger on the side of the pool and Margaret had allocated a towel for him to sit on. "Okay," said Alec, "let's recap on what we decided last night." "Right," said Diana pointing to the side of her head and running through the list of names. "Spot on," said Alec, "We're ready to rock and roll." That statement generated a severe look of disapproval from Jean, but he didn't care, he was a young person again.

Adiim told Willam where they were going and warned him not to go anywhere over the wall. He needn't have worried, Willam was going to sleep all day in the shade under the sunbed and enjoy the sudden sunshine.

The second Grace opened the door she grabbed Diana into her arms and kissed her about sixty times. They laughed and cried all at the same time, but both were thrilled to see each other. "Welcome everyone, said Grace, "please come in and meet my husband and daughter." Edwardo was visibly shaking when he met Diana, he was expecting her to be angry with him for taking Grace away. They only met a couple of times in London and hadn't made much effort to speak to one another. Instead, she wrapped her arms around him and hugged him saying "Hello my very handsome son in law." In the meantime, Grace went over to a high-chair next to the table and picked up her baby girl, handing her to Diana. "Now meet your granddaughter Valentina."

The baby went into Diana's arms without any fuss and began touching her face as though she already knew it was her granny. Diana was so thrilled she could hardly speak then she realised she hadn't introduced the others. She went through the list, Alex and Adam, Patsy, Sarah and Julia while Grace then Edwardo hugged all. Grace said she could see the family resemblance and asked how Patsy's parents were. "They're fine, thank you, and both of them are healthy and fit as a fiddle," she replied truthfully. They had cold drinks on the terrace while they passed the baby around from lap to lap then told Grace they were going shopping and would come back for Diana later in the day. As they were leaving, Patsy invited them to come over to the villa for a swim and to have a barbeque the following evening and Alec finished by saying, come over whenever you want.

For the rest of the day, they went shopping around Rio, buying very little, they had everything they could ever want. Patsy bought a hat and another pair of sunglasses for Adiim and when he wore them, he looked like one of the local boys, handsome and dark and he was beginning to tan beautifully too. Patsy couldn't stop looking at him when he wasn't aware of her and she was so impressed that he could speak Portuguese that she didn't think to ask where he learned it. Margaret commented on how handsome he looked, adding that Edwardo was also exceptionally beautiful, and Jean agreed.

During the afternoon they went for a drink in one of the many bars overlooking the busy street. Everyone else was watching people going by but Margaret was having a moment of realisation. She looked at her family sitting around the table and marvelled at their luck. Only a few short months ago they were different people with stressful lives, not badly off financially but with no real fun in their lives to look forward to. Now they were richer than she ever expected they could be, Alec Jean and herself were back to being young people, healthy and happy. They had a thriving business which was highly unconventional, but it gave much pleasure to others and it was, as Alec had pointed out, good for the environment.

They all loved working for the business without exception. Also, how many women had the opportunity to go back to be the same age as both their daughter and granddaughter? Jean had especially benefited and was more changed than any of them. Before they met Adiim she was so bored with life that all she could do was complain about the neighbours. She'd been prudish and pious and hated the relationship Patsy had with her grandma. Now she was happier than ever, beautiful and sexy and brimming with a charmingly revived sense of humour that had been buried along with her confidence. The three of them got along so well now, they were more like sisters.

Although Patsy hadn't changed physically, Margaret knew that spiritually she was far more fulfilled and she sensed a much greater affection for Adiim than Patsy cared to admit, even to herself yet. Although Adiim had only recently come into their lives, she loved him like a grandson, and she knew he would die trying to protect them all if he had to. He was special, not only for his amazing powers but for his tolerance and understanding of people who assumed he was ignorant although they had much less experience than he did. She had to admit to treating him that way herself on more than one occasion but his kindness to others wouldn't enable him to feel resentment or seek revenge. More than once she had seen a special look in his eye when he was watching Patsy; Margaret had a good idea what it meant.

After their drink, they went to collect Diana and headed back to the villa to feed Willam and unload the shopping bags. On the way back in the taxis they agreed they'd spend the whole of the next day on Copacabana beach and have a barbeque around the pool with Grace and Edwardo in the evening. Diana prepared a spare room so that they could stay over if they had a drink and the villa had a fold away cot which Diana thought would fit better in her bedroom. Jean and Margaret began to prepare food to take with them to the beach the next day. "I'm going to include two bottles of champagne in the cooler bag," announced Jean as she popped them into the refrigerator to cool for the next day. For a joke, Margaret raised an eyebrow in much the way Jean would have done herself only a few months ago. "I'm sorry if you don't approve Mother," she reacted, "but this is a once in a lifetime holiday experience and I have always dreamed of wearing a tiny black bikini and drinking champagne on Copacabana beach and that's what I'm doing." Margaret burst into laughter and dashed across the kitchen to hug Jean physically lifting her from the floor and swinging her around. "Of course, I approve, my beautiful daughter," she said, "I'm only teasing you; I love you and only want you to be happy." Jean was delighted to hear her mother say those words, but she responded by saying, "Put me down, you can't do this at your age you silly old woman, you'll do your back in." They both laughed out loud and hugged each other with happiness.

The journey to the beach took only fifteen minutes, they had deliberately set out early to beat the crowds and were soon seeking the best spot to settle into. It had to be not too far from the nearest amenities and not too close to the sea and not in a thoroughfare where everyone would be walking through them. Adiim thought they'd never find a spot and to him, one bit of sand was the same as any other. Then they had to set up folding chairs, and sunbeds, mats and towels and two large umbrellas for shade before everyone could finally relax.

Adiim could remember going to the beach with his friends when he was small and spending the whole day splashing in the water. Since that day he had never been to a beach again until now. Patsy touched his arm and said she was sorry he'd missed out on so much but he just held her hand and said, "It doesn't matter what happened before, now I am very happy being here with you." Suddenly Patsy felt embarrassed, so she jumped to her feet and said, "The last one in the sea is a camel." Then she ran for the waves as fast as she could with Margaret close behind and Alec and Adiim struggling to catch them up.

When they returned to their spot, Jean and Diana had already cracked open the champagne and had seen off the best part of one bottle. "Mother!" said Patsy in a loud voice, "what are you doing drinking so early in the day." "Shushhh," replied Jean in a slurred voice, "don't call me Mother so loudly you'll ruin my image." The rest of them roared with laughter and even Jean had to giggle. They had a lovely day drinking more champagne and beers that Alec and Adiim fetched from a beachside café, eating the delicious food that they'd prepared the day before, and alternating between sunbathing and swimming. The taxi came to collect them at five-thirty as arranged and they were soon back at the villa trying to prepare for the evening barbecue feeling worse for wear after drinking alcohol all day. That topped with a full day of the sun had ensured that none of them was fully coordinated. In the end, Adiim had to light the barbecue with Giin magic and prepare most of the other food too. By the time Grace, Edwardo and baby Valentina arrived, everything looked quite well-coordinated and Diana had drunk two strong cups of coffee.

From a fun party point of view, it was a great success but from the point of view that they were all supposed to be someone else it was a disaster. They all forgot and kept calling each other by the wrong name, especially Jean who continually said Alec Dear while Patsy called her Mother at least twice. As the evening went on Diana and several of the others went for a swim in the pool and the carefully applied makeup disappeared. Edwardo had never really met any of them before but even he thought Diana was looking and behaving like a girl in her twenties. Eventually, Valentina became tired and Grace asked Diana if she could put her somewhere to sleep. While they were in the bedroom Grace took advantage of them being alone to confront Diana. "Okay, Mother dearest," what have you and the Millers been taking?" Diana put on a shocked look and asked, "What are you implying, that we've taken drugs or something?" "I'm implying that you have taken 'A' drug, Yes Mother, one that has made you look and feel years younger, Jean and Alec too if Julia and Alex are who I think they are." That brought Diana completely to her senses and sobered her up in one second flat. She didn't answer but she couldn't lie anymore either. "It's not what you think Grace, it's far more complicated, but I can't tell you unless the others agree to it." "Oh Mother, it's nothing illegal is it," pleaded Grace, "Please tell me you're on the straight and narrow now?" "No Darling I promise you it's nothing dodgy or illegal, it's something wonderful but if the wrong people discover the secret it could have terrible consequences for Ad….," she stopped short of saying his name but Grace was no fool. "So, it's something to do with Adam," she asked? "Stay here with the baby," said Diana, "I'll go and get Alec, he'll know what to do." "So, it is Alec," Grace thought to herself and she bit her lip in anticipation of what they may say.

Diana quietly spoke to Alec and explained that Grace cottoned on because of their indiscretions and figured out that they'd been made to look much younger, but she thought they'd taken some amazing drug. Alec told her to go back to Grace and wait until he had a chance to speak to the others but mainly Adiim. Alec went from one to the other quickly explaining what had happened without drawing attention to himself, Patsy, Jean and Margaret had all said let's tell them the truth and Adiim agreed although he did worry that the more people who knew the more likely they could make a mistake. Alec went to fetch Diana and Grace back to the poolside and then turned off the music to talk indicating that it was probably better to go inside where they can't be overheard. "Oh, my dear God, your family are bank robbers," said Edwardo to Grace in Portuguese. "That's where the money for the house came from, it's stolen, and we have accepted stolen money." "Adiim immediately answered in immaculate Portuguese, "No, these people are all honest and hardworking and they have done nothing wrong, you need to sit down and listen to the entire story and then you'll understand."

The villa had a dining table large enough to seat twelve, so they all took a seat. "I'm going to tell you the whole thing from the beginning," said Patsy. "Let's get some drinks over here," suggested Margaret, "it's a long story." As they went through the series of events both Grace and Edwardo looked puzzled at first but Adiim translated anything he felt would be hard for Edwardo to understand.

Alec kept everyone's glass full and even Edwardo eventually calmed down enough to ask questions in English. "So let me just clear out this," he said, "It is true you are not the brother of Patsy but the father and Julia is her mother, she is called Jean, and Sarah is called Margaret and she is Patsy's grandmother?"

Yes, that's right" said Diana and I am Grace's mother although I am only twenty-one years old now. "Oh, my bloody good hell," said Edwardo, "I cannot believe this crazy story, but I know it is to be real if Diana says it." Grace turned to Adiim. "Can you do something to prove you are what they say?" Adiim said he would and was looking to the others for ideas of what he should do. "Adiim," said Alec," we have finished eating now, will you put out the fire in the barbecue and make it like new again,

I don't want the trouble of trying to clean it tomorrow with a hangover." He stood and walked back towards the pool and Grace, Edwardo, Patsy and Diana followed. He lifted the lid on the big barbecue and the coals were glowing hot, there were dark brown stains where the food had been and where fat had splashed the sides. Adiim closed the lid again and waved his hand slightly, more for effect than a need to do it and announced that it was done. Edwardo went over to it and lifted the lid again. The metal was still hot from the coals but all the grills, bottom and sides including the chrome were sparkling brand-new again and even the coal was new and unlit.

"So, is this what you do to the cars, make them sparkle clean and look unused?" asked Grace. "You have to admit it makes for great business and its good for the environment", said Diana. Edwardo began to laugh and put an arm over Adiim's shoulder saying, "Man you are fantastic, no wonder the family want to protect you." You never have to worry, said Grace, "We would never betray you would we," she directed the question to her husband? "Are you joke" he replied, "This man is make for us so much money that we are extraordaly rich, and we must be grateful to him and take care of him.." He gave Adiim a man hug and slapped his back hard but Adiim felt the honest spirit emanating from the man next to him and laughed.

"How amazing and kind you all are for including my Mother. I have only one other question, does Mum have to come back and work for the business or can she stay here with us?" Alec replied on behalf of them all. "Diana and I have known each other for almost thirty years and have worked closely together for the whole of that time. We are like family to each other and I think of you as part of my family too. The business is capable of making enough money for all of us very easily and if Adiim doesn't mind us continuing to exploit his powers we can continue as long as it takes for us to have a lifetime of security." "In other words, said Adiim, we have enough money for you all and if Diana wants to stay here or if you want to come back to England, we will be happy whatever you decide." No one needed to ask Diana what she wanted; they already knew she couldn't bear to leave her family behind in Brazil.

The three weeks went by quickly and soon it was time to re-pack. Jean, Margaret and Patsy went through everything they had with Diana and shared out their cosmetics and some of their clothes. It was partly to save her having to go out looking for things and partly to lighten their luggage for the journey back. Patsy reminded them Adiim could come back anytime within a few minutes and could bring anything Diana needed, including bringing any one of them for a visit. The idea was still incomprehensible to them, but it was amazing, and they knew how fortunate they were.

Willam grumbled about having to leave this lovely villa where the sun was shining during the wintertime but Adiim explained that other people would probably be moving in next week and they had to go. Adiim told him he would go back early and put on the heating so that the house would be lovely and warm. He'd already been back twice during the last three weeks and he knew it had been snowing but he didn't want Willam to know that just yet. It was a full forty-eight hours before the family would be back home in England but Adiim decided that now would be a good time to put on the heating ready for their return so away he went.

When he arrived at the house, he was dismayed to find it had been thoroughly ransacked by someone although he couldn't understand how they'd managed to get inside. He made himself invisible and searched around the entire building checking every room, the giant workshop and even the garden shed. Every part of the house had been disturbed, the main gate was broken and there had been several people there. He realised the most important things were the family books that Margaret kept in her room.

When he checked her room, everything had been pulled out and someone had gone through everything. There was no sign of the papers books and documents that held all the information about Akilah and her Giin servant. In Alec's study, the file from the Institute had also been opened and all the pages removed. Luckily, Patsy had destroyed the DNA test in a fire, but they'd searched everywhere to try and find it. Then he realised the vase may have been taken. As much as he hated the thing as it had been his prison for so long, he knew it would be bad for him if they had taken it. It not only contained an imprint of him, but it was also constructed by magic and would cause great interest.

He searched the house, but he could find no sign of it. Part of him wanted to use magic to find it and put everything back as it should be, but he knew he had to let the others know first. He quickly transported himself back to the Villa and told Alec he needed help with the heating as it wouldn't work. When Alec stepped away ready to be transported, he quickly told him there'd been a break-in at the house so that he'd be better prepared when he arrived there.

None the less Alec was physically shocked when he saw the devastation. As they walked through the house Adiim pointed out all the things that he thought had been taken, including the file from Alec's study and Margaret's documents. Neither of them could remember seeing the vase for some time but Alec knew that Patsy had kept it close to her every time they'd moved.

After a brief discussion, Alec asked if they could go back to the Villa to let the others know what had happened. When they arrived, no one suspected anything was wrong and Jean asked half-heartedly if they had managed to fix the heating. Alec asked them all to come and sit at the table and they intuitively knew there was a problem. They went through everything they'd found at the house and what they thought was missing. Margaret asked if her picture of Andrew was still there and intact and Adiim assured her it was. "In that case," said Margaret, "the documents are safe because I hid them inside the hollow frame of Andrew's picture." Patsy said, "I'm fairly sure the vase is safe, I've hidden it in clear view in the workshop and filled it with hacksaw blades, spanners and other bits and pieces."

"So, in theory," said Alec, "They only have the notes from the institute but not the DNA sample as Patsy burned it?" "Well they already knew what was in that, so they have nothing new," said Margaret. "Worst of all, they know where we are even though they may not know who we are." "They probably think Patsy has her parents and grandmother hidden somewhere, said Diana, "they certainly wouldn't have recognised you." "I wouldn't be so sure," cautioned Alec, "I read that file from front to back and the tests they did on Adiim's DNA show it has amazing rejuvenating properties, so it wouldn't take too much for a scientist to work out that the oldies have been rejuvenated." "The problem with that is, they know we have the key to rejuvenation and healing and that's exactly what they're after," said Jean abruptly. "On a more positive note," said Patsy, "they still don't know what the magic substance is, and they have no idea about Adiim." "The long and short of it," said Alec, "is that we are no longer safe in Staffordshire and they tracked our movements enough to know we are here in Brazil or they wouldn't have entered the house mob-handed." "We can't go back to the house then can we," asked Jean? "At least this time we have money," said Alec, "I arranged offshore banking with Adiim's help several months ago. We have a tidy sum in a bank in Jersey, about two million in Bermuda and a further three million in a Swiss bank account. I also followed Andrew's example and have stashed quite a bit in safety deposit boxes across the UK. Also, two weeks ago I transferred several hundred thousand pounds into

Edwardo's account, we all have considerable sums in our bank accounts and Diana has an additional sum on deposit for whenever she needs it.

We are not criminals and I have made sure the business has been run legitimately in terms of finances, taxes and wages, right down to company returns and individual expense accounts. The police and the law would have no reason to be looking for us. We've committed no crimes. If anything, the people who are chasing and harassing us are the criminals, spying on us and breaking into our homes without authority is a criminal offence."

No one spoke after Alec's speech but every one of them now felt threatened, whereas only half an hour ago they were happy and on top of the world. "Okay," said Alec, "I'll see if we can extend our time here at the villa for at least a week, preferably two, while I try to work out what to do next." "We'll have to move again there is no doubt, but I think it's better if we leave the house looking as though we'll be returning soon." "In the meantime, we can go back with Adiim in turns to collect any valuable items or personal things that we want to take with us." "I need to bring all the company accounts, for example, we must take that vase, Margaret's photograph and Jean's engagement ring."

No one really liked the idea of going back to the house but Alec and Adiim went back first and Adiim soon made everything look as it should without too much effort. Alec changed the answerphone message and the website for Classic Like New to say they were no longer trading and apologising to any customer on the waiting list who wouldn't get what they wanted. The vase was still in the workshop just as Patsy said it would be, filled with tools and with oily hand marks all over it, no one had even wanted to touch it. Alec emptied it and placed it into a plastic carrier bag, he wanted to keep it out of Adiim's sight because he knew it was a sign of bad times to him. When he went back into the main house everything was back to normal, the back door was open, and the garden looked as it should.

Adiim was in the big garden shed working his magic on the mower and clippers, shears and spades. He'd left Margaret's picture of Andrew on the kitchen worktop ready to take. Alec picked up the picture and looked at the image of the old friend he still missed.

If Andrew was still alive those events at work wouldn't have been allowed to happen. Everyone was terrified of Andrew, except Alec and Diana and everyone else knew it. "I miss you, my friend, said Alec to the photo, "It's a shame you're not here, and you're missing all the fun." Adiim was standing in the doorway respectfully waiting for Alec to have his moment thinking of his friend. When Alec turned and noticed him, he just said, "Time to go," and smiled. Luckily, no one wanted to rent the villa and it was available for the next month. Alec thought it better to book the whole month to give them time to work on a new plan. Ideally, they needed to move from there as soon as they could and go back into hiding. There was no reason to buy airline tickets, Adiim could take them anywhere they wanted to go. There was a distinct advantage to that mode of travel because there'd be no need to go through passport control, no record of them leaving Brazil or entering any other country.

That evening Alec discussed this with Adiim, and he agreed that if he transported each one of them to their new destination, it would be virtually impossible for anyone to track them. He called the family together and asked Diana to invite Grace and Edwardo to come over, they had to let them know what had happened. Willam came into the living room and Adiim told him what had happened back at the house. "I should have been there to protect the house," he told Adiim forlorn. "It wouldn't have made a difference if you'd been there, those people would have captured you and taken you and that would have upset Patsy far more," Adiim assured him. "Wherever we go now I hope the sun is shining," he answered hopefully. Adiim told the others what Willam had said and they all agreed that if they had to go somewhere new, it would be nicer if it was a warmer climate. Staying in Brazil made them realise how cold and dark wintertime back in the UK could be. After a couple of gin and tonics in the dining room the doorbell rang and a happy smiling Grace, Edwardo and Valentina walked into the room. They knew immediately that something was wrong, but all Diana told them on the phone was that there'd been a change of plans and they'd be staying longer. Alec explained what had happened and Edwardo asked if they needed to move to a new location. Alec told them he thought it would be for the best if they all disappeared at the same time. No one said anything for a while as they thought through the implications.

On the face of it - Chapter 11

It was Margaret who came up with the suggestion of moving to Florida. "I've been reading lots of women's magazines recently to keep myself up to date with younger people's fads and modern thinking," she began. "It seems that everyone in America wants to stay young looking and we have the perfect solution." Patsy began to protest but Margaret held up her hand and said, "Hear me out before you say anything against this idea." She continued, "Adiim, are you able to change only small things about a person so that they had no wrinkles around their eyes, or they were thinner or had a better-shaped nose?" Adiim said it wouldn't be a problem to do that if he concentrated on those things. "Then why don't we set up a cosmetic surgery clinic, we only need to convince clients that they are under aesthetic and make them wear bandages for a few weeks, they would have no idea how it was done."

Everyone nodded to each other approvingly. Grace then asked, "Adam, sorry I mean Adiim, could we try an experiment, could you get rid of this extra fat I've been carrying around since I had the baby." Although everyone started to tell her she wasn't fat, Adiim stood up and went around the table to Grace. His trademark swirling sandy cloud appeared; he then disappeared and within seconds Grace was looking slimmer and more youthful. When he reappeared, she grabbed him and hugged him tightly then ran to the nearest mirror shouting, "Oh thank you Adiim, now I look and feel so much better." Edwardo flashed his eyebrows at her saying, "Wow! you sexy bitch," to which first Diana, followed quickly by the rest of them, roared with laughter.

"We do have a few more issues to iron out," said Patsy sternly. "Small matters like immigration papers and green cards, bank accounts and a building, qualifications to perform medical procedures and equipment that you would have to show to anyone who was going to pay for the service. "I think we can probably fix all of those things," said Alec confidently. Are we at least in principle, in agreement that we want to be in Florida and that we think Margaret's idea is a good one? They had a show of hands and everyone except Patsy put their hand up. "Look I'm not against the idea and if you can prove to me that you can sort out that entire list of problems for us without us getting into trouble with the law, then I would be up for it," said Patsy.

Grace asked Edwardo if he was happy to go. He told her he'd always wanted to move to Florida, but he'd had no way to do it before. "Just one more person to vote," said Adiim picking up Willam from his nap on one of the other dining room chairs. Willam repeated what he'd said to Adiim before. His home is where the family is and if it's warm, sunny and safe for a cat he would be happy. Adiim repeated this and Edwardo gasped. "You mean he can talk kitty cat language as well as Portuguese?" "Yes and camel, some horse, dog and rabbit, Arabic, Greek, Russian, Chinese, Japanese, French, German, Dutch, all of the Scandinavian languages except Finnish and Icelandic,

Spanish, Italian, a few bird languages and I was just learning squirrel while I was living at Margaret's house in Edinburgh. I think there are a few more but that's all I can think of."

"Where did you learn to speak such beautiful Portuguese," asked Grace. "I spent three years on a Portuguese sailing ship with my mistress Akilah who was married to a ship's captain. I was inside the vase without any other stimulation and that is why I learned other languages that were all around me, I had no other distractions." "Wow," said Patsy, "I had no idea." "I knew some of those languages before the vase, especially camel and cat," he pointed out. "What is your true native language as spoken by the Giin," asked Margaret? "The Giin do not need language, they communicate with just thoughts, but I learned to speak Arabic at school. Mother was Giin and my father a human, I soon learned both because my mother communicated with me the Giin way. We were cast out to live in the human world as slaves. Everyone was astonished by what he said and felt guilty for never asking him about his childhood or his parents. "What happened to the Giin, where are they now," asked Grace in all innocence?

******

Adiim's Story

Adiim began a story that has been told for centuries but only from the human point of view. "I was sold by the Giin to a King when I was only nine years old to be protector and friend of the Princess Akilah." "I was taken away from my mother and she wasn't allowed to ever see me again." "I was nineteen years old when the king had me locked inside the vase as punishment for drowning a kitten that belonged to the princess. I begged to be permitted to speak to my mother one last time, but my request was refused." Adiim described the relationship between humans and Giin in those times and about a great war between them.

"It was foretold by great scholars that at the beginning of time the Giin and Mankind were created by God from different elements and lived in different realms. The Giin were jealous of the way God made man from the earth, whereas the Giin had been made from the elements of fire and smoke. The kingdom of the Giin is unlike the earth as it has no solidity and so, in the beginning, the Giin could not own or possess anything and they were aggrieved by this and some say jealous of man. God took pity on them by allowing them access to the human world and enabled them to utilise The Law of Attraction which we now call Giin magic. There was one condition, that they must help mankind and never to use their power against them or to harm any man.

Page 172

Unfortunately, mankind began to take advantage of the Giin because they had almost completely lost the knowledge of how to use the law of attraction and the GIIN were experts and could manipulate their environment. Eventually, mankind thought they held power over the GIIN because they were aware that they could never harm them. The Giin were far more powerful than mankind and could manipulate the human world and travel at whim. Eventually, it became impossible for Giin who wanted to live in the human world, they became nothing more than slaves.

Many returned to their world Deo Jagah, but many others decided to fight for the right to live in the human world in peace. Firstly, they began to amass an enormous amount of wealth so that they had no need to ask mankind for anything and also because they had a desperate desire to own precious things such as jewels, rare stones and precious metals including gold and silver. These were the epitome of precious possessions that the Giin could not keep in their world. In a cave that is accessible only to Giin, is a massive collection of treasure that still exists even today, and it is there waiting for the day Giin are released to live in peace with humans without being held as slaves.

This movement led mankind to believe that the Giin were sneaky and untrustworthy as they became more secretive and uncooperative, jealously guarding their accumulating wealth. Unfortunately, one of the Giin named Iblis became even more radical and began inciting others to take vengeance on the men that had held them as slaves and treated them badly. He wanted a war with mankind and tried to convince the Giin that all men were evil, although some had already found their way to live in peace and they tried to protest that not all men were evil.

My mother was such a Giiniri, she fought hard against Iblis until the day he exposed her relationship with my father who was a great and good Egyptian Pharaoh who wanted to find a way to live in peace with the Giin. As their relationship was considered a great sin, my mother was sold as a slave to a farmer and my father was dethroned and stoned to death by his people before I was born.

At first, the war was fought conventionally, but eventually, after many years of terrible turmoil, Iblis could not resist and allowed his anger to rule his head and he used Giin magic to burn an entire city to the ground killing thousands of humans. God had no choice but to banish all Giin back to Deo Jagah and the war ended immediately. By this time, I had become a slave and committed my crime and the king had already had me banished to live inside the vase, so my presence on the earth was overlooked by God. Therefore, I believe I am the only remaining Giin on earth." He sighed heavily as he finished, and a hint of sadness showed on his face.

******

They were all astonished by Adiim's story, it was not one they had ever heard, although Alec and Margaret had both done some recent research on Genies and what was now considered to be mere folk law. The history went back to a time long before current religions were formed. "Do you wish to find your people," asked Alec? "I am a result of people from two worlds and both are my family, but I cannot deny I long to see my mother," replied Adiim honestly." I'm so sorry about your poor parents," said Jean with tears in her eyes, "you have suffered terribly in your life, do you think we could help you to find her?" "I'm certain my mother exists still because I can feel her spirit and I'm sure she's back in the Giin world but she was considered evil for her relationship with a human so I doubt she's having a good life." "Are you able to travel to this Deo Jagah," asked Patsy? "The cave I spoke of is supposed to hold the doorway to Deo Jagah which in the oldest language means the place of the Giin but I have been there recently and could find no evidence of any doorway," Adiim told her sadly. "You have done so much for us so I give you a promise that I will do anything I can to help you to find your mother," said Alec in all sincerity. "I'm sure I can say, that goes for all of us," said Margaret holding his hand tenderly.

Several days passed and Alec kept everyone busy preparing for the next adventure. Every morning Grace and Edwardo came to help with the research needed to set up the new business. Edwardo proved to be particularly resourceful and had information on obtaining green cards that would enable everyone to work in America legitimately. The family had now grown to three men, five women and a baby girl. There was no shortage of babysitters for Valentina and even the men eagerly took their turn with her. By the start of the second week, Adiim had arranged medical qualifications and other records for all of them.

All three men were now qualified doctors of cosmetic surgery and Patsy and Margaret were anaesthetists, with papers obtained from universities across the world. The documents were superfluous because none of them would ever be holding a scalpel or administering anaesthetics. Jean, Diana and Grace were to be clinical advisors and act as nurses, cover the reception and control the administration.

The patient journey through the clinic had to be thorough, detailed and professional. Clients to be booked into the clinic first to have an assessment then photos before surgery so that later after surgery photos could be taken. Detailed information of their requested surgery to be recorded, including example images of the nose, breast types and other types of surgery. All documents including example photos to be signed by the client before any procedure could be booked. Clients would be having fake surgery, but they would have a booking date and time. They would be prepared for their operation and dressed in a gown then taken through to the theatre by two of the men. Adiim would use Giin magic to put them to sleep. While he performed the changes recorded in their file, Edwardo and Alec, assisted by Patsy and Margaret would apply bandages to them. The client would then be put into a bed on a side ward where they would sleep until Adiim came to visit and would wake them. That would enable Adiim to perform several fake operations every day based on example pictures and only wake clients when ready to deal with them.

They would stipulate that clients must stay at the clinic until it was time for their bandages to be removed even though they may feel pain-free. Adiim would use Giin magic to make removal of any bandage too painful an experience until the time decreed by him or one of the others. This would enable patients who had smaller treatments to go home then return to have the bandage removed and avoid anyone finding out that they had never been cut by a scalpel by trying to peel back their dressings.

They needed some marketing and promotional materials to show to potential clients and Edwardo had identified a way to do it. He'd arrange for members of his family and some of his and Grace's close friends to be used as guinea pigs with before and after photographs. All they had to do was convince them that Alec and Adiim were surgeons who were putting together promotional material for their new clinic which was partly true. They set up two of the rooms at the villa as a surgery and aftercare room using GIIN magic and Edwardo's mother was the first to be invited.

Lydia was still an attractive woman at fifty-three and didn't need any surgical enhancements, but Alec thought she was perfect for that very reason. Her command of English was poor, but she'd learned considerably more since her English daughter in law moved to Brazil. She didn't know anyone else, but she'd already spent a couple of days with Diana and they were pleased to see each other. She was even more delighted that the handsome young doctor spoke Portuguese and was able to explain everything. Firstly, Edwardo took several photos of her in a bikini.

Margaret soon had her prepared for her procedure and Patsy pretended to organise the anaesthetic. Within seconds she was asleep and Adiim did his thing, removing the fat from her midriff, straightening her nose, smoothing out her neck and removing a few lines from around her eyes. Diana applied the bandages to her face and head taking care to pad out her nose. In the meantime, Patsy had bound up her middle section where the reduction to her waist was quite remarkable. Grace came in to have a look and pointed out that Adiim had also given her boobs a lift, so they quickly improvised on bandages to that region also.

A short while later Adiim went to wake her and Edwardo and Grace waited with Valentina to see how she felt. She yawned and stretched and then opened her eyes and asked in Portuguese, "Is it all over?" "You are even more beautiful," replied Edwardo kissing his finger and placing it on her lips. She told Grace she felt good and had no pain. She was warned not to try removing any bandages which she agreed to. Their plan had worked, Lydia honestly believed she had undergone surgery. It would be a long wait before they could legitimately remove the bandages, but it was worth it to test the process out. In the meantime, one of Grace's friends had come in for a nose realignment and was allowed home later that day. Adiim sealed the bandage with Giin magic to make it too painful to remove and she went home to recover with an appointment the following week. Edwardo did the same thing with a few of his friends who had small changes like eye bag removal and another friend of Grace's had a breast enlargement and was allowed home two days later.

When the actual time came to remove Lydia's bandages she was delighted and couldn't believe that there was no pain and no scarring either. She looked amazing although Adiim was thinking he could have done more and made her look twenty again. She photographed well and was not afraid to show her body before and after. When she saw herself in the mirror she was delighted and ran around like a chicken making loud noises in broken English that were supposed to mean thank you and see how beautiful I am. All the others came back, laughed and enjoyed her excitement.

The other patients were equally delighted, particularly the girl with the breast enlargement who had a new lease of life and several new male admirers. Edwardo had proved to be a very skilled photographer and all the pictures he took were very professional and showed stunning transformations. During the waiting times, Adiim and Alec had been to Florida several times to arrange paperwork that would enable them to live and work there.

Alec had found a lovely house in Miami with a swimming pool and terrace which had a gauze covered framed area almost like a conservatory called a Lanai, designed to keep out insects and other creatures. It had ten bedrooms and a small nursery attached to one of the master bedrooms so there'd be plenty of rooms for them all and space for an office. It even had its own mooring and motor launch on one of the waterways as part of the rental fee. Alec had opened an account with Bank of America and was able to pay a full year's rent with his debit card which impressed the agent who asked what line of business they were in. When he learned they were plastic surgeons he immediately asked for a business card. Alec told him he didn't have any with him, but he asked for the name of their business and Adiim quickly said, "Akilah Cosmetic Clinic." Alec's eyebrows shot up when he heard it but he fully approved.

The next task was to find a place to set up the Akilah Clinic, not too far from the house, they rented but far enough away so that they could escape from it when needed. It had to be in a prestigious neighbourhood where rich clients would be happy to go. Alec went to an agent to see what was available while Adiim scanned the internet, on a laptop, checking anything out that looked vaguely suitable then invisibly going there to have a look around. Neither of them found a vacant space that was already set up as a clinic because those businesses were far too lucrative.

Alec became quite despondent and wondered if he'd put the cart before the horse by paying a year's rent on the house. Adiim wasn't so worried, he'd found a huge newly built unit with a beautiful glass façade but nothing inside. It was vacant and the builders had overstretched themselves and couldn't complete the inside. He persuaded Alec to go and have a look at it. Once in there, Adiim described how the reception could be here and behind there could be two operating theatres and several recovery wards.

Although Alec could see the potential, he still felt very despondent about the amount of work needed to get the place up and running. Adiim led him through a doorway towards the back of the first floor and closed the door. Then with Giin magic, he made alterations to the room in much the same way as he had with cars. Where there had just been bare blocks and bricks, walls were coated with decorative panels made of granite and marble and the floor was exquisitely tiled with a contrasting stone. "Amazing," said Alec, suddenly realising what Adiim could do. "That's only an example of what can be done," Adiim told him. "We would still have to arrange for all the furniture and surgical equipment to be installed because it's so specialised, but we could be ready for that in only a few days." Before they left Adiim returned everything to how it looked before. Alec agreed that this building was right, it even had a back entrance and an alley with a rear exit from the car park onto the main highway. Alec knew that not some clients wouldn't want to be seen entering or leaving the clinic, so the escape route was a perfect addition.

The businessman in him couldn't help negotiating a deal on the price with the agent because it was an incomplete unit. The developer was delighted to offload such a big space and he virtually bit their hands off. It would take some time to complete the deal, but Alec added pressure saying they had two options on the table but liked this building the most. He told them the deal was dependent on arranging the sale within two weeks or they would go with the other property. The seller reassured them and came into the agent's offices to shake their hands on it. Alec doubted anyone could arrange a property sale including all the legal work within two weeks, but he knew it would speed things up considerably.

Meanwhile, in Rio, they'd been busy back at the Villa sourcing the equipment needed, all types of furniture including state of the art beds and even anaesthesia equipment. Jean had been buying uniforms and surgical gowns. Edwardo and Grace had been putting together the publicity material and had made an amazing job of it. All they needed was a picture of the clinic and the name of the business and they would be ready to go to print. Grace suggested they needed a video to put on the website and wondered if one of them could deliver the right presentation. Patsy thought Margaret was the most eloquent of them, her lovely soft Scottish accent was nice on the ear. Since her transformation, she was exceptionally beautiful, Patsy noticed more young men staring at Margaret on the beach than any of the others. She was quite oblivious to it and was not vaguely interested in young men. The love of her life was Andrew and now he was gone she was accustomed to being alone. When Alec and Adiim appeared back in the villa, they were practising Margaret's presentation for Zum Clinic. Alec was extremely impressed with how industrious they'd been. When there was a break in the recording he asked, why Zum? "That was my idea so that we could design things and practice until we had a real name for the business," said Diana. "We do," said Adiim, "It's the Akilah Cosmetic Clinic," Patsy clapped her hands, she and everyone else loved the idea.

A few days later Alec heard that the lease on the house had completed and they were free to move in when they wanted. Adiim took him over to have a look around before the others were brought across. It was illegal to enter the country without passing through border control, but they had little choice if they didn't want to be chased all over the world forever. Adiim had made sure that all the relevant computer systems held their records and showed them as green-card holders with a legitimate business but there would be no recent record of them entering the country.

Adiim obtained diplomas and certificates from universities for everyone which Edwardo framed. The house was fully furnished and that cut down on their need to buy additional things for the move. Adiim went back to collect Patsy and Willam next. They both loved the new house and Willam felt safe being under a Lanai, partly because it kept creatures out and the baby in and clearly defined his territory, something that is particularly important to a cat. Next came Grace and the baby which was slightly more traumatic because the baby was frightened by the sensation and it scared Grace, but once they arrived, they were happy.

The rest of the family followed quickly and then Adiim went back several more times to collect the luggage and other bits and pieces that they had insisted on bringing. About an hour after they first arrived the doorbell rang, and two hired cars were delivered to them. Patsy took delivery but she was embarrassed when she went to tip them and only had fifty Brazilian Real, but Alec came to the rescue with two twenty-dollar bills.

Patsy and Jean climbed into the smaller of the two cars and went to find the nearest supermarket to stock up on food and a few basic items such as nappies for Valentina, loo roll, shampoo, soap, laundry liquids and conditioners, dishwasher tablets and cleaning solutions, cloths etc. They soon filled up two large trolleys and loaded up the back of the car. By the time they were back with the shopping, Margaret, Grace and Diana had unpacked everyone's clothes and with Adiim's help, they were all clean and pressed and hanging in the various closets. It was early evening and a delicious dinner was being prepared by Grace and would be served outside next to the pool in one hour. This gave everyone enough time to swim in the pool, get showered and change ready for the evening.

Everyone was concerned that Adiim would be worn out from travelling backwards and forwards to Brazil. He also went to Staffordshire to get things from the house and took Margaret to Edinburgh to make sure everything was alright. Jean and Patsy wanted to visit the flat in London and the House in Wimbledon but not today. Diana went back on the final visit to the Villa in Brazil with him to hand the keys back to the agent, not realising that tidying up was a three-second job to Adiim. They needn't have worried about him, he had boundless energy and loved being able to help the family. When they sat down to eat that evening Grace carried out a beautiful strawberry and fresh cream cake that she'd baked specially to say thank you to Adiim for everything he'd done.

They were settling into the new house very nicely and as Edwardo, Grace and Valentina had their own wing it was working very nicely for them. Everyone was far enough away from the baby's room not to be disturbed during the night. The central part of the house was far enough from the bedrooms, that anyone watching TV or cooking wouldn't disturb anyone in their rooms.

The two-week deadline for the purchase of the business unit passed the day before and Alec called the agent to put pressure on the seller. Remarkably he was told they were only hours away from completing everything. The agent called Alec later that morning to go in and sign the final documents and pick up the keys. The team had already pre-ordered equipment and fittings to be delivered when ready but first Adiim had to do his magic. Earlier that week they had sat around the outside table looking at samples of stone and tiles, wood and carpet, glass, metal and plastic fittings to use inside the Clinic and made several decisions. There were clinical standards relating to hygiene and health and safety so all floors had to be as free as possible of cracks and crevices that could hold bacteria. Many of the doors needed to be automatic two-way swing doors so that trolleys and beds could be easily moved through. The windows needed safety catches to prevent anyone from falling out, there had to be piped oxygen available at the bedside and special lighting in the operating theatre. Adiim had logged this information in his mind to use when he performed the transformation of the building. Patsy, forever cautious, asked if anyone would realise there'd been no materials delivered and no fitters on site to make all the changes. Alec assured her the building is on its plot of land, it's almost a small island, no neighbours and no one is watching a building that has been empty and half-finished for almost three years.

They collected the key and Adiim and Alec drove to the building to meet the others waiting outside excitedly. "Alec Dear, this is a well-chosen building in an excellent location," said Jean smiling broadly. Alec couldn't lie about it," it was Adiim who found it, and in fact, I was against it initially until he showed me what could be done with it." The building was over three floors, slightly too big but Alec had a feeling they would expand into the additional space. One inside there were various disappointed Oh's! And Mm's! as they walked around. Then when they reached the first floor, Adiim began to create the walls and floors, doors and panels they had agreed together only a few days previously. After only a few minutes it began to look like a medical facility, even without furniture. They were all excited and even Valentina was running up and down on the beautifully laid marble floor. The walls were clad in the most beautiful stone panels that gave a feeling of luxury and cooled down the environment. Within an hour all three floors looked completely different and several side rooms for recovering patients had been designed. There were three operating theatres with extremely bright lighting and worktops in stainless steel around three sides and access to all three theatres by double doors on one side. It was very professional and looked every bit like the surgeries and clinics Adiim had researched online for weeks. Grace discovered an excellent web site that identified clinics where equipment and surgeries were below the normal standards. It listed details of what is legally required from a clinic providing cosmetic surgery including standards of efficiency. They were delighted with the results of Adiim's work and couldn't thank him enough.

Over the next week they spent long days at the clinic, Edwardo designed a logo and agreed on the typeface and colour for marketing materials. He used this to commission signage for the front of the building and the entrance to the car park. When they arrived and were fixed to the front of the building and behind the reception area, the dream started to become a reality. Gradually some of the services were fitted. There were specialised laundry services, plumbing into operating theatres and the en-suite bathrooms attached to every recovery room. A specialist organisation was installing the equipment required for anaesthetics including tracks of piping to deliver oxygen to every bedside. When the beds arrived, it was beginning to look quite spectacular and Jean came out of one of the side rooms dressed immaculately in one of the new uniforms she looked every inch the professional.

Alec had arranged for a paperless IT system to be installed that would enable them to record a patient's notes and other details in the correct format. The paperwork for the complex insurance they needed had been completed some time ago, but they were still awaiting the vital certificates needed before they could begin to work with patients. A few short days and they would be ready to go but Alec dreaded the final stage which was an inspection from the Florida Medical Licencing Authority.

On the day of the inspection, they still hadn't received the insurance certificates and Alec was pacing up and down. The three men had undertaken considerable research on cosmetic surgery in case they were asked questions about procedures. Adiim didn't seem too worried but Edwardo was terrified. As it turned out they need not have worried, the inspectors were immediately convinced of their authenticity by the opulent trappings of the clinic. Only successful plastic surgeons would have been able to furnish a clinic to that standard. The only difficult question was about x-ray facilities but Adiim just told them they had made a mutually beneficial arrangement with another local clinic and that seemed to satisfy them sufficiently. They still couldn't begin without their insurance certificates and Alec was furious with the broker for making them wait.

After several days of telephone conversations and berating the agent, the necessary certificates finally arrived. It covered all of them for things like malpractice, which scared the life out of Patsy and Edwardo in particular. As soon as they were framed and nailed to the wall the website was launched and Diana and Jean, wearing pristine uniforms, sat at the reception desk waiting for calls. They had a script they would use that included the technical names for procedures and a rough price for things like breast augmentation and rhinoplasty, tummy tucks and rhytidectomy which is a facelift. They'd practised this on each other many times over but they were all still nervous including Alec until Adiim called them all together and reminded them, "What we're promising to people, we shall give to them, not only that but what we give to them will be better than any other clinic can offer. They will not need to have an anaesthetic, they'll require no drugs and their bodies will not be cut open so there'll be no pain, they'll look and feel better and I'll attempt to repair anything I find that is diseased. We aren't committing a crime we're helping people to look and feel better so we shouldn't be afraid of what we're doing." Patsy thanked him for reminding them and they all felt so much better and far less nervous.

Alec was inspired by Adiim's speech. and said, "During the last few months we've had to endure some complex and quite difficult circumstances, but we've remained in control and more importantly we've had fun." "Yes," replied Jean, "that's exactly what I was thinking, there is no danger of botched operations and if someone didn't like their new nose, I'm sure Adiim would quickly change it, so what do we have to worry about?" "Let's make it a really fun environment and a lovely experience for our customers, from the moment they walk in, to the second they leave," said Diana. "We could always play music and I could teach salsa to help them to recover," said Edwardo demonstrating his skill enthusiastically. Everyone laughed but it was the germ of an idea and it would become the signature tune of the Akilah Clinic.

Surgical times - Chapter 12

The phone rang with the first enquiry about breast reduction. Diana launched into her professional speech, but she had a big smile on her face that reflected in her voice. The second call came one minute later and soon the two women were handling a steady stream of appointments. Within a few days, the recovery rooms were full, including those on the third floor. It was then that the appointment system came into play with appointments available only for day surgery clients for small procedures and bookings stretching months into the future. The process of keeping clients in the recovery rooms wrapped in bandages was only to keep up the illusion of surgery but it was completely necessary to avoid too many questions. Patsy and Adiim helped Jean, Margaret, Diana and Grace to keep client records up to date and soon they had a routine that worked.

From day one, at least one of them had their day off every day to look after Valentina and cover all domestic needs such as food shopping, cleaning and cooking. Laundry was easy, they just collected everything in a pile for Adiim to make clean which he did daily before leaving for the Clinic. At Margaret's insistence, they were all made responsible for laundering their own underwear which they agreed would be unfair to leave to Adiim. Eventually, it became difficult to look after Valentina, they were becoming tired and needed rest. She needed to go to nursery, so they hired a nanny and domestic help to enable everyone to have free time and get some much-needed rest.

The results of the fake surgery began to emerge as bandages were removed from facelifts, tummy tucks, breast enlargements and reductions and countless other alterations. Without exception, every client was astounded by the result, including one female client named Rosetta Morgan who had already been given four facelifts previously, but Adiim had repaired her face and returned it to a more natural and youthful look. She was delighted and astounded and as an influential person within the city, she drew a great deal of attention. When she first went back on the social scene, looking so amazing at seventy-eight years of age the press had a field day. Suddenly the client list changed to include Hollywood stars, pop stars, political heads and rich sportspeople. Many of them offered to pay double the rate to have treatment at the Akilah Clinic and skip the queue. Both Alec and Adiim were keen for the business to keep a low profile and they agreed to decline all such offers, preferring instead to operate a first come first served policy for everyone. It had two effects, it deterred some of the most arrogant stars who would not be told to wait or couldn't wait. It also drew attention from the press who began to imply that the clinic had a benevolent approach that was highly unusual in that region.

Their waiting list was now so ridiculously long that Alec had to put a stop to any further bookings and gave notice on the website that their books would not reopen until the following December which was nine months away. Their reputation for exquisite work grew and grew and the few stars and famous people who had waited their turn became the focus of even more attention when they emerged with magnificent transformations.

One lunchtime a young woman named Mariana Pinto came into the clinic and asked to see Edwardo. She'd been attacked by her violent and jealous ex-boyfriend and had terrible knife slash marks across her face. She'd read the company profile and knew Edwardo was from her native Brazil, so she waited on the list for an appointment. She appealed to him for help to reduce the appearance of the terrible scarring on her face. Her one eye was badly disfigured, and her nose was virtually non-existent, but she had been an extremely attractive girl before the attack. Diana and Jean were the first people she met at the reception desk and were very sympathetic to her plight.

She inquired about the likely cost of the operation and when they told her she looked disturbed, but she said it wouldn't be a problem. They arranged for her to have a consultation with Edwardo and Adiim, just a little later the same day. She waited in the reception area and was met with stares and nudges from those waiting but she held her head up high and both Jean and Diana felt a great fondness for her. When Mariana's time came to have her consultation, Diana went into the offices to talk to the two men before they met her. She explained her plight and told them she was certain the girl had no money to pay but pleaded on her behalf for them to help her. As they were speaking, Alec came into the room and heard what was being said. He cut them off and sat down to explain to them that although he wanted more than anything to be able to help her, it would surely bring massive publicity to the door which is the last thing they needed.

Everyone knew he was right and as much as they hated the situation they had to agree. "What shall we do," asked Edwardo bitterly, "tell her to go home and pray for a miracle?" "What a fantastic idea," said Alec excitedly. "Here's what we do. We meet this girl, agree to help her and tell her she can pay for the surgery over some time, then book an appointment for her to come back in three days. I see from her file that she's staying with her friends in Miami, so we know where she'll be for the next couple of days. Then late tonight when everyone's asleep, Adiim can go to her and repair the damage to her face and leave her to wake the following day to find the change." "I like it," said Edwardo, "she'll think there has been a miracle and won't think it has anything to do with us." "I like it too," said Adiim beaming with delight. As agreed, they met Mariana and she explained the terrible attack and they examined the scars on her face. They ran through the same procedure as for all clients and recorded everything on the IT system to appear legitimate. When it came to the section about money Alec, who'd said nothing until this point, asked her if she'd find it difficult to get the money together for her surgery. She began to cry and nodded, "It will take me years to save enough but by that time my life will pass me by," she sobbed. "You don't need to cry," said Alec. "We can give you a hugely discounted operation because of your special circumstances, you need only pay for the equipment and for staying in the recovery room.

This would be at a discounted rate that you can pay back over time." Mariana could not believe her luck and was excited about the prospect of looking at least a bit more normal. She told them she didn't expect miracles and at that point, Edwardo gave her a silver chain with a medallion depicting St Peter of Alcantara. "Here you are," he said, "Pray to St Peter and you may get your miracle."

That night as arranged Adiim went invisibly to her and found her sleeping. He repaired her face and several other scars from the knife where she had been stabbed in the stomach and side of her body. As he was leaving, he opened the clasp on the little chain and medallion of St Peter and hung it gently around her neck, kissed her very softly and melted away.

The next morning as soon as she opened her eyes, she realised that she really could open both her eyes. She put her hand to her face and as she did so the chain around her neck became caught up slightly on her thumb. She thought to herself, "I'm sure I left this on the dresser, how did it get here and who kissed me on my cheek?" She pulled back the duvet and sat up then she noticed that the dull ache she'd had in her side since the attack was gone. She rubbed the area with her hand, delighted to be free of the pain even for a while. As she removed her nightclothes to get dressed, she looked closer and was shocked to see that the scar had gone. Her head was reeling, she wanted to look in the mirror, but it had become a habit to avoid it, she was almost afraid to do it.

When she did, she couldn't believe her eyes, she looked exactly as she had before the attack. She ran out of the bedroom calling to her friend Paula who assumed there was something wrong. She and her husband dashed out of their room worried. "Look at my face, look at it," she cried out. Half-awake Paula thought she was having a bad dream about the attack and told her, "Sweetheart calm down, everything will be alright." Then she noticed her beautiful face and looked shocked. "I'm not dreaming am I, tell me I'm not dreaming," she begged. Paula touched her face and stroked it. "How can it be?" she asked, mystified.

That week newspapers across the world were full of before and after pictures of the girl who was healed by a miracle. Many articles referred to the St Peter medallion and lots of paparazzi trying to interview Edwardo. He wore hoodies and sunglasses everywhere he went and now only entered the clinic via the rear alley. Alec hired a security firm to manage the door and only people with pre-arranged entry passes were allowed into the building, they were also searched and asked to leave any photographic equipment including mobile phones at the door. Eventually, the frenzy simmered down but the stress caused by the media attention had unsettled them all and spoiled the ambience of the clinic for a while.

One weekend on Patsy's day off, she wanted to spend some time with Willam because he had been left alone during the day much more since the clinic became busy. Alec told them they were making hundreds of thousands of dollars every month and would soon have enough money to close the clinic and retire without having to worry about working ever again. Willam was not himself, he seemed lethargic and listless and she noticed he was not eating as much these days. He sat out on a chair next to the pool every day and looked tired of life. Patsy tried to tempt him with a cat treat, he stroked her hand with his paw, but he didn't eat it.

That evening when Adiim came home she told him she was worried about Willam. Adiim spoke to him and discovered he was lonely and bored. He also felt trapped because of the Lanai, which was essentially a cage over the entire garden, although it kept out insects and flies it also prevented birds and other creatures from visiting. Adiim said he would gladly take him to the clinic every day but warned him that there would be lots of strange people coming through. He said he would prefer too many people than to be alone all day. Later Adiim explained how Willam was feeling and everyone made an extra big fuss of him, they were delighted that he was coming to the clinic. Adiim checked him out and discovered that he had a problem with his kidneys which he repaired along with two badly decaying teeth and a long-ago buried thorn in one of his back legs. He also turned his clock back so that he felt like a three-year-old again.

Willam's presence at the clinic had quite an effect on everyone, he was full of life and his eyes were as bright as a kitten's. Adiim had to bring him in to work almost every day by special delivery but Willam was used to this weird method of transport. He still enjoyed having a day at the house on his own now and then though. He became a great hit with clients, particularly those who were in recovery rooms on the second and third floors although he was only allowed in the lounges. Willam had taken to doing his rounds in the same way the Doctors did, helping to keep the clients happy. Adiim praised him for all his hard work and he was happy again. Most mornings he spent in the reception area, welcoming new clients as they completed the registration process. Occasionally a customer asked if the cat should be there and muttered about hygiene, but no one complained when they saw the enjoyment gained by others. He knew never to go near the rooms called the operating theatres or anywhere that clients were sleeping.

One day when Adiim was about to send a client to sleep and perform his magic on them, Willam began howling and scratching at the door to the operating theatre. Adiim was with a client and had to send them to sleep quicker than planned and go to see what was wrong. "She's here again," said Willam, "the same female as before." Adiim was confused, "which female is that?" he asked puzzled. "The same one who came to the other house and the house before it, you know the one," said Willam. "Do you mean the woman with blond hair who was with the dark-haired younger man back in England," asked Adiim with a wide-eyed look? "Yes, she's the same female but I don't see the male," said Willam nonchalantly. "Where is she now then," asked Adiim, "hurry and tell me I must warn everyone?" "Follow me," he replied and turned to head for the spiral staircase down to the reception area. Instead, Adiim stepped into one of the cupboards along the corridor and turned into the swirling cloud, as he caught up with Willam he said: "Show me, I am here but no one can see me." Willam nearly missed a step when the voice spoke but he carried on down the stairs and through to the seating area where the woman was sitting.

It was certainly the same woman Adiim recognised her and realised that neither Diana nor Jean had seen her before and wouldn't have been alerted. Adiim quickly travelled back upstairs to find Edwardo and fortunately, he was alone in a small side office entering records onto the computer. He appeared behind him so that he wouldn't be startled and rattled the door as though he'd just entered. "Edwardo, we have a big problem with security, and I need your help fast," he told him. "Of course," he responded," What's the problem?" Adiim quickly brought him up to date, explained Willam recognised the woman but Diana and Jean had no idea who she was. He needed Edwardo to let them know and then deal with the woman knowing that she was investigating them. "Wow, Willam Cat security systems," said Edwardo then ran to the elevator and set off to deal with things downstairs. Meanwhile, Adiim went to warn Patsy, Alec, Diana and Jean about the situation, it was Grace's day off so she would be safe.

Within a few minutes, they were all on their guard and Adiim suggested they keep everyone else out of sight while Edwardo dealt with the woman. Adiim changed back to the cloud and went to see how Edwardo was coping. He led the woman who called herself Miss Elizabeth Nicholson to one of the consulting rooms to see what she wanted. When she arrived in the consulting room, she began asking questions about the other doctors, who they were and where they studied. Edwardo answered a couple of questions without looking up from her notes but then he told her sternly, "I'm sure you will have a lot of questions, but I have limited time available to discuss your requirements." "I'm here for a facelift and to have my neck smoothed out as it should say in my notes," she answered almost rudely. Edwardo went through the same procedure as he did with everyone else. He was now so polished that he seemed highly confident and very professional as he took measurements of her face and nose making copious notes as he did so. "Are you the guy who gave Mariana Pinto her magic medal," she asked? "If you mean the pendant of St Peter, yes I did, but there was nothing magic about it," he responded without looking up. "Your wife is English isn't she, Doctor?" she probed? "How did you know that," he asked without looking up? She chose not to answer but went on with her questions. "Isn't she the daughter of Diana Curtis from London; I've met Mrs Curtis through my work," she stated? "No, my wife's mother is Diane Jones and she's from England but not from London, you are mistaken" he responded standing up to signal the end of the consultation.

"One more thing said Edwardo, "As you are not from the USA we need you to give us a blood sample before we can agree to operate on you and we also need your passport, entry visa for the USA and birth certificate. We can book an appointment for you to have blood taken at the hospital, the results will be sent to us so then we can decide if you would be a suitable candidate for an operation. We will send you the date for your blood test in due course and after that, we will let you know the outcome." He opened the door saying, "Good afternoon to you Miss Nicholson, we will be in touch with you soon. "Ellen Cole aka Elisabeth Nicholson had been sent a long distance to work on this case and she hated it. Her boss had the audacity to send her to get plastic surgery which the company was to pay for but only on the condition that she uncovered the truth about the miracle of Mariana Pinto, any connection to Patsy Miller and her damned cat. So far, she hadn't seen anyone familiar or even of interest, she'd learned nothing tangible, had no idea if there was any connection. She did think it was weird the way the resident cat stared at her, just the way that one in Staffordshire stared at her as she sat in the car. She hated the idea of a blood test, she hadn't expected to need one, but she had no choice if she wanted to stay close and learn anything. Most people stayed in the recovery rooms for at least two weeks so that would give her a chance to snoop around. She regretted giving a false name, she'd be berated by her boss he would either need to give her a false ID or she'd have to hand it over to her young and irritating colleague. Unless she could get her hands on that cat? As soon as she'd left the building, Edwardo went to find Adiim, but he'd been in the room the whole time with him. He handed the file to Patsy who asked what the blood test was for. "Delaying her," said Edwardo, "I was thinking we could say there's a problem with her blood and we can't offer her an operation." "Very smart thinking," said Alec. Without an appointment, she couldn't get past security and back into the building and Edwardo was certain she was working alone as she was staying in a studio apartment. Not only that but they could control the length of time before she was invited to take the blood test and delay the decision on any procedure. "I suspect she gave a false name anyway," said Alec. "Well if she has, she won't have the documents Edwardo has asked for. She'll either have to back off or produce false documents which we could seek verification on," said Margaret. "In the meantime, we should conduct our own investigation into Miss Elizabeth Nicholson, it would be shocking if the USA border discovered she'd entered using a false passport wouldn't it," said Patsy. That evening they were discussing Miss Nicholson again. "When she didn't know I was watching her she did spend a lot of time staring at Willam," Adiim told them gently bending down to stroke him as he said it. "Do you think he could be in danger again," asked Patsy concerned? "I think we may have to protect him," answered Adiim honestly. "Just a thought," said Diana, "but couldn't we disguise him in some way like changing his colour from ginger to black with dye?" "I could do it without dye, but he's a very stubborn person and may not want me to," said Adiim seriously.

Patsy loved that Willam was called a person with a stubborn personality, just as she'd always imagined. She also knew his safety was more important than his vanity. "Adiim, will you please tell Willam I want him to change colour to black for safety because I'm worried about him," she requested? Willam had no hesitation in agreeing that because he loved Patsy, he would do it. Adiim stroked his back twice and the marmalade ginger coat turned to a shiny black. Everyone agreed that he looked just as handsome in a black coat, but he knew it would take some getting used to. He was certain the woman had recognised him. "Next time I'll bite and scratch her, then she won't want to come near me," Willam told them.

The interest in Mariana Pinto had come and gone and the clinic continued changing people to make them both look and feel better. Their reputation was second to none, they had no complaints or unhappy customers and most clients reported feeling and looking better. The process worked and there was little pain unless they tried to remove the bandages too early. In those cases, the pain had been so unbearable that they just couldn't do it.

One day they were asked by Mr Joseph Rosenburg, another plastic surgeon if they could give him a facelift. It would have been his fifth and most surgeons didn't recommend it as his face had already undergone too much surgery. Alec was concerned that he was a spy trying to catch them out, but Edwardo performed the diagnostic assessment with confidence. He discussed the potential pitfalls, convinced the client he was completely competent and agreed to help him. When Adiim woke him after his pseudo operation he reported feeling extremely well. Adiim repaired the man's face but restrained himself from making changes that couldn't be explained. He tried to break his agreement to stay in the recovery room until his bandages were removed but Adiim made him feel nauseous every time he tried to leave.

One evening as Jean was doing the rounds of the side wards she checked in on Mr Rosenburg. He was trying unsuccessfully to remove his bandages a millimetre at a time and was suffering immense pain in the process. As she came into the room he cried out with the frustration and Jean went to re-check the dressing. She spoke softly and kindly to him telling him to wait until he was healed. Grace happened to be passing and knowing that Rosenburg was a surgeon himself, she gave him a telling off as he should know better. "I've performed thousands of operations myself and I've never known bandages to be too painful to remove, what have you done to me glued them on with acid," he spat out angrily? "Look here, foolish old man," said Grace snapping back, "You don't know everything even though you think you do. The surgeons in this clinic are highly skilled. Until they tell you the bandages can come off you will do as I tell you, now get into bed and shut up." He was used to people jumping around when he said jump and he was astounded by the way this young woman talked to him. Inside he knew she was right, so he climbed into bed and stayed quiet.

Adiim told them to wait at least three more weeks before removing his bandages so he'd think his suffering was longer. He asked Edwardo why the woman in the next room had already been released when she had a similar facelift. "Firstly, your face has been overworked over a long period and the new laser procedure we use is designed to ensure your scarring is minimal and the healing process is maximised. You have had deeper rejuvenation treatments than our average client owing to the terrible damage to your hypodermis, this requires a longer healing time and cannot be disturbed, or the results will be affected." "I understand you apply a thin film made of a pure amino acid after the procedure, is this true and how does it work," he probed? "I cannot and will not ever disclose our secrets as I am sure you will understand," said

Edwardo smiling. Three weeks later Adiim released Mr Rosenburg's bandages and Alec and Edwardo went to remove them. Patsy acted as the nurse for the procedure and even she was amazed by the transformation Adiim had managed to perform on the old man without making him look shockingly much younger.

Although he was almost eighty years old, he looked around fifty-five, his grey hair had grown through and was still dyed on the ends but even that didn't detract from the look. When he saw himself in the mirror, a small tear appeared in his eye and he whispered a quiet thank you. He spent several minutes examining himself and could find no scars and no bruising and there was no residual pain." You've performed a miracle that no other surgeon I have ever met would have been able to achieve these results." I've examined twenty or more people who've been operated on at this clinic and the results are always the same, astounding. I thank you for what you've done." "You are welcome," said Alec, "We hope your stay here was not too uncomfortable?" "I was a pain in the ass, but your rather attractive nurse gave me the biggest scolding I've had since my mother died thirty years ago and I thank her as I deserved it." She's quite a woman," said old Rosenburg, "I know," said Edwardo, "that's why I married her."

They all laughed and shook his hand as he packed his bag ready to leave the clinic. "If you would prefer to leave from the rear of the building, I can bring your car around for you," said Diana smiling as she handed back his credit card. "No thank you," replied the old man, "I want the world to see my new face." Then he skipped out of the clinic swinging his bag and giggling.

One morning as Patsy was lounging about and preparing for a lazy day off, Adiim appeared and asked her if she would like to spend the day together and do something fun. Margaret had noticed that neither of them really went anywhere on their time off and had suggested strongly to Adiim that he could do something about it. She was delighted. "I've lived here in Miami for months now and I have never been to Miami Beach or driven along Ocean Drive in an open-top car." "If that's what you want to do then I shall arrange it now," said Adiim buzzing with excitement at the suggestion of spending an entire day on a beach with Patsy.

"Just one thing before we do," said Patsy, making a shy little girl face, "I know I refused to let you make changes to me when you did the others but now they look so good and healthy and I feel a bit fat and old, especially when compared to Gran. Could you make me look slimmer and fitter so I can wear a bikini on the beach without feeling embarrassed?" "I'd rather do it for you than anyone else," he responded tenderly. Two minutes later Patsy looked five years younger, slim and fit, her bleached hair returned to its lustrous wavy brunette, gone was the remains of the fake tan and the Essex girl makeup that became her disguise and instead, she looked a natural olive tanned beauty who wouldn't look out of place on any beach, or magazine cover come to that. She went over to the mirror to look at herself and almost squealed in excitement with her new look. She had never looked better in her life, she felt fit enough to run a marathon. "Oh! thank you Adiim, I feel wonderful," she told him as she hugged and kissed him. "Now I understand how our clients feel when the bandages come off." I'm so pleased you're happy and I hope you like the surprise gift I've given to you also." "What surprise gift?" she asked puzzled. All Adiim would say was wait and see. Patsy went to prepare for a day on the beach and Adiim flew across to the car rental company where they had an account. He quickly chose a car and drove it back to the house tooting the horn as he pulled up. Patsy wondered who was waiting outside and called Adiim to get the door. When she eventually opened it, she was excited to see Adiim sitting in a bright blue vintage Corvette with the roof down. For the second time in an hour, she squealed with delight then dashed in to get her beach bag and lock the house. She walked out to the car wearing a wine-coloured bikini covered with the same coloured wrap-over dress. She'd bought them in Brazil, but she hadn't dared to wear them until now. Her look was completed with sandals and sunglasses and with her hair down she looked stunning.

Adiim wore the turquoise shirt and navy-blue shorts Patsy bought for him, topped with his designer sunglasses and deck shoes. Unlike Patsy, he'd long ago given up on the bleached hair because it didn't match the image of a high-flying surgeon. Together they made a beautiful couple and they knew it. Adiim was about to move over to let Patsy drive the Corvette but she declined, saying she preferred to be taken to the beach by her handsome escort. When they arrived on Ocean Drive, Adiim drove along slowly, partly looking for a parking space but also because

Patsy wanted to take in the scenery. There was loud music coming from some of the bars and restaurants as they passed by and some of the Latin music made her want to dance. Eventually, when they turned around and were driving back the other way, a woman waved to Patsy and yelled in Spanish, "If you're looking for a parking space I'm just about to leave." Without even thinking about it, Patsy replied in excellent Spanish, "Yes we are looking, thank you, we will wait for you." Adiim laughed out loud and it took her almost a full minute until she realised she'd spoken Spanish. "I don't speak Spanish, how did I do that," she asked puzzled?   "That's your gift from me," he grinned.   Although she wanted to be annoyed, she couldn't, it was done with good intentions and if she was really honest about it, she loved being able to speak another language. "Sometimes if we have a problem and we need to communicate it will be useful to speak to you in Spanish or Greek or Swedish he told her."   Do you mean to tell me that I can speak other languages," she asked astounded? "Yes, and read and write most of them too," he answered frankly.

Patsy sat grinning to herself as they parked the car. Luckily, the beach was not too crowded, and they soon found a place to settle. The sun was hot, and the beach was idyllic, there was lots of music playing and they were so relaxed. Patsy adored him and she was having the best day since they came to Miami; if she could have her wish he would kiss her, but she knew he thought of her as a sister and it would never happen. Even though he could never show it Adiim was full of emotions and very deep feelings for Patsy. He knew it was forbidden for him to fall in love with a human and he remembered only too well what happened before when he allowed his emotions to come to the surface. Both pretended their emotions didn't exist and decided instead to enjoy every minute alone together. Adiim jumped to his feet and held out a hand to her. They ran into the sea, splashing each other like kids and enjoying every minute of it. By now the sun was high and extremely hot as they both dried off back on their towels. "I would like us to do this more often," Patsy said turning to Adiim "I agree," he responded, "every week?" When they were dry, they decided to go back and put their towels back in the car and have lunch at one of the restaurants on the other side of the road.

While they were waiting for their food to arrive, they discussed the clinic and the people who left feeling happy, not to mention those who'd been sick and Adiim had made well again. "I wish we could help more people in the world. Those who need your help, those who are sick and poor and can't get anyone to help them," said Patsy deep in thought. "That could be our adventure every week on our day off," said Adiim enthusiastically. "We could travel anywhere and seek out people who need help to get well." "Could you change our appearance so we can't be recognised," asked Patsy?" "We could become angels and it would be seen by some as the reason for their miracle cure for their sickness." Patsy loved that idea and was so excited she suggested they should try it out that afternoon. When they finished eating, they drove home and logged onto the internet to try and find an idea for their first adventure. Only the day before there had been a terrible earthquake in the Philippines and many people were still trapped, particularly in remote regions. Hundreds had been injured and many thousands had been left homeless. "This is it." Said Patsy. Adiim changed them both into albino versions of themselves dressed entirely in white to match their gleaming white hair and transported them into the heart of the earthquake aftermath.

Several people noticed the swirling cloud arrive and two, glowing, whiter than white beings, stepping out of it one male the other female and both about twenty-two years old." Adiim quickly began locating trapped people and spiriting them out of their tiny prisons repairing their injuries as he did. He then laid them out in a row next to each other for Patsy to care for. Within two hours they had rescued seventy-nine people and a small crowd was watching. All of those rescued had their injuries repaired, many of them would have been fatal. As this happened the angels spoke to them in their own language. When the authorities arrived on the scene equipped with television cameras Adiim held onto Patsy's hand and they disappeared into the cloud.

When they arrived back in Miami, they were exhausted, but they were both satisfied with what they'd achieved. "I think it should be our secret," said Patsy looking directly into Adiim's eyes. He nodded and was about to discuss things further when the others started arriving home from the clinic. They were all hungry and wanted to know what wonderful delicacy Patsy had prepared for their dinner. Adiim went into the kitchen and a moment later walked out with a chicken casserole that anyone would swear had been in the oven for at least four hours. While they were eating, the others complimented Patsy on her new look and asked them what they'd done during their day off. They talked about the Corvette, the beach and lunch on Ocean Drive but that's where they ended their story. Patsy remembered her gift from Adiim but decided to keep it as a surprise. Jean and Alec decided they should take their next day off together and do something similar. Grace didn't say much for a while but when the opportunity arose, she told Patsy how beautiful she looked and they both grinned at each other.

Margaret had also noticed the twinkle in their eyes and Patsy's physical changes but for now, she decided to stay quiet about it. By the end of dinner, it was decided that the married couples should take time off together, Patsy and Adiim said they'd be doing that weekly from now on and Diana and Margaret were planning some fun days out too. Adiim went out to the pool deck to look for Willam and Edwardo turned to Grace and asked her in Portuguese if she wanted to come to the bedroom while everyone was clearing up and the baby was sleeping. "What for?" asked Grace, teasing. Before either of them could do anything more, in perfect Portuguese Patsy said," I think you should try being a little more discreet when you discuss your personal love life in future." The looks on their faces were a picture and they couldn't believe what they were hearing. Patsy roared with laughter and proceeded to tell them in Portuguese that Adiim had given her the gift of languages.

Edwardo enjoyed having another person to communicate with using his native language and although like Adiim, her language references were sometimes a little old fashioned, her pronunciation and grammar were excellent. The rest of the family were equally as impressed to hear Patsy suddenly speaking Portuguese, but only Grace and Edwardo understood what she said. When Adiim came back from the pool deck holding Willam he was amused by the conversation taking place and explained to the others about the special gift he had given to Patsy. Alec was interested, he'd always struggled to try to learn a bit of French and German and told Adiim he was envious of her new ability.

Jean had learned French at school and had gone on to study the language to A-Level, but she'd never really been in a position to use it. Diana, like Alec, had studied both French and German for work but would not consider herself proficient. Margaret, on the other hand, was a real scholar and was particularly good with languages. She was a history teacher and studied archaeology and Egyptology throughout her career. She read and understood Latin, ancient Greek, Hebrew, Arabic and could read some ancient hieroglyphics. She was thrilled to have conversations with Adiim in Greek and Hebrew and when she first met him, they'd studied and translated ancient Latin text. However, like the others, she was not particularly proficient in any of the modern languages although she'd studied Italian for a time. They were all inspired by Patsy's new ability and vowed to use their language skills much more in future. Adiim was trying to decide whether to give the gift to them all but for now, he wanted Patsy to be the one who enjoyed it. Instead, he made the four older family members fluent in French and German, Grace fluent in Portuguese and Edwardo completely fluent in English, which they were all thrilled about. By the end of the evening, they were all planning their next day off.

A number of them had already begun messing about on the water as the house came with a launch although none of them was secure enough to try moving it alone, Alec had arranged for them to be taught piloting skills by a local professional called Dylan. He was a charming man, a native Floridian with years of experience a great sense of humour, and they all enjoyed his coaching. Alec had shown a flair for it and was already moving on to some more advanced training. Margaret also had excellent sea legs and Dylan had told her she'd learned faster than any other woman he'd taught. Although Margaret thought him slightly sexist, she couldn't help feeling flattered by the comment. Jean, Diana and Grace had done well but were on more basic levels and Edwardo, Patsy and Adiim were on middle ground. On their next day off Alec and Jean were planning to go sightseeing because they both had a penchant for the beautiful Art Deco buildings that Miami was famous for. They also decided to have either lunch or breakfast at Jerry's, a famous deli which itself was housed in a beautiful example of that type of architecture. Patsy was already scheming to arrange a fun day out for Diana and her Gran as she believed they both needed some male company. Edwardo planned to take Valentina to the beach and Grace was planning a shopping trip at the same time. Patsy looked forward to her next day off with Adiim because they could be alone together and because of the amazing things they could do to help sick and dying people.

During that week at the clinic, everyone was happier because of the new arrangements. With an established new pattern of working, it was easy to deal with. Alec had even begun talking about the day when they could sell the clinic and all retire, which was not too far away given their current rate of earnings.

On Wednesday a new client came in for an assessment and asked specifically for Doctor Adam. This was not unusual except this young man didn't appear to need any surgery. Jean took his name and asked him to take a seat in the waiting room, then let Diana know she had a weird feeling about him. Diana noticed Willam on the back of the seat facing the young man, he stared and hissed at him. They needed to let Adiim know but he was inaccessible for a time as he was busy performing miracles. Diana knew Willam was watching the young man for a reason and guessed he was the partner of that Nicholson woman. By telephone, they quietly let everyone know what they suspected. Grace and Edwardo were on their day off, but Jean contacted them anyway so that they were alerted. Eventually, when Adiim and Patsy left the theatre, Alec was waiting to tell them about the visitor.

Adiim quickly disappeared and went to have a look for himself. Willam was completely stoic and continued his long, fixed stare at the man. Adiim whispered to him that he was there. "It's the male this time," he told Adiim. "Yes, I recognise him," Adiim responded, "we need to deal with him now." Adiim went back to where Patsy and Alec were waiting and told them his plans. "It's the young spy as we suspected, he's seen most of our faces before, but he has no idea what Adam Osman looks like does he?" said Adiim.

At that, he changed himself into a middle-aged man with greying hair, a slightly broader middle and a large moustache. Patsy hooted with laughter at his new image, mainly because his trousers didn't fit, and his jacket was so tight. She laughed even louder when he spoke in a cross between an American and German or Yiddish accent. She twiddled his moustache and gave him a little kiss on his forehead. Then she phoned Diana and Jean to ask them to show the client to the first floor and warned them about Adiim's appearance. When Diana came into the consulting room to introduce Mr Malcolm Bird to Doctor Osman, she had to fight hard to keep herself from laughing. As soon as she closed the door, she ran down the hall into a store cupboard and let out an enormous laugh that lasted several minutes.

The consultant facing Mr Bird was not the Adam Osman he was expecting but he went along with his plan anyway. He showed his documents which included his actual passport, entry visa and his birth certificate. He'd been pre-warned by Ellen Cole alias Ms Nicholson, what to expect. Adiim asked all eligibility questions then came to the main one which was, what actual surgery he wanted to be performed. Malcolm blushed a deep shade of red before saying he wanted pectoral and bicep implants. Dr Adam rose to his full height and told him he had no desire to begin implanting fake muscles into men who were too lazy to go to the gym. However, he told Malcolm to take his shirt off and proceeded to measure the circumference of his arm and his upper chest. "In my opinion," said the good Doctor in his stilted German voice, "you have perfectly normal body mass although it looks a little flabby because you need to exercise the muscle." Wow, that stung Malcolm because he considered his body to be quite well defined. "I'm willing to pay whatever it takes to have an operation here," he blurted out.

Adiim knew that was a desperate attempt to get into the clinic and nothing at all to do with needing the surgery. "Here at ze Akilah Clinic ve pride ourselfs on ze selection and filtering of our clients and ve help only those who need it. I have turned away Hollywood stars and American footballers because vot zey ask for woz not necessary." Malcolm was angry now because of what the old man said about his body and because he'd failed his mission. He told himself, "This clinic is nothing to do with Patsy Evans it's a boring legitimate glory hole where the surgeons like to play God." He stormed down the stairs and dashed out of the front door, throwing his security badge at the guard on the way. Adiim watched from the office window as he climbed into his car looking up for one last time at the clinic. The stupid old man in the first-floor office window waved at him which only added to his anger, he slammed the door and drove away.

Past catching up - Chapter 13

During their day off Alec and Jean decided not to go on their skipper training and instead went to look at the wonderful Art Deco buildings nearby, as previously planned. They stopped for a brunch and Alec was delighted to find a newsagent that sold newspapers for ex-pats. He'd managed to get copies of the Mail and the Times that were only a day old. They sat in the sunshine enjoying their day and relaxing until Alec turned to page four of his Daily Mail to find a picture of his old self, staring back at him. Next to it was a picture of him with Diana at a conference they attended several years previously. He read the piece in silence without alerting Jean and was horrified to find that he'd been branded a thief a liar and a spy who'd embezzled millions from his country with the help of his sidekick and then disappeared with said proceeds. His stomach went cold and at the same time, his face grew red, partly from the humiliation and more so from anger.

There was a fee of fifty thousand UK pounds for information leading to their whereabouts. The report said they were known to have been in both Yorkshire and Staffordshire before they went to Brazil using fake passports and accompanied by Miller's wife, daughter and mother in law. There had been no record of them crossing any border from Brazil, but it was believed that they were making their way north and that they were expected to illegally enter the USA at some stage. Alec was completely disturbed after reading the article and didn't want Jean to read it so he purposely spilt his coffee over the newspaper and then made a big fuss about screwing it up and putting it into a bin in the street. Jean thought he was a clumsy so and so, but she suspected nothing.

They continued with their day out and Alec tried to remain smiling and relaxed, although his mind was racing through solutions to their latest problem. His only change to their agreed schedule was to call at the bank where he spent at least twenty minutes in a private interview room while Jean sat in the main lobby waiting. She was a bit narked when he returned but he smiled and told her the good news, they'd finally made enough money for all of them to retire and live comfortably for the rest of their lives. Although Jean loved the idea, she couldn't help thinking how much she would miss the clinic in the same way that she'd missed the cars, both gave a great deal of pleasure to the customers and made her feel worthwhile.

Later that evening Alec decided he had to tell Diana about the article so they both went out in the car under the pretext of getting a few things from the supermarket and Diana saying she would come along for the ride. No one paid any attention, so Alec drove two blocks down the road and pulled into the car park of an Italian restaurant. Diana knew something important was coming so she stayed quiet until Alec was ready to talk. They'd worked together for so many years that sometimes Diana recognised stress in Alec before Jean did.

He slowly went through the story he'd read in the UK newspaper and Diana's eyes went wide with a mixture of anger and fear. When he'd finished, she just said," Who are those people Alec and how did they manage to infiltrate the organisation the way they have. No one seems able to stand up to them and they just overrode or undermined everything anyone with any authority tried to do. I never saw another senior manager again after they arrived and although I am not normally a violent person, I couldn't stop myself from wanting to smash that vile woman's face in." Alec nodded, "I've asked myself that same question and I imagine they're so high up in security that they outrank everyone working in the department." They were both completely silent for a while and eventually, Alec said, "I suppose we will have to tell the others, it's only fair." "Will we have to move again," asked Diana? "The good news is that I've been working with an offshore banking advisor, we've squirrelled away millions in bank accounts that could never easily be traced back to Alec Miller or Diana Curtis and we have enough to retire on and none of us ever need to work again." "I don't know how I feel about the idea of becoming a rich recluse," she answered with a wry smile. She hugged Alec and he kissed her forehead; they were like sister and brother.

Back at the house, they told everyone about the newspaper article. Initially Jean was cross that he didn't tell her earlier, but he explained that Diana had to know first as she was implicated in the story. Patsy forever the practical one said immediately, "We have to move again but this time we will just have to stay completely low key." "I feel very sad," said Edwardo, "I was enjoying being taken seriously by people for a change." "Better to be safe than sorry," said Margaret frankly. "Anyhow," said Jean, "Alec already told me we have made enough money for all of us to retire very comfortably, so what's the problem?" "Think of how wonderful it would be to spend any time we wanted with Valentina without sending her to babysitters or nannies," said Grace grabbing Edwardo's hand.

Only Adiim stayed silent and eventually went outside to tell Willam what was going to happen. Patsy noticed his solemn mood and followed him out. "What's wrong Adiim," she asked him? "Are you unhappy about having to move again?" Adiim looked as though a tear was forming in his eye when he turned to Patsy. "I was just beginning to enjoy our time together and our secret adventures as the unknown angels." Patsy took his hand and smiled, "We don't have to be living here to have those adventures, we can go from any place and anyway it's our day off tomorrow so let's start planning our next one." It cheered Adiim when he realised that the adventure was equally as important to Patsy and he squeezed her hand. "There's a terrible drought in Ethiopia and everything is dying for lack of water but there is plenty of water buried under the ground, they can't reach it, but I can," he told her. "That sounds exciting," said Patsy, "I can't wait for tomorrow."

That evening when Valentina had gone to bed, they all sat around and discussed several scenarios that included where they could live that would be safe and what they would need if they were going to retire. "Just list all the things you could need, an art studio, music room, exercise gym, swimming pool, and IT equipment, media centre, the answer is yes to anything you want," said Alec frankly. "We need to move to a remote but beautiful part of the world where we can have all the luxuries we could ever want, but with the type of security that would enable us to relax fully," he added. They all knew this was not something they could arrange overnight but with Adiim's help to scout for appropriate places, it would take a lot less time. Willam didn't mind the suggestion of moving but he asked if they could go somewhere without a Lanai this time.

The next morning Patsy was up early even though it was her day off. She made coffee and breakfast for everyone and even offered to take Valentina to kindergarten. Grace thanked her but said she had a routine and preferred to see her settled in before going off to work. Adiim was messing around the pool with the skimming net pretending to be busy. He offered to take Willam to the clinic for the day, but he declined, saying he would have a quiet day at home and for Patsy and Adiim to go and enjoy themselves. When he asked where they were going Adiim told him the truth and he was intrigued saying he wished he could come too.

Adiim explained that this trip could be too risky for him as they were going to a part of the world where cats were as big as, or sometimes even bigger than a man and he could easily be killed and eaten. Adiim promised to find a different kind of venue like a hospital or orphanage for the next adventure and he would be welcome, and children would love to see him. When Adiim told Patsy, she agreed that it would be fun to take Willam along and she knew he would be very welcomed anywhere that children may be. She picked him up a hundred times a day and kissed him, but she was getting worried that he could be very bored with life. "Maybe we could find a girlfriend for Willam," she asked Adiim? "Well he had a big crush on the girl next door when we lived in Staffordshire, maybe I could go and get her," said Adiim? "Well that sounds easy but what about the people who she lives with, they love her like we love Willam and they would miss her terribly," Patsy responded. They agreed to keep an eye open for a likely girlfriend for him and then prepared to set off on the latest adventure.

They arrived in a small village where it was clear that everyone was dying for lack of water. Before they left Patsy knew where they were going, she insisted they bring as many bottles of water as they could carry. They had managed six gallons which were a start. As they materialised in the village dressed as two shiny white people, the villagers were afraid but Adiim began to try speaking to them in a variety of languages and eventually found several people who spoke Arabic. He explained to them that they were here to help and not harm them and had brought water from their land for them to drink now. Everyone gathered around and took cups full of the cool sparkling freshwater and said it was water from heaven because it was so clear, cool and tasted so good. Patsy continued to make sure everyone was given water and paid special attention to the children.

Meanwhile, Adiim was talking to some of the elders to find out where their normal water source was. They told him it was a one hour walk from the village and it was now only a drying muddy pool full of dying fish and animals. Adiim asked one of the elders to let him borrow his wooden ceremonial staff and walked a few paces towards the outer limits of the village. In his mind's eye, he could sense the water so far beneath the ground and used Giin magic to begin putting pressure on it while at the same time he pushed the wooden staff into the parched ground so hard that it was buried almost to the end. The villages who were not too sick to walk came to watch what he was doing. Then Adiim shouted in Arabic, "let the water come here," then he deftly drew the stick out of the ground. At first, nothing happened but then there was a sound like steam coming from the hole in the ground and then suddenly a giant spout of water shot into the air like a fountain.

The people were shocked and delighted and could not believe their eyes as the water cascaded over the dry ground and turned into a gently babbling stream that had already found a course along the side of the village. The villagers came and drank from it and bathed in it and let the animals free so that they too could drink and join in the celebration. After only a few minutes a large pool was forming on the lower ground only a quarter of a mile from the village and from nowhere, flocks of birds began diving down to drink and swim on the newly formed mass of water. Adiim could sense other animals heading towards what was now becoming a lake and soon the sounds of elephants could be heard, and other large game animals began to appear on the horizon.

The Elder of the village who had given his wooden staff to Adiim began shouting and waving his arms about. When Adiim asked him what was wrong he told him he was trying to form a hunting group to protect the water from the wild thieves and to stop other men coming to take their water that was a gift to their village from the white spirits. Both Adiim and Patsy chastised him and told him the water was for everyone, man and beast and did not belong to them. Patsy asked him to imagine how they would feel if the next village had found so much water and would not share it when their people were sick and dying from thirst. The old man fell to his knees and apologised saying he had not been thinking straight because of the excitement of it all.

As the warriors began to gather around, he told them he was mistaken, and the white spirits wanted them to make sure the water was given to any man, beast or bird that needed it. By now Adiim had begun already to learn a little of the Oromo language and he tried to explain to them that they had come to help but now they had to find others who needed help. As a parting shot, Adiim turned three pieces of land on the other side of the village into fields of maize, one of them was already ripening and could be harvested. He told them they must not fail to water it and they should be certain to withhold some of the corn to plant for the next crop. Adiim asked the old man if he may keep the wooden staff which he first took away then bowing and holding it horizontally he presented it back to him as a gift of honour. The women gathered around Patsy and one poor sick little girl that she had been feeding and giving water to, somehow found the strength to leave her bed and walk outside to hug her legs. The women wanted to give her some beads they had made, and they even thanked her for the bottles that they had brought the water in. Everyone looked more alive and as they were getting ready to leave, more people began to arrive dragging and carrying sick and older people with them to drink from the new and amazing water source. The birds were chattering, donkeys and cows were wagging their tails and even elephants and zebras were making loud splashing noises downstream. Most amazing of all were the Antelopes, casually drinking in the water next to lions, hyena and other big cats. There was an unwritten treaty for the moment as the neighbourhood took advantage of the water.

While the villagers were busy tending to their sick and thirsty neighbours, Adiim took a large piece of woven material from one of the village houses and laid it on the ground then with Giin magic he produced a large pile of fruit, vegetables and bread, enough for everyone to eat now and enough for the visitors to take some away. While no one was looking, Adiim took Patsy's hand and they disappeared, this time travelling only a few miles away to the dried-up riverbed the elders mentioned earlier. They were both shocked by the number of dead or dying animals, birds and fish, many of them half-submerged in the heavy mud choking and desperate for water. As before Adiim used his senses to locate the water deep below ground and using Giin magic put pressure onto it. Then as before he pushed the wooden staff deep into the muddy riverbed. This time the pressure was so great that an immediate spout of water gushed out about twenty feet into the air and took the staff with it and within seconds it was nourishing the dried-up riverbed. Patsy stood to the side sadly stoking what appeared to be a dead baby elephant, his exhausted mother on her knees stroking his furry little head. Adiim came over to him and within moments had revived mother and baby who both waded into the rapidly growing pool of water. Patsy walked among the sick animals carrying water in an old tin bowl she had found and was giving each of them a drink. Adiim followed behind her reviving those that were still living including tiny birds and fierce-looking cats. They spent hours caring for all the sick animals they could find and during that time another large lake was forming, and the spout of water had reduced to only three feet above the surface. Animals were appearing from everywhere and the sky was full of birds of all sizes.

The first people started to arrive and for a few moments Adiim disappeared as he went to look for other people and creatures in the vicinity to let them know about the water then he returned for Patsy. Adiim found her tending to an antelope with a small calf lying on the ground several hundred feet from the water. She was trying to encourage the mother to get up and walk the last few feet to the water so that she and her baby could drink but she just didn't have the energy left. In a desperate attempt to help her Patsy used all her strength to lift the female and managed to carry her several feet nearer. Adiim went directly to them and spoke softly to the animals in the only antelope language he had learned but they understood and then he healed the mother and she gently stood and walked to the edge of the water to drink. When she was satisfied, the mother returned to Patsy and nudged her gently with her head to say thank you.

Adiim took Patsy's hand and they disappeared, arriving back in the house in Miami only a few moments later. They were both exhausted and Patsy felt as though she was waking from a strange dream although she knew everything she had seen was real. Without really knowing why she began to cry so Adiim hugged her tightly. She told him she realised how much suffering there was in the world all the time and people like her family didn't even realise. She was also saddened by the fact that not all the people and animals had survived, and she knew there were others as desperate as the antelope mother who would never make it to the water. Adiim explained that he'd scouted the area and helped many creatures to find the water although most of them knew by instinct where it was. Those who needed were given extra strength to reach the lake including a sick family in a small village who would have reached the water in less than an hour. Although she understood she still held on to the sadness brought on by all the suffering she had seen. When the others came home from the clinic Patsy was taking a long bath and kept out of their way for a while as she tried to get her head together.

As if he knew something was wrong, Willam jumped up onto her bed giving one of his tribbling sounds and rubbed his head against her tenderly. Patsy was hugging him and kissing his head when another little visitor arrived. Valentina had drawn a lovely picture of Willam that she proudly presented to Patsy. She was quite touched by it and picked up the little girl, twirling her around as she giggled and giving her ten kisses. "Let's pin it on the fridge door," said Patsy and Valentina set off for the kitchen with Willam rubbing around her legs the whole way. How could Patsy be anything more than happy with the life she had, she walked into the sitting room with a beaming smile.

From that following week, they had begun the work of closing the business by ending the waiting list. Anyone who came to the clinic from that point onward would be already on the list and no exceptions would be made. There were difficult telephone calls every day from people desperate to have modifications made. Occasionally people with facial disfigurements needed help and the team were always going to plead a case for them. In truth it wasn't the amount of time required to operate because Adiim could repair most things in only a few minutes, it was the length of time needed in the recovery rooms. This additional time was only needed so that everyone would believe they had been through a surgical procedure, patients, their families, friends and observers alike. When the volume of patients dropped enough, they could secretly squeeze in special cases.

During the evenings, Adiim and Patsy had taken to searching for the next place to go. Collectively the family had determined that a private island of their own would be ideal and Alec confirmed that there was enough money in the pot to make that happen. Although Patsy was shaken by their last adventure, she had told Adiim to look out for the next one and he was pleased that she still wanted to continue with it. Although he was a very caring being in his own right, his love for Patsy and her love for everyone and everything had made him feel just as passionate about their adventures. Most of all he loved spending time alone with her doing something that was theirs and no one else.

Cat Island - Chapter 14

One evening after work Alec asked Adiim if they could go and look at one island that they'd identified in the South Pacific nearer to Australia and New Zealand than the Americas and called Ngeru. The island was comparatively large compared to some at 75 acres, it had several dwellings including one quite large Dutch-style colonial house, a helicopter pad, a landing strip for a small aircraft and a large marina. Needless to say, none of them could fly either a helicopter or an aircraft and Alec had only recently begun taking his Yachtmaster's Offshore Licence in Miami and he knew it would be at least a couple of years before he could complete it.

Patsy had suggested they should employ a few staff to live with them on the island including security and housekeepers, a Governess for Valentina perhaps a cook and especially a pilot for their yacht and or a helicopter pilot. Although everyone hated the idea of more people infiltrating the small family unit, it did make perfect sense. Of course, Adiim questioned the need for either form of transport as he could take them anywhere but as Patsy pointed out, it was not so easy for Adiim to carry them all together and moving large scale items such as furniture was impossible. Adiim knew it was possible, but it was more difficult, so he agreed with her.

Alec and Adiim flew off to scout around Ngeru Island and were both amused when they arrived to find the shoreline or outline of the island looked just like a curled-up cat with his tail hooked beneath him. Adiim used his thoughts to communicate it to Alec but he had already noticed for himself. Where the tail of the cat hooked beneath it a beautiful natural marina was formed, there was a stripe down the cat's back which was a landing strip and the current owners had even installed the helicopter landing pad right where the cat's eye would be.

The island was lush with vegetation and it was obvious that the people who lived here took great care of the environment. At one side of the land, there was a cultivated area growing vegetables and corn, including tomatoes, even pineapples, bananas and other exotic fruit trees. The land was relatively flat apart from one large mound in the middle which was probably the remnants of the volcano. The centre of this dead volcano held a crystal-clear pool of water and several streams and waterfalls were running down the sides of it. It took Alec's breath away. It was so beautiful and caused a tear to form in his eye as he imagined Jean, Patsy and the others living here peacefully. He imagined Patsy married to Adiim with new grandchildren to play with Valentina who already called him Grandpa. Adiim took them silently closer to the several small houses within the walled-off area and there was staff living and working there just as Patsy had suggested. Inside the big house, they swept through each room and Alec fell more and more in love with the place. When he had seen enough, he signalled to Adiim that it was time to go and they swiftly rose above the Island for one last look before heading back to Miami.

They were so excited when they returned and couldn't wait to tell the rest of the family what they had seen. When they explained the shape of the island was like a cat, Margaret said it was an omen and was a good place for them to be. Diana told them that she'd been reading a bit of information online about those islands and Ngeru was a Polynesian word for cat. Adiim went to find Willam and told him all about the cat island. He was fascinated and wanted to go and live there immediately. "We have to buy the island first before we can live there," said Adiim. Willam still found the concept of paying for things a little difficult to understand but then again, there were certain things that cats did that humans didn't understand, and he didn't worry about it.

"This time when we move, I think I would like to have some company of my own," he told Adiim. "Patsy has already been speaking about this and she is going to find some girls for you," he replied patting Willam's soft black furry head. "I think we can give you your natural ginger hair back when we are on the island," said Adiim. "Thank goodness for that," said Willam with a serious face, "The girls prefer me that way."

By now the work at the clinic had declined until they were waiting for just a few more people to reach their desired length of time before the bandages could be removed. The entire family were sad to be leaving it as it had been a real business that hundreds if not thousands of people had benefited from. Some had been cured of terrible sickness, some from minor ailments but all of them had gone away feeling completely well and looking good.

Alec had begun the process of winding up the business and the lease on the building was up for sale. Considering what they had paid initially, the improvements made by Adiim to the inside, coupled with the massive interest in their business had quadrupled its worth in just under three years. There were several local plastic surgeons interested in taking on the building which was a state-of-the-art clinic filled with equipment that had, to a large extent, never actually been used. Whenever anyone asked where they were going, they had agreed that the party line to use was that they were going to retire but hadn't settled on anywhere yet.

Alec had arranged for the purchase of the island to be managed by a third-party investment company, a man he and Adiim had checked out thoroughly and knew to be completely honest and trustworthy. His name was Steve Neilson and he and his brother Martin had been handling monetary matters for the family for several years now. Alec had treated them well and had made sure they were well rewarded financially. They were delighted to be involved in buying the island and quickly set to work on it. By now the profile of the family was more legitimate as they had made so much money through the clinic.

The Neilson brothers had no problem convincing the local authorities in Australia of their suitability as a rich family to buy the island and began negotiating with the seller. She turned out to be a young widow named Jan Manolis, whose husband had been a talented broker on the Australian stock market and had died suddenly from a massive and unexpected heart attack. She had stayed on the island for the first four years alone but eventually decided that she was too isolated and needed to move back to the Australian mainland to begin living again. When she heard about the small family who wanted to buy the island she was pleased because she knew they would love and care for it and most importantly it needed the children that sadly she had never had.

The sale went without any difficulties and there was plenty of money available. Jan had already purchased a large house near Brisbane a couple of years before so moving there permanently would not be too traumatic. Unexpectedly, the negotiations on the sale had taken an unexpected slant and she had found herself a lot more than just attracted to Steve, the older of the two American Neilson brothers and the feeling was mutual. She may have left behind her wonderful cat island, but she had hope again and a new life and a new love. As soon as Jan had moved and there had been a respectable time elapsed, Adiim began to transport the family to the island two at a time. The remaining security guard who was fat, lazy and quite useless, was shocked when he realised all these people were walking around and he hadn't seen them arrive. It was hardly surprising as he had been too busy looking through the kitchen and helping himself to any food left behind that he fancied. Alec took an instant dislike to him and bluffing, asked him where he had been when their helicopter arrived. He muttered out a few excuses and Alec tore a strip off him and told him to get his things together as he was fired and would be going home as soon as the next boat arrived. Patsy and Adiim spent a whole day interviewing potential staff as they arrived by the boatload from Australia.

It was Jean's idea to invite people in that way because they would see the place for themselves and everyone would be able to better judge their ability to fit in with the family. A few of the existing staff returned to ask for their old jobs including one young girl called Emma who had been a sort of cook and housekeeper for Jan. Patsy and Adiim both liked her personality and there were other advantages to recruiting her in that she already knew how things worked. She told them she had to come back even if it was only to see the island one more time and to collect her cat Dotty who had gone missing the day she had to leave. When Patsy saw Dotty the deal was clinched, she was a beautiful white cat with smooth fur except for slightly tufty ears and a fluffy tail and furry feathers down the inside of her legs.

Patsy asked to hold her and Adiim asked if she liked living on this island. She was surprised that the man could talk to her but pleased and told him it was a beautiful place to live although a little lonely at times as she was the only cat here. Adiim asked to be excused and went into the study closing the door. As fast as he could he flew over to the house in Miami and appeared in the Lanai next to a sleeping Willam. He stroked him, "Come with me my friend," said Adiim, "there is a new place for you to live and someone I want you to meet." Willam could hardly get his eyes open when he was suddenly travelling at great speed. Before long he could see the cat island getting closer and then they arrived back in the study of the big house. "Are you ready for this," asked Adiim? "I'm always ready," responded Willam with a slightly spinning head. Adiim walked out into the daylight and found Patsy still chatting to Emma and holding Dotty in her arms. When she saw Adiim approaching holding Willam in his finest ginger coat, she was delighted. In their language, Adiim introduced the two cats and they sniffed each other in a way that showed they were more than interested. "Dotty, meet Willam," said Patsy excitedly. They set both cats on the floor and they brushed against each other tribbling as they did it. Emma clapped her hands with delight. "I was always worried that Dotty was lonely but now she has a boyfriend to play with, I just wish I could see them play together every day," she said happily. "You can," said Patsy, "we'd like you to stay."

When the Neilson brothers had been travelling back and forth to negotiate with Jan, they had used her Australian Helicopter pilot called Jeff Richards and found him to be professional, helpful and friendly. Jan didn't have any need to employ him anymore so Steve Neilson had recommended that Alec should have a word with him. Alec interviewed him and with Adiim's help checked him out for credentials, honesty and integrity, he passed with flying colours in more ways than one.

Jeff could fly almost anything and what's more, he enjoyed it. On the island, there were seven other smaller houses in addition to the big mansion the family were moving into. The staff would be staying in their own completely private homes as part of their employment conditions. The family were keen not to employ too many people as they wanted to remain as contained as possible and the fewer people around, the less likely they were to see Adiim doing something that the family now considered normal, although it would shock someone without that prior knowledge. Margaret, Jean and Diana were working out schedules for shopping, cooking and cleaning, gardening etc. so that they would know exactly when the staff would be around. Compared to the smallish house they had been renting in Miami the mansion house was enormous and they all had a suite of rooms.

There were some communal areas such as the large kitchen, a formal dining room, several living rooms and a cinema that had already been taken over almost completely by Valentina. She had already watched two Disney cartoons and she'd only been in the house half a day. Edwardo had drawn the short straw and was busy making popcorn and good-naturedly selecting ice-cream from the machines and gadgets installed along the wall. He was desperate to explore the island and the house, but his little girl had her own agenda and that was more important to him than anything else.

Diana had taken it upon herself to make sure that all the staff who had already been recruited, were comfortable in their allocated house. She went with Jeff Richards to check out his Billet and he explained to her that he'd lived in the same house before while working for Jan, so he knew it well. Although they had not purchased a helicopter or aircraft, Alec had taken Jeff's advice and hired just a helicopter for a month to see if their need was for more. As they walked together, Jeff told Diana that he was happy to be called at any time of day or night to fly for the family and he smilingly told her that he wasn't prone to bad moods, didn't have a bad temper or anything like that. He also told her that he'd been working on growing a few vegetables at the far side of the island in his spare time for the main kitchen and was hopeful that the family wouldn't mind if he continued with that. Diana told him they would be delighted, and she hoped he wouldn't mind if she joined him because she loved gardening, especially things that could be eaten. He said she was welcome to come and dig and told her of his ideas for growing aubergines, melons and a particularly good strain of potatoes. Diana left him to unpack and walked back to the main house with more than a little sparkle in her eye. Jeff was also quite taken with this young woman although he was certain she was completely out of his league and far too young and beautiful for an old ocker like him.

Margaret wasn't keen on flying at the best of times and the thought of having to go everywhere in a helicopter left her feeling sick inside. Patsy knew this and had already talked to Alec about getting a motor launch just like the ones they had been training on back in Florida. He asked Margaret if she would come to the Australian mainland with him to choose one and arrange for it to be delivered to them on the island. She was thrilled and excited and immediately went to find her laptop to start researching them.

Two by two - Chapter 15

Alec walked into the large main kitchen and almost laughed out loud. Jean was standing on a set of step ladders wiping the tops of the kitchen cabinets while Emma passed the washed and rung-out a cloth for her. Emma was trying to protest that it was her job, but Jean was having none of it. "I have my standards Emma Dear," said Jean frankly. "However, I have to admit so far everything has been extremely clean and well cared for." "That's because like you, Mrs Manolis had the same standards," said Emma slightly frustrated. "I'm sorry but I won't feel comfortable until I've been through everything and I know it has all been cleaned and checked over." "Don't feel annoyed or insulted," said Alec grinning from the doorway, "she would clean Buckingham Palace from top to bottom if the Queen ever sold it and Jean moved in." They both laughed but Jean was unperturbed.

Then Emma looked puzzled and asked, "Should I call you Julia or Jean?" At the same time, Alec said Jean and Jean said, Julia. "My name is Julia Evans, but my husband always calls me Jean; don't ask why," said Jean. Emma shrugged and said, "Julia it is but I'd still prefer you to let me climb the ladder, especially as you're pregnant." "What me, pregnant," said Jean, almost laughing and having to stop herself from saying," at my age." "I may be a glorified housekeeper now," said Emma, "but I trained in midwifery for seven years before moving to this island for a more luxurious lifestyle and I know a pregnancy when I see it." Jean put her hand on her stomach and carefully climbed back down the steps. Alec's face was a picture, both knew instinctively that Emma was right. "Do you mean to tell me you didn't know you were pregnant?" asked Emma. In your professional opinion, how pregnant do you think I am?" asked Jean. "I'd say probably five or more months, but that's just a guess and I'd need to examine you properly to be certain," she responded. "I think we should ask Doctor Adam to take a look at you, he'll know for sure," said Alec in quite a shaky voice. Part of his head was telling him they were far too old to be parents again but the rest of him was excited by the prospect. He went off to look for Adiim while Jean and Emma carried on with the cleaning but this time with Emma up the ladder and a shaky Jean standing in a dream world on the floor.

Emma was silently thinking about the name confusion and wondered if they were lottery winners who want to remain anonymous. Alec discretely explained to Adiim what Emma had said and asked him if he would wait in their suite of rooms for him and he would bring Jean up to be examined. Ten minutes later Adiim reappeared out of his swirling cloud having examined Jean. "There is no doubt you have a baby inside you, and he is almost ready and will come out in the next three weeks," said Adiim excitedly. Jean sat down with a thud onto the bed and Alec crashed down next to her. "Three weeks, him, is it a boy?" asked Jean. "Yes, he is a fit and healthy boy," said Adiim, smiling. "We have to tell Patsy first and then my Mother," said Jean dreading the conversation. "I'll go and get her now," said Alec as he tore down the stairs calling her. Three minutes later a worried-looking Patsy was standing in front of them. "Darling I have something shocking, surprising but quite amazing to tell you," said Jean looking directly into her eyes. "Okay," said Patsy, "nothing you two do could ever surprise me anymore" "Well this might," said Alec grimacing. "I've just found out that I'm pregnant and almost full-term, Adiim thinks the baby will be born in three weeks and he's a healthy boy," Jean spat the words out like a machine gun because she didn't want anyone to stop her until she'd said it all. Patsy didn't say anything for a full minute, but you could almost see the cogs whirling in her head as she processed the information. "A baby brother, a baby brother," she repeated, "I always wanted a baby brother and now he's here." "Are you okay with it then," asked Jean? "Okay, okay, it's the most wonderful news ever," said Patsy dashing over to kiss Jean and Alec. "We wanted you to know first but we now have to tell your Gran," said Alec knowing that Jean dreaded the very idea. "I'll go and get her now," said Patsy dashing off to find her.

Margaret's eyes were a real picture when they told her, but she was ecstatic and couldn't wait for her new grandson to be born. Soon the whole household knew, and everyone was jumping around with the excitement of it all. "How could you be so near your time and not know you were pregnant?" asked Diana. "I had the most terrible time with both my pregnancies, but you seem to be sailing through it." Valentina was excited when they told her a new baby boy would be coming to play with her soon.

Edwardo and Grace went over to the corner of the room whispering to each other for a few moments before returning to the group to announce another new surprise. "it's early days yet," said Grace," but I am a few weeks pregnant too. The champagne came out and Adiim went to let Willam know the news. He was snuggled up to Dotty on one of the sunbeds out on the terrace. He was delighted to hear the news and came in to see Patsy and let her know he was happy about her new brother. Jean was sitting on the sofa when Willam jumped up and rubbed his head under her chin in his "I love you" way. Jean was delighted and hugged him, kissing the top of his head as she did so. Everyone toasted everyone, the parents, the grandmothers, the sisters and the uncles and aunts. Except for Jean and Grace who had only taken a tiny sip of their champagne and Valentina who was drinking lemonade, the rest of them were getting drunk and rowdy, especially the grandmas.

During the run-up to the birth, Adiim read everything he could on human childbirth and set up a sterile room at the top of the house for them to use and also to show the staff that the mothers were safe and would be looked after by a trained Doctor. Emma offered to help out with things if they needed her to but as most of the family were medically trained doctors, nurses and anaesthetists she stuck to offering advice on things like diet and breastfeeding to the two mothers which were extremely beneficial. During the last week, Jeff and Diana had taken the helicopter to the mainland to buy supplies for the new baby including nappies and milk formula and had also collected a few pieces of medical equipment for Adiim's tiny surgery, mainly to keep up the appearances needed. Now that everyone knew that Jean was pregnant it was so obvious that they couldn't understand why they hadn't noticed before. One evening they were all sitting outside and there was a warm wind blowing across the island. Diana had invited Jeff to join them for a drink and the rest of the family had already noticed the spark between them. Jeff warned them that a warm wind coming from the south-east meant a storm was on its way. Since the family had moved to the island, they had only known beautiful warm sunshine and a few refreshing showers that kept the landscape green.

We could be in for a bumpy ride tonight Jeff warned them, so make sure anything outside that could blow away is taken in especially those two lovesick cats. It's probably going to rain hard too but we should be alright because the island has been fortified against mudslides after a small disaster a few years back. All the houses are fitted with hurricane shutters and it's best if we shut them all tonight. Alec counted the staff who would be staying on the island that night and there were seven in total including Chris, the security team, Jenny and Lisa who were the cleaning and laundry team, Emma and Jeff. "We have plenty of room in the main house for everyone so I think we all should spend the night here rather than have each of you on their own in the smaller houses, what do you think," he asked Jeff. Jeff thought it would be better for everyone if they were kept together so he went to fetch Chris who was trying to secure the motor launch, Emma and the two security guards, Mike and Jane.

By the time they'd collected anything loose from outside and closed all the hurricane shutters the rain was pelting down hard. All the staff were relieved to be staying in the main house and thanked the family several times over. Emma made a massive supper that she could leave for everyone to help themselves to whenever they wanted, including lots of bread and cheese, a pasta dish kept in a warmer, a chicken casserole in a slow cooker and lots of fruit, cake and other sweet things. She even opened a tin of salmon for the two cats to take their minds off the distant thunder that was beginning to move ever nearer. The rain was lashing down so hard that it made a roaring sound outside the shuttered windows. Alec suggested they should all go down to the basement cinema and watch a film together while they waited for the storm to pass.

They all agreed and trooped down the stairs excitedly until Valentina decided the film would be Disney's Dumbo. "We already saw this film one hundred times Poopie," said Edwardo in a frustrated and already defeated way. "I know but Jane hasn't seen it yet," she responded turning to the smiling security guard. "I've seen it already," she pleaded mainly for the others, "let's go and see what other films there are in the cupboard." Try as she might, there was nothing she or anyone else could do to dissuade the little girl that Dumbo was the only thing worth watching. "Don't worry folks, I have a plan," said Grace jumping from her seat. She was back just as the film began with a large baby bottle of milk formula. "I know Mummy told you you're too big for a bottle now, but this is a special one," said Grace loudly so that everyone could hear. She sat Valentina on her lap with the bottle in her mouth and her eyes glued to the screen.

In only five minutes Grace gave the thumbs-up signal that Valentina had fallen fast asleep. Then the fun started as the rest of them fought over which film to watch. Eventually, they settled on The Hunger Games, although Diana was concerned it would scare Valentina if she woke. After they'd watched a couple of films several of them went to bed leaving only Edwardo, Jeff and Mike to burn the midnight oil.

Adiim checked the weather report for the region and was shocked to see a red alert being sent out to all the islands. Jeff had been right to get everyone and everything inside when he did. The wind was building up and Adiim could feel the building shuddering slightly from the force of it. Not only that but the rain hadn't slowed down and was still making its thundering noise at it hit the ground and other buildings. He peeked out of the shutters and was surprised by the density of the rain. It was so heavy it appeared like a thick fog, blotting out the darkened landscape beyond the main garden. Adiim was just about to climb into his bed when there was a gentle tap on his door. Excitedly he rushed to open it, hoping it was Patsy asking if she could stay with him during the storm. Instead, it was Alec looking serious. "I think Jean has gone into labour a few days early, probably because of the storm, can you come and look at her," he asked? Adiim was sitting in his boxer shorts and a white T-shirt so he pulled on a pair of jeans and a cotton sweater, socks and deck shoes and followed Alec back to their suite of rooms.

Jean was in labour and Adiim asked how she wanted to do things.

They'd discussed it many times and Jean insisted she would give birth naturally unless there was a problem and then Adiim could do whatever he needed to make sure both she and the baby were okay. Hours went by and Jean paced up and down in the room periodically looking out of a small gap in the shutters at the pouring rain. Suddenly the process stepped up and the baby decided he was coming out, Jean panted and pushed in order just as Adiim asked her to, she steadfastly refused to allow him to intervene and suffered the pain of childbirth with great dignity. Finally, the baby boy arrived, and Jean forgot the pain instantly.

Alec checked his watch and it was six forty-five in the morning, he picked up his new son and looked him over with wonder and awe. "Whatever shall we call him," he asked Jean? "Noah," she replied without batting an eyelid, "because of the great flood out there." "I love it," said Alec proudly. "So, do I," said Adiim laughing, now let's go and tell the others. Patsy dashed up the staircase two steps at a time and was the first to cuddle baby Noah. Margaret was three seconds behind her, and she hugged both Patsy and the baby at the same time. "My grandchildren," she spouted. "Who thought of the name Noah, asked Margaret? "It suits him wonderfully." "Jean did," said Alec, "he was born during the great flood." They all laughed affectionately, and Margaret carried him over to the window to look at the rain, but it had stopped. "Well would you believe it, Noah, the storm has ended now you're here," said Margaret kissing his tiny head. The rest of the family and the others were equally as excited and in turn, they all came to have a look at the new baby, including Jeff, Mike and the two security guards. Valentina came back twice to see baby Noah because she couldn't believe he'd been hiding inside Jean's tummy all that time. Even Willam eventually came upstairs to see the new kitten and find out what all the fuss was about. He bounded onto the bed and butted Jean under her chin in his usual way then stepped up to the side of her to look at the new baby in her arms. He smelled new but he was certainly the same family and Willam thought his tiny face even looked a bit like Patsy's. Dotty suddenly appeared next to him on the bed and Jean couldn't help singing out loud, "The animals came in two by two Hurrah! Hurrah!" Alec, Pasty, Margaret and Diana were all there with her and they rolled about laughing.

Family business - Chapter 16

In the six months since Noah had been born the time seemed to fly and it would soon be time for Grace and Edwardo's baby to come. Alec and Jean went to the mainland and registered Noah's birth a week later. They also took him to a paediatrician for a thorough check over, not because they didn't trust Adiim, but they wanted him to have a medical record and registration numbers he would need to obtain a passport later. Emma was a great support to Jean although she was confused about names, but she eventually became used to them calling each other different things. She thought about it long and hard and decided they were probably trying to disguise their identity after winning a massive amount of money on the lottery. When any of the other staff mentioned the confusion, she told them her theory, so eventually, it became generally accepted that the family were lottery winners who wanted to keep their identities secret. They all decided that the family were lovely to work for, they were treated so well by them, so they used the names they were given and ignored any other names they used for themselves.

Margaret arranged for the specially commissioned motor launch to be delivered to them later that week. She'd also secretly arranged for their old tutor Dylan from Florida to come and stay on the island for six months to continue with their skipper training. When Dylan arrived in Australia she asked Jeff to take her to collect him but not to tell any of the others just yet. When Dylan arrived and waved at Margaret she noticed her heart quickened slightly but she dismissed it as pure excitement at the thought of restarting her skipper training.

Dylan was delighted to see Sarah which was the only name he knew her by. He couldn't help thinking how beautiful she was; to him, she was an old-fashioned girl with a good brain and experience beyond her years. He had to admit he was very attracted to her, although he knew he was too old for her and not in her league. They hugged and kissed each other affectionately in a friendship way. She introduced him to Jeff, and it was clear that the two men liked each other immediately and they chatted away together as they headed back to the helicopter. When they reached the Island, Margaret pointed out its cat shape and Dylan said it was more beautiful than anything he'd seen in Florida. When they landed Adiim and Diana were in the garden discussing the possibility of growing more plants and trees. They were surprised and delighted when they saw Dylan and they welcomed him to their home. They went inside and Diana called Patsy, Jean, Alec and the others to the main sitting room to meet Dylan. They were all surprised but delighted to see him and even Valentina remembered his name. Jean carried in baby Noah and Dylan smiled at him and spoke a bit of Floridian baby talk to him. Alec was particularly delighted because he was desperate to recommence his skipper training before everything he'd learned became out of date and invalid.

Margaret was furious when she received a telephone call to say the boat would not be arriving for another three weeks. She decided to use the time to show Dylan around the island and she knew it would allow him more time to acclimatise and research maps of the local waterways. Chris, the skipper who'd been recruited under a temporary contract to manage the rented launch, sadly bade goodbye to them all as he left to take it back to the mainland. He was sad to be leaving but happy to have had the privilege of spending time on the beautiful island with people who he now thought of as friends.

Two weeks after Dylan arrived on the island Grace went into labour but unlike Jean, she asked Adiim to stop the pain for her and to make the birth as relaxed and comfortable as possible for her baby and herself. Within an hour, baby Carlos was born and as Grace felt so fit and able, she took him downstairs herself to introduce him to his sister Valentina. She was delighted to see her new brother and asked if Noah could be her brother too. Edwardo was thrilled with his son and wanted him to meet his grandmother Lydia as soon as possible. Grace cautioned against bringing Lydia to the island the unconventional way by Giin magic, so Edwardo booked her a flight from Rio. She was to be picked up in Brisbane by Jeff in the chopper two days later. He knew Lydia was scared to death of heights and although she'd be okay flying on an aircraft, she'd be terrified in the helicopter. He asked Adiim if he could do anything to help and he suggested sending her to sleep but as Jeff would be there he'd pretend to use hypnosis. On the way to collect her, they explained the plan to Jeff. He completely understood and had experienced several people screaming with terror as they gained altitude. Lydia looked completely worn out when they met her as she hadn't managed to sleep during her journey. She was delighted to see Edwardo and kissed him almost to death asking a million questions about baby Carlos, Valentina and Grace as they walked along.

When they were near and it was obvious where they were headed, Lydia began to whine about the flying death machine. Edwardo and Adiim led her along and held her arms as Jeff quietly pushed a trolley containing her suitcases and the three giant teddy bears perched on top. Jeff gave them all headsets with microphones attached and they lifted into the air. Lydia began screaming in Portuguese that they would crash and burn to death or fall into the sea and be drowned, that this was a death machine and Edwardo had arranged it to torture his poor Mama.

Jeff turned off Lydia's microphone so he could concentrate but Adiim told her to sleep. For the rest of the journey, she was silent but fully awake although now the experience had become a normal journey like travelling in a car. Within a few minutes, she fell fast asleep as she was already exhausted from her incredibly long journey. Jeff was impressed and asked Adiim if he could teach him how to make yacking women fall asleep. Edwardo laughed but the joke was completely lost on Adiim. They arrived back at the island at midday and Grace and Valentina were out in the garden waiting to meet her. Adiim released her from his spell just as the helicopter engines were switched off. Lydia had no idea what had happened, but she felt nice and rested after her short nap. She virtually ran up to the house screaming in Portuguese and grabbed Valentina kissing her a thousand times. Then she took baby Carlos from Grace and kissed him gently, she was in heaven.

As they were all celebrating Lydia's arrival in the main house a loud tooting noise started sounding outside. Margaret and Dylan knew exactly what it was, and they dashed for the door and set off like rabbits down to the marina. As the beautiful motor launch docked, Margaret jumped up and down clapping her hands with excitement. Alec was delighted too, and he expected there would be a bit of a fight over who would be the first to take her out on a run. They went aboard and the guys who delivered it showed them around almost inch by inch. Dylan was the expert so he spent his time learning about the state-of-the-art navigation equipment and sonar that would help them to avoid the hidden reefs that were a problem in the region. Then he spent time in the engine room and was shown all the additional equipment that covered everything from cleaning out the heads to cleaning the more difficult to reach windows and portholes.

It came with a brand-new radio and satellite navigation system, tons of local maps and charts and even fishing equipment. Alec had said yes to everything listed as extra on the options for a bespoke vessel. The rest of the family were aboard now as were Jeff and Emma, but they were more interested in the lounge area, the cocktail cabinet and the sun deck. Jean found one of the bedroom cabins and tried the bed out for size, laying Noah next to her on the soft clean linen. She almost had to pinch herself when she thought about how lucky she was. Before Adiim came she was a bored and frustrated middle-aged woman with nothing really to look forward to. Now she was a new mum with an exciting new life and a young fit and healthy body. Just for a moment, she wondered if they were now truly safe and could forget about being pursued across the world. She decided to put such ideas out of her head and picked up baby Noah kissing him and heading back to find Alec.

A few days after the new launch arrived Patsy woke one morning to the sound of tiny meows coming from somewhere in her room. She knew immediately that it was kittens, but she could find them nowhere. As Willam and Dotty were the only cats on the island she knew the kittens had to be their offspring, but she'd seen no sign of Dotty. She went to find Emma and the two of them went back to Patsy's rooms to listen for the noise. They waited for ages and there was nothing then suddenly Patsy heard the faintest squeak. Luckily, this time Emma heard it too and they both began trying to fit a direction to the sound. After almost an hour they found Dotty and her three kittens in amongst Patsy's shoes right at the back of her wardrobe. One was white one was ginger and the other was tortoiseshell and all three of them were huge like Willam. Valentina came to see the new kittens and Dotty didn't mind moving away from them so that she could see clearly. She'd already been told she wasn't allowed to touch them yet but when they were bigger, and their Mummy brought them out to play she could stroke and hold them. Valentina named them Buddy, Max and Alice, which amused Emma completely. Although she and

Valentina were both excited, Patsy was certain that Emma would burst with the thrill of it.

Alec received a reminder that the helicopter lease was up for renewal, but the hiring company had a special deal they thought he could be interested in. For what seemed not much more than the cost of renting the helicopter, he could rent a small private jet with seating for twenty passengers. There was a usable runway on the island and flying in a jet was both more comfortable and faster, so he asked Jeff what he thought about it. Jeff thought it was an excellent offer and was worth trying out, even if they decided to go back to the helicopter when the offer ended. Everyone was pleased, especially Lydia who would be returning home to Brazil before too long. The thought of climbing back into the helicopter still scared the life out of her despite Adiim's best efforts to allay her fears. When the day came to change them over Alec, Adiim and Patsy went with Jeff to collect the aircraft and were delighted with the faster smoother ride back to the island. When they returned, Patsy walked around the island with Adiim before returning to the house. "I think it's time we had one of our adventures again, don't you," she asked him? "I would love to do it again," said Adiim, "but I thought you were happier staying at home on the island." "I was for a while," she responded, "but now they're all like couples and I feel like we're left out a bit." Adiim frowned because he wasn't as perceptive as Patsy so the relationships forming between Jeff and Diana and more recently with Dylan and her Gran, had not even registered to him. When Patsy spelt it out the light went on and Adiim suddenly realised what she meant. "Are you feeling lonely," he asked tentatively? "I'm not lonely because I'm surrounded by my family and friends, but I miss having a special relationship with someone, you know the way we used to spend time alone together." Adiim didn't dare to believe she could mean she wanted to be intimate with him so instead, he decided she just wanted to spend private time together as friends. He longed to be allowed to show his real feelings for Patsy, but he knew it was forbidden for his kind to be in a relationship with a human. Patsy was also longing to get closer to Adiim, but she saw only a childlike friendship with him and when she tried to suggest she would like to be more than friends, he just assumed she meant a closer friendship. Whatever it was it would be fine for now if she could be with him. "We will have to tell the others where we are through, it's not like it was in Florida when we could pretend to be at the beach or something," said Adiim. "We can always tell them we are going to explore the other small islands and we can do that on the way back from our adventure," Patsy suggested. They agreed on it and went back to the house to check the news and see if there was anywhere in the world that could need their help. As they walked through the kitchen Emma was clearing away some dishes and watching TV as she did so. On the TV was a news report showing some devastating bushfires that were raging through the Australian countryside. Patsy grabbed Adiim's hand and held him there as they listened to the TV news flash. They turned and smiled at each other then ran upstairs to Patsy's suite to make sure they could not be seen leaving.

Just before they went Patsy knocked on Jean's door and was told to shush as the baby was sleeping. She whispered to her mother that she and Adiim were going to explore the nearby islands as they were slightly bored, just in case anyone wondered where they had gone. Jean was about to say what a weird idea but thought better of it when she realised, they probably just wanted to spend some time alone. "Well don't be late for dinner," she warned, "or Emma will start asking where you are," Patsy whispered her agreement and Adiim nodded his head silently as Jean closed the door again.

A few moments later they were there, white hair white skin and white clothes, standing in front of the burning trees. It was so hot that Patsy put her arms up to shield her face and Adiim moved them further away. In amongst the burning trees were frantic creatures trying to get out but trapped in the fire. Adiim moved between them carrying the smaller ones and herding the larger ones through gaps in the wall of flame. Patsy had laid down some soft branches and leaves on the ground and she gently tended to the smaller animals and birds that had been overcome by the smoke or the flames.

Occasionally Adiim appeared with a small wallaby or koala and handed them to her before disappearing back into the flame. A small group of Aboriginal people watching were convinced that they were seeing white angels. One of the older women quietly asked her if they could help find her grandchildren who were lost in the fire. At first, Patsy couldn't understand her but when Adiim reappeared he understood and asked the old woman where the children could be. Before he left again, he touched Patsy on her head, and she immediately understood the language and could speak to the old lady who said her name was Marcie. When Adiim found the two children they'd been overcome by smoke and would have burned to death within the next five minutes if he hadn't rescued them. He quickly healed them both and then spirited them out of the fire back to where Patsy and old Macie were standing. The old woman stood solid as a tree with just a small tear in her eye and put an arm around each of her grandchildren. She thanked Adiim and told him she knew who they were because the ancestors spoke about Numakulla the two sky Gods who had created every life on earth. Then she pointed to a place in the distance where the fire was raging more than ever and told them, "That the place where the white folks live, they in danger and will be burned." Patsy kissed Macie and the two children, and all the other Aboriginal folks stepped forward and bowed heads to them, then she took Adiim's hand and they disappeared.

One second later they were in front of a small town where several hundred houses were in line with the raging fire. People were fleeing in their cars, women and children were crying and everyone was shouting. Adiim sensed an elderly couple trying desperately to round up all their cats although many of them had run away in fear several hours before. He led Patsy to them and told her in her mind to help them. When Patsy walked up to their house the fire was close and she could hear them speaking to each other in their native Hungarian. They were shocked to see this completely white vision calling them to follow her. She was carrying several of their cats in baskets and some in her arms, wrapped around her body. As she loaded the cats into the car she spoke softly to them in their language. She told the old man to drive as fast as he could to the main road away from the fire and to keep going until he met the rescue teams who would be waiting for them. She assured them that her partner would rescue all the cats and any other creatures that could be in danger.

Thinking she was a spirit or an angel they did as they were told and as soon as they were far enough away, Adiim stopped the fire in its tracks. Luckily, they had arrived just in time to save all the houses even though some of the surrounding land and fields had been turned to black ash. Adiim collected all the wounded and sick domesticated animals including the two remaining cats that belonged to the old couple and four other cats from neighbouring houses, a tiny dog, three horses, a pet rabbit and two guinea pigs. Adiim made sure they were all safe and completely well and they left them in a stable block to look after each other and wait for their owners to return.

Patsy arranged water for them all and Adiim provided a variety of food from meat and fish to carrots and hay. Next, he collected all the sick wild animals and birds including everything from frogs and lizards to koalas and a couple of large kangaroos. He took them back to the Aboriginal people who had been watching when the great fire suddenly went out. He asked them to care for the animals until they could return to their homes and the people agreed. They were just about to leave when Patsy shook Adiim's arm and they turned to see the elderly couple followed by a fire truck, a police car and a TV crew racing towards them across the charred earth in their convoy of odd vehicles. Adiim took Patsy's arm and they disappeared just in time before the cameras were close enough to capture them.

There was a huge amount of speculation about who they were, from angels to aboriginal spirits and even a theory that they had been kind aliens who had been travelling nearby and saw the fire. The news stories were rife with speculation, but no one could say for certain who or what they were, and the crowds of animals gathered in safety from the fire only bred more rumours. The elderly Hungarian couple had reported that they spoke their language beautifully and the Aboriginal woman had reported that they spoke her tongue, just like they were born in the bush.

Meanwhile back on their safe island, Patsy and Adiim were changing ready for dinner and smiling to themselves about the adventure. When they went down to the dining room to eat, Emma was full of stories she'd picked up from the TV about aliens landing and putting out the raging bushfire, saving the lives of people and their animals and homes. As she was dishing up the food she asked if anyone else could smell eucalyptus wood-burning and both Margaret and Grace said they thought they could. Alec pointed out that the smoke had probably carried in the air and that was what they could smell but Alec was sitting directly between Patsy and Adiim and he had a vague idea who the aliens could be.

Jean testing - Chapter 17

Over a period, Diana and Jeff had formed a strong relationship, initially based on their love of gardening but eventually, they had admitted their feelings to each other. They tried to remain discreet and were not physically demonstrating their feelings in front of the others. Grace was no fool and several times she'd seen Diana creep out of her rooms during the night to stay with Jeff in one of the other houses. She discussed it with Edwardo, and they'd decided it was up to them to decide when to tell everyone else. When they did make the great announcement the whole family already knew and were relieved to be able to be open about it. They'd decided to do things properly and get married, so Alec was asked to give Diana away as he was her best friend.

He took her aside and asked her if she'd thought about telling Jeff about Adiim. She said she was waiting for an opportunity to discuss it with everyone else first when Jeff was away somewhere. "I think it would be wise to ask Adiim before you do anything," Alec told her. Diana knew that Adiim had a way of delving into a person's head to help determine how honest they are. "I feel confident that Jeff's a good person and would never do anything to harm any of us," she told Alec. Alec told her he would speak to Adiim as soon as there was an opportunity. Later that evening Adiim went upstairs and then descended on Jeff without anyone being aware. Jeff did have a vague sense of memories flashing by, but he couldn't think why. When Adiim emerged and went to speak to Alec not all the news was good. "I think he is a good and honest person, but he is hiding something, not only from us but from himself," said Adiim. Alec tried to work out what that meant but he couldn't rationalise it so instead he decided to be honest with Diana who was, after all, his best friend. She was upset but she accepted it because she knew that Adiim was unlikely to invent a problem. Instead, she decided she would work on Jeff to uncover his hidden side. In the meantime, the information about Adiim would be kept a secret and the wedding would be on hold.

It was over a year now since they had moved to the island of Ngeru and they had finally begun to feel safe. They had a total of four security guards who took turns to look after them alternating their time on and off the island. Dylan and Jeff had become firm friends, and both were willing and ready to take anyone in the family anywhere they asked at a moment's notice.

The new jet plane was a great hit and saved so much time whenever there was a need to go to the mainland. Everyone enjoyed the ride and wanted to go on shopping sprees for clothes, groceries and other provisions. Today it was Patsy and Adiim's turn to go shopping for groceries. They had a long list from Emma and the rest of the family that included everything from nappies and baby clothes to chocolate and even melon seeds for Diana and Jeff's garden. As usual, Jeff stayed with the aircraft to save having to go through border control and Patsy and Adiim took a taxi to the massive supermarket on the edge of the town. Patsy was feeling particularly romantic at that moment for some unknown reason and longed to have Adiim as her love and not just as a friend.

As they walked around the cavernous store Adiim saw a flower stall selling the most beautiful red roses. He couldn't resist the urge to take one and present it to Patsy. She was completely overwhelmed and looked into his eyes before suddenly saying what she'd wanted to say for so long. "Adiim I am so in love with you, I wish you could be mine." Adiim was reeling and didn't know how to react, but tears fell from his eyes. "Have I said something bad," asked Patsy? "No," he replied, "what you've said is beautiful, but I'm Giin and it is forbidden for me to love you." "Do you love me though," she asked? "Yes, I love you more than anything," he responded. She hugged him in the middle of the giant supermarket and told him it was alright for them to love each other. "We are living in a completely different time," she said, "and no one can do anything to us." "I am afraid the others won't approve, your father in particular," he admitted. "I understand why you feel this way, so maybe we should leave things between the two of us until we're ready to tell the rest of the family?"

Adiim was relieved and they decided to try to spend more time alone so that they could talk and get to know each other more intimately. Patsy suggested it could be a good idea to explore some of the other islands, they'd already told the family they were doing so. They continued with the shopping, held hands and smiled at each other at every opportunity. When they returned home to the island Margaret could swear she could see an even bigger sparkle in Patsy's eye than usual.

That evening, Diana and Jeff drank slightly more rye whisky and ginger than usual and found themselves in Diana's rooms lying on the bed and giggling away at trivia. He asked her about her ex-husband and Diana described him as a good man who couldn't help taking things that didn't belong to him. Jeff was fascinated and asked for more information and was surprised when she told him he'd run away with the local Vicars wife. He couldn't help but laugh and Diana joined in. She took the opportunity to delve further into his background. "Sometimes, I feel there is a big part of you inside that I can't reach, almost as though it is hidden." It was a low-down thing to say, she was using information that Adiim gave to her, but it created an unexpected reaction. "I knew you could see right into my soul," he responded. "I do have things inside that I find difficult to face but I feel I could tell you anything." She kissed him and looked into his eyes. "There's no time like the present." He wriggled about on the bed as he tried to decide how or if he should tell her. He sat upright and took both her hands in his and looked into her eyes. "I did something terrible when I was a boy although everyone would say I had no choice." "I know you're a good and kind person so whatever you did I know there was a good reason for it," she told him. Here it was, the time he thought would never come, the time to admit to someone else what he'd done all those years ago. "I killed my own father," he told her without blinking or moving any muscle on his face. "What reason did you have to do that, "asked Diana?

Jeff then began to tell her a sad story about a poor Australian family living in the outback, getting by from scratching the earth to grow what crops they could. He had been taught to fly by his only friend, Jonty, the old man who lived nearby. He had a small plane that he used to spray local crops that included the pitifully few fields grown by his own family. The farm had seven dogs to protect them and a few chickens and ducks in the yard that provided eggs and meat now and again. His favourite dog was a bitch called Penny but one day she contracted a form of rabies from one of the wild Dingoes that frequently tried to raid the local farms. His father wanted to shoot Penny and three of the other dogs, but Jeff had pleaded and begged him to spare Penny's life. Even though both his mother and father had explained what would happen to her and how she'd suffer, he insisted she would be okay.

His father attempted to keep her alive for him, but she bit the old man on his hand. His mother treated it with boiled salty water; they had no form of antiseptic except for a bottle of whiskey and couldn't afford to buy any. After several days of suffering, Jeff eventually agreed to allow his father to shoot Penny although it broke his heart. Not too long after that, the old man became ill and eventually became delirious and violent.

His mother managed for a few days but eventually, she was so afraid of him that she locked herself in an upstairs room and wouldn't come out. Jeff didn't know what else to do so he ran the five and a half miles to old Jonty's house to tell him what happened. Jonty grabbed his shotgun and two of his dogs and ran with Jeff to jump into his pickup truck. He went at top speed to get to Jeff's parents driving in a direct line through the bush while Jeff and the dogs tried to stay in their seats. The front door to the house was swinging open and Jeff's dad was nowhere to be seen. He ran upstairs and banged on the door to tell his mother to come out and get into the car. She opened the door trembling like a leaf and walked carefully down the stairs with Jeff holding her arm tightly. Jonty was looking into each of the outside buildings as Jeff put his mother into the vehicle and told her to lock the door. Suddenly to his left he heard Jonty shouting and his dogs barking and saw his father beating him and tearing into him like a bear biting and kicking his poor friend and kicking out at the two dogs. Jeff knew his father was completely demented and would kill old Jonty and probably turn on his mother and himself immediately after. Without another thought, he ran back into the house, reached down his father's shotgun, loaded it and ran outside to where the two men were still struggling on the dusty ground.

Suddenly they fell backwards, and Jonty's head hit the corner of a drinking trough and Jeff knew he was dead. Both dogs were gravely injured and were whimpering and trying to pull themselves away from the madman on their broken legs. His father turned to him with red eyes and a wild look on his face. Jeff pleaded with him not to attack him, but it was like talking to a wild animal. He reared up and went for Jeff with his teeth and claws bared and without thinking anything more Jeff fired the shotgun twice into his father's chest and he fell dead on the ground.

His mother drove them silently to the next farm which was almost thirty miles away and broke down wailing when the women on the farm came to see what they wanted. The police were called, and his mother never admitted that Jeff had been the one to shoot his father and everyone assumed he was too young to have done it. His mother never recovered from the terrible event and she died less than a month later. Jeff was sent to live in an orphanage and only discovered later that Jonty had left his farm and the old plane to him in his will along with a large bundle of Australian dollars that he'd kept under the floorboards. When he was old enough Jeff sold both farms and the old plane and bought himself a shiny new crop sprayer with the proceeds. For several years after that, he had made a good living from dusting the farms across Australia.

After hearing the story Diana hugged him tightly while he wept for his father and mother and his friend Jonty for the first time in his life. "So, no one knew it was you who shot him but, he was already dead, and you probably saved him from a great deal of suffering. Jeff continued to weep and eventually fell asleep in Diana's arms. Later, Diana told Alec what she'd learned and when Adiim next looked inside Jeff's head he knew, just as Diana did, that he was no longer keeping any secrets.

Jeff was astounded when Diana and Patsy sat him down and told him about Adiim. He was difficult to convince until Adiim took him on a short trip to one of the local uninhabited islands. He found the thrill of flying without any aircraft to be the most exhilarating experience of his life. He immediately understood the danger to Adiim and by default to the family if the truth ever leaked out. He swore on his life that he'd do everything to protect Adiim and the family no matter what the danger may be. Adiim knew instinctively that he meant every word.

One morning Patsy woke to hear a light tapping on her door. She looked at her clock and it was five thirty-eight in the morning. She climbed out of bed and opened it to find Adiim waiting outside. "Come in and don't bother knocking my door in future, just come in," she told him. "Patsy, I was up early and looking at the news on the internet when I read that a terrible landslide in China has trapped hundreds of people, many of them will die unless we rescue them. She was about to get dressed when Adiim took her hand and within only a couple of minutes, she was in the middle of a terrible moving mass of mud and tangled houses. Adiim began collecting trapped people and bringing them out for Patsy to care for.

She found a strip of dry land with coarse grass growing over it, then began to get the survivors to sit or lie next to each other. When people began to approach her, she spoke to them in their dialect asking them to go and find blankets or even curtains and bedsheets to wrap the survivors in so they wouldn't be sitting out in the cold air. Slowly the number of survivors grew as Adiim worked quickly digging them out from certain death in the thick mud. Their numbers included children and babies, men and women of all ages, shapes and sizes. The crowd grew and everyone wanted to look at the white spectres who'd been sent to rescue people from the mud. As always the crowd eventually grew too big and too curious so Adiim took Patsy by the hand and they disappeared. Back in her bedroom, they checked the time and it was still only ten past eight. Adiim was about to leave the room but Patsy held him tightly around his waist. He kissed her but still, she knew he was desperate to leave before anyone knew he was with her. Reluctantly she let him go but she knew it was the way things had to be until she could convince him that no one would mind that they wanted to be together.

During the following weeks, they spent as much time together as they could including visiting the local islands to explore and another two angel adventures that included rescuing people from a fire in a tower block in the Netherlands and helping to rescue survivors of a shipwreck in the middle of the Atlantic Ocean. One day she asked him to take her to the places he'd lived when he was a boy. Adiim explained that most of those places no longer existed but she wanted to see them for herself. The ruined palace of Malkatah was disappointing because there was nothing left. They sat on a rock in the sand as Adiim tried to project an image of the beautiful palace to her and Patsy put her head on his shoulder as she listened to his voice.

He was running through some Giin history again when he happened to mention the cave where the Giin had stored all their treasure. Patsy asked if he would take her there and he agreed on her understanding that the place was cursed, and she must not take anything from there. She agreed and before long they were flying low over the

Dead Sea towards the craggy point of a mountain range. There was a tiny hole in the top of the mountain that no one would have known was there but Adiim slowed down and they gradually poured through the hole like sand in an hourglass until they were both standing inside the massive cave. As her eyes grew accustomed to the dim light, Patsy was astounded by the huge pile of treasure that almost filled the entire space. Even in the space directly in front of her feet, she could see golden chains and deep red rubies, sparkling diamonds and emeralds so green they looked endless. "My God," said Patsy, "I know you said the Giin had accumulated incredible wealth, but this is almost obscene." "There is a curse on any human who takes any of the treasure from this place so please don't be tempted to remove anything," Adiim begged her. "Don't worry," said Patsy, "we have all the wealth I could ever need in my life."

As they were about to leave Patsy asked, "Is that the doorway that leads to the Giin world?" Adiim was surprised, he'd visited the cave many times before, but he'd never seen any doorway. "Which door would that be," he asked her puzzled. "This one here in front of me," she replied pointing directly at it. Adiim was completely bewildered, for once in his life a human was able to see something that he couldn't. He admitted he wasn't able to see the door and so Patsy began to describe the size and shape of it and the designs that ran around three sides of it. By the time she'd finished he did not doubt that she'd just described the entrance to the Giin world Deo Jagah. They spent the next hour or so trying to find a way to open the door, but nothing worked even though they pushed and pressed all sorts of buttons and any nail heads protruding from it. Eventually, Adiim collapsed to his knees with despair in his eyes. "I just want to see my mother again," he told Patsy. "We'll figure out the way to open this door," she told him, "it's meant to be, it was only by bringing me here that we found it at all." She took her mobile phone from her pocket and tried taking a picture of the door although the image was very dark and blurred. Adiim thought about what Patsy had said and began to realise that a Giin would only bring a human to this place if they knew without a doubt that they could trust them forever. The thought gave him hope that perhaps their relationship was meant to happen. He took her hand and before long they were back on their lovely island.

As they strolled gently on one of the beaches of the island, Patsy gently tried to persuade Adiim it was time to tell the rest of the family about their relationship. "I know instinctively my Gran is fully aware of our feelings for each other," she told him. "Have you noticed she sometimes gives me a secret smile when we're sitting together," she asked him? "I'm not afraid of what Margaret will say because she's also an Akilah, but your father wouldn't approve of his only daughter wanting to be with a Giin," he told her, believing every word. "My Dad is one of the kindest people in the world and he would not only be pleased for me but for you too, he thinks of you as part of our family already and if we married you'd be exactly that,"

Adiim quickly answered her, "Long ago the king would also tell me I was part of his family but when his only daughter was hurt, he no longer considered me a son or nephew." "Times are changed now, and we even have laws to prevent people from being discriminated against, even recently a law was passed to allow gay couples to be married just like everyone else," she suggested. "What if we have children who are like me, we can't hide them away from the rest of the world for the whole of their lives can we," he asked her? "Well Valentina, Carlos and Noah have been hidden away and they seem to be doing just fine if you ask me," she responded sarcastically. "They are normal children, but our children would not be," he responded. "They are not normal children, they have privileged lives and live on a private island with a jet plane and have an uncle who can take them anywhere they want instantly by magic," she pointed out. "Our children are likely to have the same abilities as me and will have to be taught to control them," Adiim pleaded. "It's simple," said Patsy, "we keep them on the island and arrange their schooling here until they're old enough to understand the danger of showing their abilities to anyone outside the family. Both my mother and my Gran are trained teachers. When they're older, they can go to school or University, anything they want, and no one needs to know anything about their special talents." "What if they are asked to take a medical examination or provide a blood sample and someone checks their DNA," Adiim argued.

Patsy couldn't think of an answer to that just now but in the back of her mind, she knew it could be possible to deal with it. "Our children are likely to have a mixture of human and Giin DNA as I am sure you have. I'm certain it would be possible to separate their human genes and keep them and any blood sample we could require ready for when it's needed. It would be a simple case of using Giin magic to swap the samples over." Adiim was silent for a moment as he thought through everything Patsy had said, then he suddenly laughed out loud and lifted her off the ground kissing her. "It could work," he admitted.

The next day Patsy spoke to Alec, Jean and Margaret about setting up a laboratory to continue her work on genetics in the hope of isolating the parts of Adiim's DNA that could heal sick people. They all thought it was a marvellous idea and Alec agreed to buy whatever she needed. Jean and Margaret were both interested, and Patsy suggested she could teach them some of the techniques used in her research so that they could be involved. They were excited by the suggestion, both had become bored with retirement and wanted something more to occupy their minds. Adiim wanted to know more about Patsy's work and he knew the other reason she wanted to set up the lab. "There's no time like the present," said Alec.

They soon identified two basement rooms in the house that would make a perfect research laboratory and Patsy went online to identify the equipment she needed. Although some of the equipment was available in Australia and New Zealand, Patsy had been trained in the UK using specific systems and needed them to be imported. Some of the more state-of-the-art kits had been only recently designed and tested in the USA and Alec suggested it would be prudent to keep up to date and order those that were most relevant to Patsy's research. It would take some time for some of the things to arrive but in the meantime,

Adiim set about the design of the basic rooms to Patsy's precise requirements.

The equipment arrived over a long period, beginning with isolating units and specialised refrigeration, workbenches and chairs, powerful microscopes with cameras and video capabilities, a centrifuge and boxes of miscellaneous glass and metal items. Adiim had installed a glass wall at one end of the main room with entry to a scrub room like an operating theatre where those entering and leaving the lab could shower and change into sterile clothing. Although Patsy didn't expect to need these types of sterile conditions for her work, Adiim designed it anyway and she didn't argue. She did insist on an intercom at the glass wall so that entry to the lab could be minimalized and anyone just needing to speak to them wouldn't need to go through the whole clothes changing process. Adiim also knew how to keep the room sterile and clean using Giin magic, which was extremely beneficial to her work. She began to teach the basic skills they would need to work in the lab and was amazed when Alec, Diana, Grace and Edwardo asked if they could attend. It would mean eight of them could be working in there and there wasn't room.

None of them had given enough thought to child-care issues and so it was agreed that Adiim and Margaret would be trained fully, Jean would have training arranged around a childcare schedule and the others would have ad-hoc training. There was no urgency to the work, and everyone wanted to be a part of it, so Patsy was delighted to involve them. Although Alec was highly intelligent and was quick to learn, his head was currently filled with sailing and he was afraid that Dylan would return to Florida before he had gained enough skill and experience to attempt his skipper licence. Grace, Diana and Jean agreed to share the childcare and Edwardo took his turn with the children but as Valentina was getting older, she needed schooling and so Margaret's time in the lab was also compromised. Margaret didn't mind, she was a natural teacher and Valentina was an excellent pupil who was hungry to learn. In less than five months Patsy had begun to gather momentum in her research of Adiim's DNA and both Adiim and Margaret had become quite proficient in several processes. More than anything Patsy was delighted to find that Jean was a natural in the lab and for the first time in their lives Jean was delighted to have found an affinity with her daughter that she never even knew existed. Like Patsy she was intuitive and could spot patterns in their research that passed the others by, this skill often saved a great deal of time and was valuable.

Patsy was proud of all of them and was thrilled to be able to chat with Grace or Diana about gene sequencing over a glass of wine in the evenings. After years of everyone thinking discussions about her work was too highbrow, it seemed almost surreal to be talking to them all in such detail about her work now. Mapping Adiim's DNA was much harder than she'd expected, Giin cells behaved in such a bizarre way but that did make isolating the human side of him a lot easier. Patsy estimated that less than thirty per cent of Adiim was human which didn't surprise anyone. He asked her secretly one evening if she had any idea what percentage of their children would be human. Patsy discussed some of the random possibilities of genetics, they could be almost entirely Giin, entirely human or a complete mixture of both depending on how nature threw the dice. As she'd never encountered Giin DNA before she had no idea how dominant the genes were. They'd long ago stopped referring to the Giin as Genies but Adiim couldn't help referring to Genie genes for a laugh.

After several more weeks, they'd successfully isolated the human side of Adiim's genetic makeup which was a milestone for Patsy in terms of convincing him that having children of their own could be managed safely. However, they had a long way to go yet if they were ever going to isolate the parts of Adiim's DNA that could cure illness. They often had discussions in the lab about what they will do if they find a safe and stable way to fix some of the major illnesses in the world such as cancer and heart disease. Edwardo had an interesting idea about releasing it into the water supply so that it couldn't be traced to any specific person or location. Patsy agreed it was a great idea in principle, but she pointed out that it would need considerably more testing and research to check for any likely impact on the environment.

Margaret suggested manufacturing a brand of aspirin or even vitamins that could hide the secret ingredient which would lessen the impact on the environment. Again, Patsy pointed out the pitfalls of trying to release a drug of any type that had not been tested and approved by the correct authorities. If they tried to hide that special ingredient it would no doubt be found by the authorities during testing and that would cause the same interest in them as before.

It was quite a dilemma, not only trying to isolate the magic cells but packaging them and distributing them without causing any attention to be focussed on their laboratory. For now, the research would continue, and everyone involved enjoyed the challenge.

Off the latch - Chapter 18

One morning the children were playing outside, and Diana was sitting at one of the tables with her laptop watching over them while Grace had a shower and Jean was preparing breakfast. The younger boys were easier to control as there were gates on the edge of the terrace and they were far too small to reach them, but Valentina was becoming a handful. She was growing taller and could open most doors and cupboards in the house, which was a hazard. She'd recently worked out how to open the gate on the terrace which was a complete disaster. The steps beyond it led out to the rest of the island, down to the swimming pool, the marina and the sea. Every one of the adults spoke to her about the danger of going through the gate without an adult present but nothing had been done to secure it.

As Diana was on child-minding duty this morning, she found a long bootlace and tied the gate tightly to the gatepost to secure it temporarily. Willam and Dotty were both sunning themselves out on the terrace and the kittens were playing with small table tennis balls that Carlos loved to throw around for them. The most adventurous of the three kittens was Max and he liked to climb trees and fences and had even appeared on the roof a couple of times. Dotty tried to control him, but he had a mind of his own and he'd only behave if Willam gave him a biff around the ear. Just when everyone else was busy, Steve and Martin decided to contact them on Skype. Diana answered them on her laptop then dashed off quickly to fetch Alec.

During the one minute and thirteen seconds that she was gone, Max climbed over the gate although Valentina tried to stop him and scolded him for being naughty. It was not her intention to break the rules, she only wanted to rescue Max from the dangers that were beyond the gate. She made short work of unpicking the bootlace and easily flicked over the catch holding the gate closed. She ran through and slammed it behind her running down the steps at full speed to catch Max. Willam saw what happened and as he dashed to climb over the fence and chase after Valentina, he told Dotty to go and fetch Adiim. When Diana returned, she was busy telling Steve that Alec was on his way and was distracted, so it took her a few moments to realise that Valentina was missing. She ran to the gate and immediately saw the bootlace was untied.

Dashing back into the house she yelled for help and Emma dashed out to her first. "Quick, please watch the boys for me, Valentina has gone through the gate," she shouted to her. "Go!" said Emma and rushed out to gather them both up. Dotty had located Adiim in the lab with Patsy, but he was behind the large glass screen and she couldn't get to him. She made all the noises she could think of to attract his attention, but it was only when Patsy looked up and saw her frantically pawing at the window that they realised something was wrong.

Assuming it was one of the kittens, Adiim dashed through the door without bothering to change and when she could be heard Dotty told him about Valentina. Adiim repeated what she had said to Patsy, they both dashed upstairs in their lab gear and ran outside to the terrace.

By now Diana, Dylan and Alec were dashing around the pool and the marina calling to Valentina, Grace had Carlos in her arms and Jean was holding Noah, Jeff and Alec were over by the landing strip and Edwardo and Emma were dashing frantically along the strip of beach. Adiim stretched out his senses and suddenly heard Willam's thoughts. He had located her in the water under one of the smaller boats in the marina. In front of everyone he called out loudly," Valentina, I am coming." Then he turned into his trademark swirling mist of sand and smoke and moved at incredible speed to find her. Emma, Dylan, the two cleaners and even the two security guards were out searching, and they all saw Adiim disappear.

A few moments later Adiim and Valentina appeared on the quayside, she was crying but otherwise unhurt. Grace, Edwardo and Diana hugged her tightly and thanked Adiim for saving her life. Until now, only Alec had realised that Adiim's powers had been exposed and the shockwaves it had caused. The two guards and the two cleaners were discussing what they saw and none of them could believe their eyes. "Do you think they're aliens or something," asked Jane? None of them could speak and they saw Alec walking towards them with a serious expression on his face. "What you saw just now can easily be explained but we need to sit down together so that you will understand fully," said Alec. They all nodded but they looked at him curiously, trying to work out if he too was an alien.

Dylan was nearest to Jeff and Patsy and stood with his mouth open for a while. Patsy took his arm to reassure him and told him, "Don't worry Dylan, I'm sure my Gran can explain everything to you, it's nothing bad. "Your Gran, who's that," he asked, and Patsy realised she had further complicated things. Jeff cringed when Patsy referred to her as Gran, but he could do nothing to help so he stayed silent. Emma didn't say a word either, but she went and stood next to Jean and Noah. Jean put an arm around her and told her not to worry as everything would be alright and she would understand when they had a chance to tell her everything.

As they walked back to the house Alec gathered Patsy and Adiim together for a chat. "This is a disaster, there are too many people involved now and I don't like it," he said. "Adiim, I was wondering if you could erase certain things from someone's memory," asked Patsy? "Of course, I can," said Adiim, "but I think it is probably morally very wrong to mess with people's minds." "That may be the case but knowing things about you could put them in danger so perhaps you'd be helping them, the way that you helped Lydia cope with her helicopter flight," said Patsy. Although he didn't like it, Adiim agreed that they'd gather all the staff and Dylan together to change what they'd witnessed.

As this was an important discussion, they called everyone into one of the smaller houses and Patsy went to let the rest of the family know what was happening. Margaret objected to Dylan being included with them and said she wanted time to talk with him first, particularly after Patsy referring to her as Gran. They all agreed, and Margaret assured them that if she had any doubt after she'd spoken to Dylan, Adiim could change his thoughts. Adiim changed the meeting into a vote of thanks from the family for their loyalty and help in trying to find Valentina. He explained that he was glad he had trained as a lifeguard and knew how to rescue and resuscitate people who had been in the water. The thoughts penetrated them and immediately they knew that to be the events as they happened. Only Emma looked troubled after Adiim's speech, but she smiled when Alec told them they were all getting a two-thousand-dollar bonus in their next salary as a thank you.

Later when the family discussed what had happened, they criticised each other for not making sure the gate was childproof. Jean suggested they may need to employ a handyman to deal with things like gates and anything that could break down or need fixing up. Jeff asked if they'd allow him to take charge of those things. He'd been brought up on a farm and he knew how to do most things including growing good vegetables and he would enjoy having something else to keep him occupied when he wasn't flying. Everyone thought it was an excellent idea and Jean asked him if he would make child security his priority.

Old youngsters - Chapter 19

Margaret took Dylan down to the basement cinema to talk to him privately. She ran through the whole story starting with her family history and ending with Adiim rescuing Valentina with Giin magic. It took almost two hours to cover everything, but Margaret wanted him to have no doubts about what and who they were. He was astounded and a bit angry that Margaret hadn't told him her real name because he'd always known her as Sarah. Now she seemed like a completely different person, not to mention the fact that she was a woman in her early eighties. He did understand that it must have been exceedingly difficult for her to tell him everything, the mere fact that she had done meant she trusted him, and he knew he must mean something to her. He loved how she looked no matter what her true age was and more than that he loved her mind and intelligence. If he hadn't seen Adam, no Adiim change into a swirling whirlwind, he would have found it much more difficult to believe. It also helped to know that Jeff had only recently learned the truth, but he was fine with it all. Margaret explained what Adiim was going to do with the staff.

Although he hated to change people's thoughts, Patsy and Alec had persuaded him that it was for their safety. Dylan could see the logic to that, although he didn't feel that his safety was at all compromised. As they were near the end of their conversation, Adiim came to find them and make sure that both Dylan and Margaret were okay with everything. He asked Adiim about many things including several questions about Patsy's new ability to speak foreign languages. Unlike the others, Dylan asked point-blank if Adiim could give him the ability to play the piano, he'd always wanted that skill. Adiim didn't hesitate and just touched his head with one hand telling him it was done. Margaret was slightly annoyed with his attitude but decided that perhaps unlike British people, Americans didn't consider it rude to be more direct. They went back upstairs to find the others who were anxiously waiting to see how Dylan felt.

They were relieved to hear that he was fine with everything and had understood the need for their secrecy. He explained the most difficult thing was remembering the truth about the family and their relationships. Secretly he was disturbed by their revelations, but he didn't feel threatened and couldn't find anything bad about Adiim, he'd never known a kinder being. He'd seen for himself Adiim's reaction to the little girl drowning and he realised he'd sacrificed his safety without a thought to save her. "Do you mind if I go to your music room?" asked Dylan. Only Margaret and Adiim knew the reason but no one minded if that was what he wanted to do. He reached into one of the cupboards along the walls and retrieved a wodge of sheet music, flicking through it until he chose the piece he wanted. He opened it as he sat down at the beautiful Steinway piano and began to play.

He couldn't believe the music that seemed to flow from his fingertips and Margaret was mesmerised by the sheer beauty of it. He stopped playing, turned to Adiim with tears in his eyes and said thank you to him humbly. "My mother was an amazing concert pianist," he told them, "She tried everything to teach me to play but my brain was not capable of absorbing the information." I have to go back to Miami soon and show her while she's still here, she's eighty-nine years old," he explained. "I can take you there immediately and you can show her," Adiim told him. "She is in a nursing home so I don't know how I could arrange it," he told them sadly. "Then perhaps we can bring her here," said Adiim enthusiastically.

Dylan couldn't believe it was possible, but he loved the idea and so did Margaret. "Okay, let's go and get her then," said Dylan laughing. Adiim showed him how to prepare and suddenly they were flying high in the air. In only a few minutes they'd located his mother and were descending into the private gardens at the rear of the building. It was the evening in Miami and already dark. They walked into the reception area and Dylan signed them in as visitors to see Molly Morden. They located her suite and Dylan tapped the door before walking into her room.

Molly was born in Amsterdam to a Dutch mother and an American father, she was a beautiful young blond woman. When they moved to America, she met her beloved husband Michael and gave birth to her only son Dylan. Until around eight months ago, she and Michael had managed perfectly well on their own, living in their beautiful little house on the outskirts of Miami. That was until Michael went strange and before long the doctors had diagnosed Alzheimer's and Molly had to cope with his aggression. Things had finally reached a climax when he pushed her down a set of steps in the garden fracturing her pelvis and putting them both into care. Dylan visited them every day initially, but he had to go away for work and was now living and working somewhere in Australia.

She was delighted to see her lovely son's face as he appeared in the doorway. "Oh my," she cried out, "what are you doing here and me looking so untidy?" Dylan laughed and kissed her several times then introduced Adiim. "This is my friend Adiim," he told her. "He's a Genie and he's going to fly us both to Australia for a visit." "Is he now," said Molly not believing a word of it, "and how am I going to get there on my broken hip?" "Just do everything we tell you and you'll be alright," said Dylan laughing.

Firstly, Adiim disappeared and went into Molly's hip, repairing the bones and while he was there giving her a good overhaul in several other departments but taking care not to change the look of her age too much. Then he reappeared and asked her to trust him and to stand up. Molly was shocked by all of this and looked at Dylan who simply smiled and nodded to her. She stood without any pain and in fact without any problem at all, better than she'd been able to in several years.

Adiim wrapped his arm around their shoulders and before long they were flying in the air and heading to the island. "Weeeeee!" said Molly suddenly and unexpectedly. "I'm having the best dream ever." Eventually, they landed on the island and appeared back in the music room in front of a smiling Patsy. "Hello dear," said Molly excitedly, "welcome to my lovely dream, I hope I don't wake up before I get to know you." "Look, Mom, you're not dreaming, what I told you is true, I'm friends with a Genie, and this is his girlfriend Patsy." Patsy was slightly embarrassed at being called his girlfriend but neither of them said anything. Margaret introduced herself and Molly said, "Molly Morden, pleased to meet you, my dear." Without another word, Dylan sat at the piano and began to play. Molly was shocked and enthralled by his ability and so proud and delighted that her smile lit up the entire room.

They listened until he had finished one of Chopin's nocturnes and Molly clapped her hands. "That was note-perfect and in perfect time," she told Margaret, "I always knew he had it in him, it just needed to come out." Everyone was charmed by Molly; she had such a beautiful character and even the children were interested in her as old as she was.

On the Island, it was still only eleven o'clock in the morning and Jean had prepared a nice lunch for everyone. Emma asked who the old lady was, and Jean quickly told her she was Dylan's mum. "Jeff collected her from the mainland late last night in the helicopter and she's just woken up." They'd forgotten to let the staff know because of the trauma earlier that morning with Valentina nearly drowning. It seemed to satisfy her questions for now and she helped Jean set the table outside.

In the meantime, both Molly and Dylan took it in turns to play the piano as everyone gathered around. Molly ended it by playing Gershwin's Rhapsody in blue followed by Scott Joplin's maple leaf rag, to the absolute delight of everyone including Valentina who performed a special dance to it as though nothing had happened to her earlier.

Molly hadn't had so much fun in ages and didn't know where her energy had come from. Dylan calculated the time difference and wanted to make sure she was safely tucked up in bed by morning when the nurse came to check on her. They had lunch on the terrace and Molly was impressed with the beauty of their small island. They had delicious fish and pasta accompanied by some of Adiim's bread and pastries that he made almost every morning before the rest of the house had risen. Molly's appetite had returned with gusto and she ate more than she had for years. Patsy discovered she liked a Cosmopolitan, so she went into the bar next to their dining room to make her one and a jug of Pimm's for the others. Dylan was completely sold on this wonderful family; they treated his Mom as though she was part of their own family. Any doubts he had about Adiim or Sarah-whoops Margaret had now disappeared, and he was glad they'd let him in on the great secret.

After lunch, Dylan took her out on the boat for a trip to look at some of the other small neighbouring islands. While they were alone, he tried to explain everything about Adiim and this time she listened. She was completely calm and only fascinated by the story. She asked him if he would be asking Margaret to marry him soon and he laughed loudly. "She's nearer your age than mine," he told her. Molly thought about this for a moment and then asked if he thought Adiim could restore her and make poor Michael young again instead of an aggressive old lunatic. Dylan could only suggest that she should ask Adiim when he took her back. Molly had been on the island for seven and a half hours and as they left Miami at around eight-fifteen in the evening, it would be almost four o'clock in the morning if they left now. As she prepared to leave, Valentina gave her a picture she'd drawn of Molly playing the piano. Jean packed her some tasty goodies including one or two of Adiim's pastries. Alec took a selfie of them all on his phone and went off to download it and print it off for her. Margaret gave her one of her handbags that she'd taken a shine to and then put both pictures and all the other goodies into it for her. Even Willam jumped onto her lap and butted her under the chin with his head. "What a lovely boy you are," she told him stroking him gently and passing him on to Patsy.

Adiim and Dylan stood with her and in seconds they were flying back to Florida. When they arrived back at her room, Molly took Adiim's hand. "Adiim, I know I've only just met you and already you've done the most wonderful things for me, but I wonder if I can ask you for one last thing. My poor husband Michael developed dementia and I lost him and could never even say goodbye to him because he has no idea who I am. Would you please arrange for us to have just one more day together as we once were, so that I can tell him I love him, and we can say goodbye to each other properly. After that, I won't mind what happens to me." Adiim smiled and sat her down on the bed. "I can do more than make you and Michael young for one day but there are certain things we have to arrange first. No one can ever know how you did it, or I will be in great danger.

We need to get you and Michael out of the nursing home and say that you're being taken to Australia to live with Dylan. Then we'll arrange new identities for you, a new home and a new life for you both. I will take you both back to twenty years of age and you can live your lives together again. It must be kept a secret, or you'll never find peace and my own life, and my family will be in danger."

Molly fully understood the implications and was excited and happy with what Adiim said. "Dylan and I will make all the arrangements, and in the meantime, I've healed you of all your ailments, so you'll be more comfortable," said Adiim. "Before I leave here, I'll go with Dylan to see his father and reverse the sickness that made him confused. It will be a surprise to the nursing staff, but it will enable you to speak to him about what we're planning." Molly clapped her hands with excitement, and they had to tell her to be quiet. They tucked her up in bed and kissed her then Adiim looked to find Michael. He was fast asleep, so they didn't wake him as Adiim performed his magic without him knowing, then they left for the island.

When Molly woke the next morning, she thought she'd been dreaming but she soon realised her hip no longer pained her and she felt quite well. She reached down the side of her bed and there was the handbag that Margaret gave to her. Inside was the picture that Valentina had drawn and the photo of the lovely family on their island. Smiling and happy in the middle of the photo she saw herself with Dylan holding her hand.

She put both pictures on top of her locker and tucked into one of the pastries Jean had packed for her. A few moments later there was a knock on the door and the nurse came in with a smiling Michael, his arms reaching out to her.

On their return, Dylan told the family what Molly had asked for, and they were delighted Adiim was giving them a new life. Dylan suggested they keep their real names and Adiim arranged documents to show their new ages and their wedding date of a year ago. Alec asked Steve Neilson to buy them a house like the one they'd left behind a few months ago but in a different neighbourhood. Steve also set up a trust fund for them with a regular income. The next day Adiim and Dylan went back to his house in Miami, picked up his car and drove to the nursing home to collect Molly, Michael and their belongings.

The nursing staff weren't concerned when Dr Osman produced paperwork that reassured them that they were moving to a home with trained doctors and nursing staff in residence. They drove to Dylan's house and once inside Adiim performed his miracle and they both became twenty years old again. Dylan decided to stay with them for a few days to help organise their new life, to update their clothing and help them to prepare for the move while they waited for new documents to arrive. They couldn't believe what had happened to them, but they were grateful for the second chance at life and promised never to tell a living soul.

Back on the island everything soon returned to normal, none of the staff remembered anything about Adiim's unconventional rescue of Valentina and the gate had a new childproof catch fitted. Only Emma was changed by what happened on that day, but no one had noticed. The cats knew why. Willam had spoken into Emma's mind to ask her to help Dotty who was frantic with worry and trying desperately to attract Adiim's attention in the lab. Meanwhile, he was desperately trying to locate Valentina down at the harbour. Although she chose to think she'd imagined it, at the back of Emma's mind some things nagged at her every day and she couldn't forget them. She thought she was going crazy, but she was sure Willam asked her to go and help Dotty to find Adiim. Then again, it had been a very frantic few moments and she may have just imagined it in the heat of the terrible moment.

Wedding planning - Chapter 20

That week Diana and Jeff's wedding was to take place on the island. Alec had spoken to Jan who'd helped them to arrange for an official from Brisbane to come over and perform the ceremony. Jeff had no living relatives, but he wanted his best friend from the orphanage to be his best man. Like Jeff, he'd remained single all his life but for a different reason. Ronnie had been born with a spinal deformity that meant he'd spent his entire life in a wheelchair. It didn't prevent him from living the life of a wildcat. He'd performed parachute jumps and even bungee jumping, all to raise money for children's charities. He didn't need picking up, he'd be piloting a helicopter himself.

Edwardo invited Lydia back for the wedding and she screamed with excitement over the phone when he told her about Diana and Jeff. Diana wanted her son Clive to be at the wedding, but no one seemed to know where he was. Both Diana and Grace had tried desperately to find her brother for several months but none of his old friends knew where he had gone since he left London over a year ago. Grace spoke to Patsy about her dilemma and Patsy suggested Adiim may be able to help to find him. Apart from Dylan and the staff, the only other people invited were Emma's boyfriend Eddie, Steve and Martin Neilson and Jan Manolis. Diana had suggested bringing in caterers to arrange all the food, but Margaret, Jean and Emma had insisted they could do a much better job themselves as there would be less than thirty people even if they included the children.

After looking at a few family photo's showing Clive's face, Adiim offered to take Grace to try and find him. They tracked down several his old friends but none of them could give any more information than they already had except that his last address had been in Wood Green. They visited the house and found it was divided into five flats over three floors. The current occupants of his old flat had no idea even who he was, but they suggested speaking to Miss Clarke, the old lady who lived in the basement. She was delighted to meet Grace and thought she looked a lot like her brother. This sweet old lady must have appealed to Clive's softer side because she told them how exceedingly kind he was, and what a good friend he'd been to her. She asked them to sit down and offered them tea which they declined politely. Then she opened a beautiful antique bureau and carried an airmail letter back to the table. It was a short note from Clive to let her know that he was now in the army, had been stationed in Afghanistan, but he was perfectly fine. The letter was dated three months earlier and was the only one she'd received. They wrote down as much information as they could glean from the letter and thanked her for her help. She sent her best wishes to Diana and Jeff for their wedding and said she hoped Clive would be able to attend. They both kissed her and went down the hallway waving until she'd closed her door, then Adiim transported them back to the island. They found Edwardo and Patsy and let them know what they'd discovered about Clive being in

Afghanistan. Patsy had a great idea. "Let me speak to Dad, he has friends with senior positions in the army, he may know someone who could arrange a pass for Clive to attend the wedding." Alec took all the information about Clive Curtis from Grace and went to make a phone call to his old friend Lieutenant General Douglas Marklew. In less than two hours he'd found Clive and arranged for him to be taken to RAF Akrotiri in Cyprus. Alec was arranging for him to pick up airline tickets to take him to Brisbane where Jeff would collect him.

When Private Curtis was called out of parade by the Staff Sergeant, he racked his brains to try and think what he'd done wrong. When he reached the office, he was informed that he'd been given special dispensation and two weeks leave to attend his mother's wedding to Mr Jeff Richards. He'd be flown to Cyprus where his airline tickets to Brisbane Australia would be ready for him to collect.

He asked for permission to speak which was granted so he asked the staff sergeant if he was sure they had the right soldier because his mother never had any time for men or her children, only her job. The staff sergeant scoffed at him and told him not to lie. "You must have some pretty powerful friends or relatives high up to be given this special treatment Private, so I suggest you get moving and pack your wedding suit, you leave at 20 hundred hours tonight."

They decided not to tell Diana about Clive but to let it be a lovely surprise when he arrived. Jeff was trying to coordinate the collection of the wedding official and his wife, Jan, Steve and Martin Neilson and the arrival of both Lydia and Clive in Brisbane. Dylan was going to pick up a few of the others in the Motor Launch but Chris, who had been their temporary skipper, had been invited to the wedding. Instead, he arranged to bring everyone who was not flying to the island in one of the rented launches, to save Dylan having to go back twice.

The wedding was arranged to take place the following day so most of them were up at daybreak getting ready for everyone else to arrive later that afternoon. Jeff left at eight-thirty and Edwardo went with him to meet Lydia and his brother in law Clive who he'd met briefly once before in London. Less than an hour after they'd left, a small helicopter arrived and with only a little struggle Ronnie dropped down a ramp and lowered himself out of the pilot's seat and into a wheelchair then came racing down the ramp. Diana and Grace were the first to greet him and let him know that he'd just missed Jeff. He wasn't worried at all and spent the next few hours exploring the island, playing with the children and talking to the cats. Diana secretly wondered if it would be possible for Adiim to heal Ronnie's legs and spine, but she decided to wait for the right moment to ask, possibly after the wedding.

Early in the afternoon, the sounds of jet engines attracted everyone's attention and an excited Grace ran outside swiftly followed by Patsy. Jean and Margaret had been tipped off and were keeping Diana distracted with thousands of questions about the preparations so Grace could meet her brother and prepare him for how young his mother now looked. Luckily, Edwardo and Lydia had already been talking to him and Lydia was a prime example of the cosmetic surgery performed by Doctor Adam. When Clive's face appeared in the kitchen doorway still wearing his army uniform Diana burst into tears and hugged him tightly. She knew her son resented her for giving more attention to her job than she had to her home when they were children, but he hugged her and told her he loved her anyway.

Edwardo and Lydia came in behind them and Lydia shrieked in her usual way and kissed everyone almost to death. The sounds of Jeff and Ronnie meeting up outside almost drowned out Lydia's shrieks and Diana couldn't help laughing with the thrill of it all. Then, to top the bill, there came sounds of trumpets and singing coming from the marina as Chris arrived with the rest of the guests in the other motor launch. As a surprise to Jeff and Diana, the staff had clubbed together and hired a Mexican Mariachi band and they all marched together towards the house singing "Do you come from a land down under" but Mexican style. They had the most amazing evening, and everyone became quite drunk, including Aubrey and Gwen the wedding registrar and his wife. When Clive met his little niece and nephew and baby Noah, he fell totally in love with all of them and within an hour had captivated Valentina, which she loved.

The wedding went without a hitch and everyone enjoyed themselves completely. Diana looked stunning in an ivory coloured dress and a beautiful fascinator with ivory and black feathers curling out of it. The Mexican band was fantastic, and they played again for the entire evening much to the delight of the guests and Valentina in particular. The food prepared on the island was delicious and included a barbecue in the evening as if everyone had not eaten too much already. Even the cats had a good time gobbling up all the bits of chicken and meat dropped around the lawn by tipsy wedding guests.

Eventually, everyone had to go to bed and without realising, Adiim followed Patsy to her room and climbed into her bed fully dressed falling asleep immediately. Patsy changed into a respectable pair of pyjamas and snuggled up next to him enjoying the opportunity to be close to him for a whole night. When he woke the next morning Adiim was horrified to find himself in Patsy's bed and sat bolt upright. Patsy grabbed onto him tightly so that he couldn't just jump out of bed. "We have to let everyone know about us so that we can relax and enjoy being together," she tried to tell him. "I'm afraid they'll say no to us and then what will we do," said Adiim, genuinely afraid? "If by some remarkable chance they do say no, I will tell them it's none of their business and we will be together anyway," she assured him.

"I just want everything to be right and as it should be with your father and mother's approval," he explained. "Okay well why don't we just go and tell them that we love each other, and we want to get married too," she replied shrugging and holding her palms out. "No, I must ask your father for permission first," Adiim insisted. It was agreed that when the right opportunity arose Adiim would ask Alec, he was a complete bag of nerves and dreaded the moment arriving, but he would do anything for Patsy.

It was a beautiful warm and sunny morning and despite the varying levels of a hangover, everyone was happy as they ate breakfast and discussed the incredible wedding. Diana managed to talk to Clive and apologised for all the years she allowed her work to take control of her life to the detriment of her family. She even went as far as telling him about Adiim and Alec promised that when he'd completed his time in the army there'd be a place for him on the island. He was completely shocked by the revelations and felt incredible sympathy for Adiim for his time trapped in the prison of a small vase.

He didn't tell Diana, but he let Adiim know he had been captured by the enemy several months ago and was kept in a small cage with not enough room to stand or move around. Although it was only five days before the British army rescued him, the fear of being trapped had never left him. Adiim hated war, he remembered only too well the terrible things that could happen. He told Clive he would visit when he could but he promised it would be when no one else could see him and that would enable him to bring letters and other small things to him, such as the pictures Valentina had already drawn for her newly discovered uncle. Lydia had also taken a shine to Clive but instead of being flattered, he was slightly afraid. Grace and Edwardo thought it funny because they knew she was teasing him, and her flirting was harmless. She frequently winked her eye at Grace as she suggested he should marry her and then he could be uncle and grandpa to Valentina at the same. Clive just squirmed in his seat and said he was dedicated to the army and didn't have time for anything else right now.

Jean, Margaret, and Emma were exhausted from all the work of preparing for and executing the wedding plans, but they'd thoroughly enjoyed it. Emma's boyfriend Eddie turned out to be a real godsend, he was a trained chef and whipped food together quicker than any of them could. He'd been grateful to be invited to the wedding on such a beautiful island, he'd never had a chance to visit Emma at work previously. Jean and Margaret asked him if he wanted to come and work for the family, but he was tied into a contract with a hotel in Canberra, although the training he was receiving made it worthwhile. Jean suggested he could come and visit whenever he had time off and when he was free from his contract to let her know.

Jeff, Dylan, Ronnie and Alec were doing the man thing and wandering around the gardens together cracking rude jokes and telling anecdotes to each other. Dylan broke off when they were near the marina and went to check on the motor launch but the other three continued towards the small runway where the small jet plane was parked up. Ronnie asked Alec if he could have a look inside and Alec told him he was welcome to do it anytime. When they reached the small plane, Jeff lifted Ronnie over his shoulder and carried him up the steps into the cockpit. Alec asked if he needed the wheelchair bringing up, but they told him just to leave it where it was.

Patsy had been watching everything from the terrace, she grabbed Adiim's arm. "Look Dad's finally alone, now's our best chance to go and talk to him," she said. Although he was shaking with nerves, Adiim walked with her over to the small runway where Alec was wandering around the aircraft looking at the nuts and bolts of it.

When he saw them coming, he smiled and held out his hands to Patsy. "Dad, I hope this is a good time because Adiim has something he wants to ask you." Alec wasn't stupid and he had a good idea of what was coming next. His wicked sense of humour kicked in as he waited for a trembling Adiim to speak. "I would like to ask you if you will give me permission to marry your daughter, Patsy?" Adiim mumbled nervously.

Alec kept him waiting for a few seconds to help build the tension before saying, "I can't let you do that Adiim-." He hadn't finished his sentence when Adiim suddenly sobbed and turned into the swirling cloud of sand and smoke that enabled him to fly away. Inside the cockpit, a curious Ronnie chose that precise second to start up the jet and Adiim's essence was immediately sucked into one of the jet engines and scattered into the hot air behind it.

"No! No! No!" shouted Patsy through the roaring sound of the engines. She banged on Alec's chest asking why he did that to Adiim. Alec was in shock and told Patsy "I was only going to say I can't let you marry her you're much too nice a man and she's far too much trouble." "You can't joke about things like that with Adiim, he was terrified you'd say no and that's exactly what he thought you'd done," cried Patsy sobbing.

The sand and smoke that had been Adiim Ben GIIN Labet was scattered far and wide and was unable to respond but a cat named Willam was still able to sense his dear friend so there was hope.

Willam & Adiim as depicted by my lovely sister,
talented artist Jan Jones.

Thank you to everyone who helped me to prepare this book for publication, including those who read it and gave feedback Hazel, Sarah, Aleksandra, Sharon, Sam, Jan and Steve and my husband Rafaël.